Scheme

Scheme

AN ON THE SHELF OMEGAVERSE BOOK

COLETTE RHODES

ISBN 978-1-7386105-0-1 (paperback)

ISBN 9781738610518 (hardcover)

CONTENT WARNING

SCHEME CONTAINS REFERENCES TO SEXUAL ASSAULT (SIDE CHARACTER, OFF-PAGE), AS WELL AS THE DEATH OF A SIBLING (OFF-PAGE).

WHAT IS OMEGAVERSE?

WHILE THERE ARE MANY DIFFERENT INTERPRETATIONS OF "OMEGAVERSE" IN FICTION (AND THIS ONE HAS A FEW QUIRKS OF ITS OWN), THE BASIC CONCEPT IS A DOMINANCE HIERARCHY AMONG HUMANS WHEREBY EVERYONE IS EITHER BORN AN ALPHA, A BETA, OR AN OMEGA. A PERSON'S DESIGNATION IMPACTS THEIR PLACE IN SOCIETY, AS WELL AS THEIR ROMANTIC AND SEXUAL RELATIONSHIPS.

OMEGAVERSE INCLUDES KNOTTING, HEATS, SCENT MARKING, AND OTHER ANIMALISTIC BEHAVIORS.

AUTHOR'S NOTE

WHILE I USUALLY WRITE IN US ENGLISH, SCHEME IS SET IN LONDON AND I COULDN'T IN GOOD CONSCIOUS HAVE A BRITISH CHARACTER SAY "MOM", SO THIS BOOK IS WRITTEN IN BRITISH ENGLISH.

IF YOU'RE WORRIED THAT MY BRITISH ENGLISH WILL BE WORSE THAN MY AMERICAN ENGLISH, PLEASE REST ASSURED THAT I AM FROM NEW ZEALAND AND PROBABLY UNFIT TO WRITE BOTH.

"Love yourself first and everything else falls into line. You really have to love yourself to get anything done in this world."
—Lucille Ball

Prologue

"Do you think this will actually stay in place?" I asked Layla nervously, turning my face from side to side in the mirror and then rechecking the waterproof claims on the make-up I'd ordered just for today's party. "It says waterproof, but that probably means 'will survive a light drizzle' not a whole day in the pool."

"You're overthinking it," my sixteen-year-old younger sister advised, adjusting her royal-blue bikini top in the mirror. "Fraser won't be paying attention to your face anyway, not with that swimsuit on. Can't wait to hear him mention a million times how excited he is to go into your nest with you." She gagged dramatically, cutting me an impressively judgemental side-eye. "You absolutely reek of impending heat, by the way."

"That's not exactly surprising, it should be here any day now," I murmured, running my palms over my hot-to-the-touch skin, amazed and a little terrified of the changes my body was going through in the lead up to my first heat. The past few days had been incredibly uncomfortable—like the worst fever I'd ever had, except *everywhere*. Hopefully, my heat would properly kick in tomorrow. Fraser and I would go into my nest together, and I wouldn't have to panic about him seeing me without make-up on ever again.

"Surely, you could just go into your nest now?" Layla pressed, undoubtedly sick of the syrupy pre-heat scent that I'd been sporting for the past few weeks. I'd initially been excited about the signal that my first heat was approaching, but I was finding the scent a little nauseating now too. It didn't help that I was basically stuck at my house or Fraser's, unable to go out in public unless I practically bathed in scentshield lotion, and I always missed a spot.

I shook my head. "It's still too early. You know Fraser could *die* if he bites me before my heat has set in properly."

Before now, the toxin in my blood, in all omegas' blood, had always been a blessing. It kept us safe from alphas who would take us and claim us against our will. But now that I had an alpha who I actually *wanted* to bite me, the idea that I might kill him was terrifying.

"But how do you *know*? There's no light that goes off on your forehead saying, 'Hey, my blood isn't poisonous right now, claim me, alpha.'"

"I just know," I insisted, choosing to be optimistic. "I'd never risk Fraser. I'll know when it's safe to invite him into the nest."

She didn't look entirely convinced, but Layla was still two years away from her first heat. She'd get it then. Her instincts would guide her like mine were guiding me.

"I hope you don't kill him," Layla mumbled. "We'd definitely have to move."

That was probably true. Fraser was my boy-next-door love story, and if anything bad happened, living right next to his parents would definitely have its downsides.

No. Nothing bad is going to happen. You love Fraser, and he loves you. We'd been together for two years, since we were sixteen, and that had to mean something. Two years was *so* long.

There was a low ache just south of my belly, and I rubbed at it absently, willing it to go away. Mum had warned me that this heat would be the worst. That after Fraser and I were mated, my heats would be regular, shorter, and less agonising. Right now, it felt like my uterus was punishing me for being single.

"Are we leaving or what?" Calum demanded, throwing open the door to Layla's room with a bang and glaring at us.

"Knock next time, would you?" Layla huffed, glaring at our younger brother. "What if we were getting changed?"

"Lock the door then." Calum shrugged, unrepentant. He'd been such a sweet kid, but now he was fourteen, and since his alpha dynamic had emerged last year, I recognised less and less of my gentle, mischievous younger brother in him.

That he was chaperoning us to a pool party when he was only fourteen and I was eighteen was beyond insulting. Alpha privilege, I supposed.

"I think we're nearly ready," I murmured, trying to keep the peace. Layla finished primping, finger curling the ends of her hair and shooting a confident smile at her reflection. She didn't have a stitch of make-up on, of course. She didn't need it.

With a tight smile, I moved away from the mirror. Next to her, I looked ridiculous in my attempts to highlight the passable features I had and disguise the less attractive ones.

I must have done something bad in a past life for all of my siblings to inherit my parents' good looks and for me to look like my seventy-something-year-old Nana, minus the wrinkles. The big, bleached blonde curls I spent hours on each day sort of distracted from the general lack of symmetry and non-existent jawline, but they couldn't work their magic if they were soaking wet. My make-up gave me the impression of cheekbones and sultry eyes—without it, I looked like a sickly wraith.

Shit, shit, shit. A pool party was a terrible idea.

"Maybe I shouldn't go," I hedged, pulling on my white cover-up. "I feel crampy and gross and *so* hot. Those are very legitimate reasons *not* to come."

Calum groaned, flinging himself down in an armchair and pulling out his phone. "I think it's stupid for you to be out of the house at all when you stink of pre-heat, but Dad says it's fine because Fraser will be there and he'll protect you. Whatever. Just decide already."

Layla turned to face me, her natural, lustrous-brown curls bouncing with the motion, and glared at me with pale hazel eyes, startlingly light against her tanned skin. Why couldn't I have inherited at least *one* of those features? Instead, I'd got dishwater hair, brown eyes, and a face full of broken capillaries.

I was the oldest of six and somehow the runt of the litter.

"You're being so dramatic, Margot. Fraser doesn't care what you look like without make-up on. He's literally in love with you, you've both been counting down to your first heat for over a year now. Your scent is ridiculously appealing to every alpha, way more than any of the other mature, single omegas we know. You'll have fun today, you'll invite him to your nest when your heat arrives, and then emerge a mated lady. Stop feeling so sorry for yourself, it's annoying. Some of us are still looking for our alphas, you know."

"Right. You're right. I'm sorry." I swallowed thickly, snatching up my canvas bag and shoving the make-up on top to reapply after. I didn't share her confidence. It was easy to think no one *really* cared about appearances when you were as beautiful as Layla. When you hadn't gone through life being overlooked in favour of your prettier siblings by everyone from the postman to your own fucking parents.

Layla didn't *get* it. Fraser was gorgeous, the perfect alpha in every single way. I'd been in love with him since the day he and his family moved in next door. Now we were finally eighteen, my heat would be here at any moment, and we were going to make everything official.

I'd never recover if he changed his mind.

But it was selfish of me to think about myself when Layla was still looking for the alpha who'd make her dreams come true. Every omega dreamed of inviting an alpha they loved into their nest at their first heat. Dreamed of being cared for and supported through what was a physically demanding time.

Fraser would be at my side through this heat and each one that followed. I was one of the lucky ones. I shouldn't be complaining. I had *nothing* to complain about.

"Fucking finally," Calum muttered, shoulder-barging me to get out the door first and knocking me into the frame. "Let's get this shit over with."

"You tricked me."

Chapter One

FOURTEEN YEARS LATER...

Dad: Come downstairs.

I narrowed my eyes at the message on my phone, trying to will it away with my mind. My parents *never* came into the city. They'd certainly never been to my flat before.

I quickly changed my status to 'away' and hoped my colleagues didn't ask questions, before slipping out of my spare-bedroom-slash-office, grabbing the keys on my way downstairs.

The old terrace house I lived in had been split into two flats years ago, and I had the upstairs while the Clarksons, an elderly beta couple, had the downstairs. The sounds of their favourite game show filtered through the wall to the stairwell, but it was the murmured voices on the other side of the exterior front door that had my attention.

I took a fortifying breath before opening it, bracing myself to see my father.

"Margot!" Asher said with a beaming smile, throwing himself at me for a surprise hug. Chelsea followed with a soft smile, shyer than our baby brother.

"Upstairs," Dad barked, barely keeping the alpha command out of his voice. "I need to talk to your sister."

I pressed the keys into Chelsea's hand with what I hoped was a reassuring smile while Mum suddenly burst into tears. It wasn't totally out of character for her, but it always made for awkwardness.

"Head on up, make yourselves at home."

"Oh, we will," Asher promised, already jogging noisily up the stairs. Good thing my downstairs neighbours were hard of hearing.

"What's going on?" I asked the moment the top door closed behind them.

Mum let out a full-blown wail, and while Dad *could* soothe his omega with a well-placed purr and a hug, he unsurprisingly did neither.

"Calum's dead."

I blinked at him, certain I'd misheard. Calum couldn't be dead. He'd messaged me asking for money just yesterday.

"*Poisoned* by some omega," Dad added viciously. My blood ran cold. "Chelsea and Asher don't need to know that, though."

"He was such a good man, a good alpha," Mum rasped, half-collapsed against Dad, who barely spared her a glance.

"Do they know he's dead?" I asked bluntly. Calum was a dick who'd grown more dickish each year, and he'd been particularly awful to Asher when he'd presented as an omega, instead of an alpha like we'd all expected, but they'd been surprisingly cheerful, all things considered.

Maybe they didn't know. They *must* not have known. And the *cause* of death being what it was...

Deaths like that didn't happen very often these days. Alphas were educated about the risks now. They *knew* not to lose control.

Only the worst of the worst did.

"You can tell them." Dad's voice was hollow and distracted, his mind very clearly somewhere else. "Tell them it was a heart attack. That's what we're telling the neighbours, but we wanted the youngest out of the way in case rumours spread. We need to go to the station, sort some things out. We'll be back for them later."

How incredibly typical of them to not only drop this horrendous bombshell on me with the least amount of compassion possible, but to also expect me to relay it to my siblings. No, not even relay it. *Lie* about it.

The moment I realised I didn't respect my parents at all had been a life-changing one, freeing me of all the expectations I'd put on myself as a daughter and allowing me to be unapologetically myself.

And yet, despite having zero faith in them to begin with, they still found ways to disappoint me.

"Where's Jules?" I asked.

"With her future alpha," Dad replied. "She's eighteen, that's who she needs to be relying on now in the lead-up to her heat."

He and Mum exchanged a look that I *knew* was about me and my failure to do just that. How fortunate for them, that they had three beautiful omega daughters to follow the path that I'd spectacularly diverted from.

"Alright, well, I'll see you when I see you, I guess," I said, already closing the door, eager to get rid of them. There was a reason why I'd moved out of the little village I'd grown up in over a decade ago and only went back when my youngest siblings or my nana needed me.

I took a steadying breath on the top stair, assembling my expression into something that I hoped resembled calm. I wasn't sure how Chelsea and Asher would take the news, and I didn't want them to feel as though they had to manage my emotions as well as their own.

Chelsea let me in when I knocked on the door to my flat, and I was totally unsurprised to see that she was in the midst of going through my make-up bag on the small dining table.

"This stuff is so bougie," she said, admiring the absurdly expensive bottle of foundation. It was a perfect shade match for me and actually felt comfortable to wear, and one didn't wear as much make-up as I did without developing some pretty strong preferences about it.

Asher had made himself at home on the small two-person sofa, kicking his feet up, sketchbook and pencil in hand. He'd only been here once before because my parents so rarely came into the city, so I didn't know why he felt so comfortable putting his feet all over my furniture.

"So," Asher began, all traces of cheerfulness gone. "Are you going to tell us how Calum really died?"

And here I'd been, worried about how they were going to take the news. "You two should really consider careers in espionage."

"Does it pay as well as being a lawyer?" Chelsea asked, admiring my most expensive tube of rosy pink matte lipstick.

"I don't know," I replied, filling the kettle to make us all tea. "It might come with a wardrobe allowance, though."

"Come on," Asher whined. "You're changing the subject."

I sighed, turning to look at them and leaning back against the bench while the kettle began to boil in the background.

Looking at Asher and Chelsea next to each other was eerily like looking at Calum and Layla side-by-side back in the day. The same chocolate brown curls, tanned skin, light hazel eyes, and perfectly symmetrical faces. Except where the oldest trio was rounded out by me and my unfortunate collection of scrap genes, Jules, the oldest of these three, was also stunning.

"Margot," Asher began, sitting up and setting his sketchbook aside, all teenage confrontation. He was only fourteen, and like all teenagers coming into their dynamic, he *reeked*. I vaguely wondered if there was a tactful way of giving him an industrial-sized tub of Om-Guard, my favoured brand of omega scentshield lotion. It wasn't as though I was short of bottles—if I had my way, no one would smell my scent ever again. "As our oldest and most likeable sibling, I think you have a responsibility to tell us the truth."

"Is that so?" I replied, amused in spite of the dire circumstances. This is why my youngest siblings were my favourites.

"*Yes*. Everyone is lying to us. They tried saying that Calum was sick and that's why we had to come to the city, which is some serious bullshit—" *Was I supposed to stop him swearing? Surely he was old enough for curse words.* "—because they've been on the phone all day, and they must think we're deaf or stupid not to hear what they've been saying."

"Plus," Asher continued. "Layla showed up sobbing with all her dependents in tow—"

"Her children, you mean."

"—but she was so hysterical that Dad sent her away," Asher continued. "Which is odd since she wasn't even close with Calum and never missed an opportunity to tell us all how irresponsible he was for not taking a mate yet." He paused to take a breath while Chelsea nodded along enthusiastically.

"The compassion is really rolling off the two of you in waves."

"We get it from you," Asher shot back. He was such a sassy pants, this youngest brother of mine. I hoped he never lost all that spark, even though I knew Dad was trying to snuff it out. "Come on, Margot. We three are all omegas. We have to stick together."

The kettle beeped, and I considered my next words carefully while I set out three cups and dropped the teabags in, pouring the water and letting them steep.

"If it helps," Chelsea said quietly. "You won't be shattering any illusions about Calum in our eyes."

"Yeah, he had some pretty fucked up views of male omegas, which he was *more* than happy to share with me after I presented," Asher added bitterly.

I didn't need to ask if Mum and Dad had done anything to reel Calum in. They'd made no secret of how ashamed they were to have an omega son.

Assholes.

Recent research suggested that male omegas weren't actually becoming more common over the past few hundred years, as had been previously assumed, but that they'd always been around. They'd just been killed by their families the moment they presented. They still faced prejudices today, and it was heartbreaking that Asher was experiencing them from his own fucking parents.

"Calum is dead," I said decisively, looking between the two of them. "I'm meant to tell you it was a heart attack—that's the story everyone else will get."

If Chelsea and Asher were old enough to deal with the side effects of being an omega, then they were more than old enough to understand the dangers too.

"And what's the real story?" Asher challenged.

"Well, Dad said he was *poisoned* by an omega." I swallowed, forcing down the bile that threatened to rise at the thought of that poor omega and how terrified they must have been. "His phrasing places blame on the omega, but my guess is that Calum lost control and tried to force a claiming bite on an omega who wasn't in heat."

Chelsea paled.

"Mum said that it was dangerous for alphas and they didn't do that," Asher said, suddenly unsure and reminding me of just how young he was. "That we had nothing to worry about."

"Spoken like an omega who has been safely mated for decades." I sighed heavily, pulling the milk out of the fridge. "Mum's scent is intermingled with Dad's, so it's off-putting to any alpha except him. As unmated omegas, we don't have that kind of protection. It is *rare* for an alpha to attempt a claim outside of heat—they're educated on the dangers of it from the moment they present. The toxin that the heat hormones neutralise is well known to be incredibly poisonous."

"So maybe it was an accident then?" Chelsea suggested hesitantly. "Maybe the omega just cut herself and snuck him some blood to get him to back off?"

I gave her a sad smile, understanding the impulse to concoct a less horrifying reality. To not want to believe that Calum was capable of such monstrousness.

After living in London for well over a decade now, I'd seen all kinds of things and met all kinds of people. I knew that alphas like Calum existed, and I knew omegas who suffered because of it.

I wanted to educate Chelsea and Asher on the very real dangers of our designation, but I didn't want them to be as jaded and bitter about the world as I was. Where was the line?

"If the omega had just cut themselves and swiped some blood on Calum's mouth in self-defence, he'd have been sick, but he'd have lived. For him to have died, he must have gulped it down from the vein," I told them gently.

They were both palming the unmarked spots on their necks where a claiming bite would sit one day if they went down that path. Which they almost certainly would, since most omegas did. My lifestyle was the exception, not the rule.

"He would have been aggressive," I added. "Aggressive enough to tip himself into rut and then possessive urges would have demanded the bite. I'm sure I don't need to tell you that Calum was always entitled, you would have seen that for yourselves. Entitled and angry when he didn't get his way, swinging around 'instinct' as an excuse to behave like a brute with no consequences. Daddy's little alpha, you know?"

They nodded, lost in their thoughts as I distributed the cups of tea. I returned to my leaning spot against the bench to drink mine, watching them process and trying to sort out where my own grief began and ended.

There was a not-insignificant part of me that was *glad* that Calum was dead, but that carried a heavy dose of guilt with it since he was my brother, after all.

But then I thought of some poor omega, forced to carry the trauma of an attack as well as a bite mark for the rest of their lives. Even though I was one hundred per cent confident that they'd done nothing wrong, they would still face judgement and recrimination from small-minded assholes because the world was not a fair place.

"I wish we could live with you," Asher said wistfully. "I hate it at home. I hate being a male omega."

Every time I spoke to Asher since he'd presented, I was crushed in a swell of helplessness. He wasn't happy, and he never would be because our parents would never accept him as he was, but the situation wasn't bad enough that I had any legal recourse to get him out, and they'd never let him go voluntarily.

It wouldn't be a good *look*.

I'd been in the middle of delicate negotiations with our parents to let him go to the Sutton-Harris School—a boarding school for those who showed artistic promise. He'd already got through the application round, and next up was the interview.

But Calum, ever the centre of our parents' world, had rudely gone and died, so we were probably back at square one. Mum and Dad would be more conscious of their reputations than ever.

"I know you do, and I'm sorry. Maybe if you were born into a different family, you wouldn't have minded it so much."

Asher looked doubtful. "Unlikely. They only stopped executing male omegas after King Jasper took the throne. It wasn't even that long ago."

"Two-hundred years or thereabouts," Chelsea offered, intently examining a tube of mascara.

"Right. And that was because King Jasper was better suited to rule than his alpha brother," I pressed. "Because being an omega was nowhere near the most important thing about him. We are more than just our designations, and we're no less valuable or capable just because we're omegas," I reminded Asher, hoping he'd remember those words the next time Dad said something wildly offensive. "I haven't given up on the Sutton-Harris School."

Asher snorted. "You should. Dad didn't like the idea before Calum died, he's not going to consider it now. What would the neighbours think if they sent me away? There might be *gossip*, Margot." He gave a look of mock horror that was eerily reminiscent of Mum's face whenever we did something she didn't approve of.

"If you still want to go, then I'll keep pushing for it." Chelsea nodded supportively, though I knew she'd be devastated if her favourite sibling went away. She'd be *okay*, though. Chelsea and Jules were beautiful female omegas, blessed with the same flattering combination of genes that Layla had got. Our parents were pretty good to *those* omegas.

"You know, Layla was mated at eighteen, and Jules is pretty serious about that alpha girl next door, right? You might meet the love of your life in your teenage years too," I teased, attempting for levity so I didn't weigh Asher down with my own frustration at the situation.

Asher wrinkled his nose while Chelsea laughed. "Taytum's a snob. Her and Jules are already talking about going into Jules' nest together at her first heat."

My smile grew a little strained at that. I'd been eighteen once. I'd made plans too.

Eighteen-year-old me wouldn't have imagined I'd be single at thirty-two, that was for sure.

Happily, intentionally, permanently single.

"Me and Chelsea aren't going to be like that," Asher continued. "We've made a pact."

"What kind of pact?"

"We're going to be unmated omegas, just like you," Chelsea said, grinning at me. "We're going to have cool flats in the city and go to yoga class and buy nice shoes and purses, and *not* ask for a double stroller for our twenty-first birthdays like Layla did."

That got a genuine laugh from me. "Don't let Mum hear you say that," I warned, grinning at them. "You never know what the future will bring, but if you *do* choose to follow in the family spinster's footsteps, I'm here for you every step of the way. I need to send my boss a message, then I'll get my laptop, and we can watch a movie and order a takeaway. Sound like a plan?"

"And this, Margot, is why you're our favourite sister," Asher sighed.

It was dark by the time the buzzer for my flat went off. I left Chelsea and Asher watching the awful horror movie they'd talked me into putting on and jogged down the stairs.

I was steeling myself to confront my dad about the way he'd dropped it on me to tell Asher and Chelsea about Calum, which was something I never did. No matter how much my confidence had grown since leaving home, my dad still made me nervous. But when I opened the front door, I was presented with an entirely different alpha.

He was older, at least in his sixties, and from his wet cardboard scent, unmated. The look on his face when he saw me wasn't entirely lecherous, but it also wasn't quite un-lecherous enough to have me relaxing.

"You must be Margot," he said before I could shut the door in his face. "I'm here to pick up the two little ones."

"I'm sorry, I'm not sure we've met," I replied, wondering in what world a fourteen- and sixteen-year-old could be considered little ones.

"That's Jimmy," Asher yelled down the stairs, having opened the door impressively quietly to eavesdrop. "He's dad's golf buddy."

"Get your things," Jimmy instructed, leaning past me. "Your parents are still held up at the station, and they asked me to drive you to Layla's house since your lovely sister here doesn't have a car or room to put you up for the night."

He gave me an appreciative look, and my ovaries curled in on themselves.

Asher and Chelsea grumbled at each other before shutting the door to get their things, probably not enthused at the idea of spending the night at Layla's house. Something I was rather smug about, though it seemed a little petty and beneath me to admit it, even to myself.

I was the cooler sister though.

"You've got a lush pair of tits, you do."

I startled, finding Jimmy's gaze firmly fixed on the outline of my breasts in the loose grey blouse I'd been wearing all day for a work call.

"I do. How very forward of you to mention it," I replied coolly, taking a step back and crossing my arms over my chest. "I'll be honest, Jimmy, I'm not feeling great about sending my siblings anywhere with you."

Jimmy laughed awkwardly, rubbing the back of his neck. "That was a bit much, wasn't it? I'm out of practice at pursuing omegas."

Pursuing omegas?

No, surely not.

"I'm not interested in being pursued—"

"Your parents wanted us to meet." He adjusted his stance, exuding the kind of obnoxious confidence that alphas swung around like a weapon. "Your old man said he'd introduce us, but I doubt he'll have a chance any time soon, circumstances being what they are. Terrible shame about your brother."

Jimmy gave me an appreciative look that made my skin itch while I was momentarily too stunned to respond. "Your mum mentioned your heat was coming up. She said it's been real hard on you all alone these years. I had an omega once—she died years ago, may she rest in peace. Took me a while to get to a point where I was ready to find a new mate, but now that I am, well... Your dad has been saying for years that it'd be a good idea, you and I. He called me earlier and said, 'Jimmy, it's time. My family is overdue for a bit of good news, Jimmy.' He's not wrong about that, is he?"

For a long awkward moment, I just stared at him, baffled by this whole interaction. Was this my parents' plan? Sell me off to take the heat off Calum's actions?

I wanted to tell him to go fuck himself—or that this whole conversation was making me feel genuinely ill—but a mixture of alpha wariness and ingrained politeness had me tempering my words.

"I'm not interested in finding a mate."

Asher and Chelsea were coming down the stairs behind me, bickering with each other about who would sleep on Layla's couch and who'd be stuck in the nursery with the six kids.

"Course you are." Jimmy flicked his hand dismissively, and I felt my eye twitch. "Like I said, I had an omega once. You don't need to play coy with me, I know how all the mechanics work. Mighty uncomfortable time for you, during heat, if you don't have a decent alpha there, making you feel better."

Ew, ew, ew. My eye twitch grew into a full-blown spasm.

"Ew," Asher said loudly, coming to a stop behind me, reading my mind. "Jimmy, you're well old. You can't mate my sister."

To his credit, Jimmy laughed rather than responding like an alpha with wounded pride and a point to prove like I'd braced myself for.

"I can see why you'd think that, young Asher, but things are different when you're an omega Margot's age. Can't be choosey about little things anymore." Jimmy winked at me, setting off another round of general nausea. "Kids, eh? I've got grown ones of my own, so I know the drill. We won't let ours be as lippy as your brother, that's for certain."

"I'm not lippy," Asher shot back, genuinely affronted.

"And I'm not choosey, I don't *want* a mate," I said, articulating each word clearly in case he'd misheard me the first time.

That my parents had a problem with my dedication to staying single forever wasn't surprising. That they'd sent my dad's sixty-something-year-old golf buddy after me *was*.

I shouldn't be surprised.

Jules' heat was approaching soon, and she already had an alpha lined up to invite into her nest. If they managed to pair me off too, that would be a great distraction from The Calum Problem.

Jimmy gave me an indulgent smile like I'd just said the cutest thing he'd ever heard, and it immediately set my teeth on edge.

I wasn't a *cute* little omega. I was a grown-ass woman. I was accomplished. I had at least eighteen different knot-simulation dildos that would get me off with more success than this obnoxious alpha.

Chapter Two

"I appreciate you coming to collect them, but I'd be more comfortable keeping Chelsea and Asher here for the night. They've just gone through a tremendous shock, and I'm sure my parents would appreciate the break," I said stiffly. Who the fuck was this guy? I wasn't sending my baby siblings off with him, that was for sure.

"Oh yes," Asher added solemnly, valiantly attempting to look mournful. "I'm *very* sad on the inside. That's why I'm being so lippy. To cover up the pain."

I shot Asher my best *be quiet* look out of the corner of my eye, and he wrapped his arms around my waist with a dramatic sigh, leaning his head on my shoulder.

Jimmy grunted in acknowledgement, annoyance written all over his face. "Well, I suppose that makes sense. It's a credit to your maternal instincts that you take such good care of your siblings, Margot. I'll be seeing you soon."

And just like that, Calum dying suddenly wasn't the worst part of my day.

"You really are my favourite sister," Asher said around a mouthful of pancake. It was as though he hadn't demolished an entire pizza on his own last night. Teenagers were bottomless pits. "These are so good. I didn't know you could cook."

"I can feed myself," I corrected, because *cook* seemed like a bit of a stretch. I didn't make anything that didn't come with instructions—pancakes included.

The buzzer went off five times in quick succession, startling all of us.

"That's definitely Dad," Chelsea sighed, glaring at Asher until he started chewing with his mouth closed. "This will be fun."

"I've got this," I assured her, pushing away from the table as the buzzer went off again. "Get your things together, though. He's clearly not in a patient mood."

He was never in a patient mood, I added mentally, jogging down the stairs to meet him at the front door.

Dad usually looked perfectly put together at all times—built like a superhero with the overly polished aesthetic of a supervillain—he was a larger-than-life figure that loomed over me, both physically and metaphorically.

He didn't look like that today.

While Calum had acted mostly as a tormentor in mine and Asher's life—and Chelsea's to a lesser extent—he'd been my parents' most beloved son.

"They're just coming now," I said, breaking the tense silence when it looked as though Dad wasn't going to. "Are you, um, okay?"

We weren't a family who talked about feelings. I felt as uncomfortable asking as Dad looked at being asked. At least it had startled him out of his weird funk, and he was back to wearing the usual you-are-my-worst-daughter face he usually had around me.

"The situation with Calum has come at an unfortunate time. Your mother is very busy with the PTA at the kids' school, there are a lot of end-of-term activities she's involved in. And I'm up for a promotion, and you know my boss lives down the road. He'll hear about this."

"Yes," I agreed, confused about where this was going. "I imagine so. Speaking of school, the Sutton-Harris School is still really keen to interview Asher—"

"The scandal could ruin *everything*," Dad continued as though I hadn't spoken. "And while I'm doing my best to ensure the more, er, *unsavoury* elements of Calum's passing don't become public knowledge, I think it would be best to distract from it entirely."

"I'm not sure that's possible—"

"Jules' first heat is due soon, and Taytum seems certain that she'll be accompanying Jules into her nest." He paused to cut me a side-eye, a silent reminder of my failure to deliver on that front. "But Jules and Taytum have been together for so long that their mating is entirely expected."

The alarm bells in my head that usually operated on a low steady hum whenever I had to interact with my parents were now blaring at full force.

"What *would* be unexpected would be *you* inviting an alpha to your nest, Margot, after your failure with Fraser and your, shall we call it reticence, to pursue anything with an alpha ever since. It's been fourteen years, Margot. You need to stop pining over him. He's a happily mated alpha now."

I gaped at him for a long moment, too stunned to speak. Pining? *Pining*?

"I am not *pining* after Fraser," I spluttered. "That's not the reason—"

"Fortunately for you, Jimmy is willing to take you on. His omega died ten years ago, and it's taken him a while to feel ready for another mate, but now he is and I've assured him you'd be a manageable one."

"Manageable?" I choked out, more affronted than I'd been in years. "*Manageable?*"

"He also has grown children already, so if you're barren because of your advanced age, I doubt it will cause too many issues."

"People have babies at thirty-two all the time. Not that I will be having babies with him. I'm not mating him—"

"If you want Asher to go to that ridiculous art school, you will settle down and mate an alpha, Margot."

Shit.

Dad had me there and he knew it.

Before I could propose getting that in writing, the door at the top of the stairs opened, Asher and Chelsea's voices filling the stairwell as they bickered about who knows what.

"You will arrive together at Nana's 90th and announce your intention to go into your nest together there. The whole village will be there, and it will be an excellent distraction from Calum's absence."

"Ready," Asher said, stumbling into the wall as Chelsea elbowed him in the ribs, stomping past with her nose in the air. They were best friends and worst enemies, those two.

"Don't embarrass us again, Margot." And with those delightful parting words, my dad was gone.

There was no outfit that transitioned seamlessly from daytime funeral to eighteenth birthday party, I thought to myself, quickly stripping off my black sheath dress. Not that I had to get super dressed up for tonight, but I was going to help my friend Violet out with her hosting duties. The birthday girl was her little sister, who I barely knew.

I wasn't exactly in the mood for a party after Calum's rushed and uncomfortable burial, but I promised Violet I'd help. Of all the friends I had, Violet asked the least of me and was more than generous with her time. I couldn't disappoint her. Like me, she was the oldest sister, and having mated into money, she was always the default party host.

She'd never expect me to show up if she knew about Calum, which is why I hadn't said anything. I didn't want to put her out.

I put on my dressiest jeans, a slinky black top that I could still comfortably move around in and some sandals, adding enough make-up to look like I was making an effort but not so much that I couldn't get to work without worrying about turning into a shiny mess. On the way out the door, I grabbed a cardigan, since the unpredictable spring weather had swung from blistering hot afternoon to chilly evening, and made the familiar five-minute walk to Violet's home as the sun was setting.

"There you are!" Violet said, pulling the door open before I could even make it up the path. "I'm so glad you're here, I'm frantic."

"I'm so sorry, I should have come earlier—"

"No, no, I'm grateful you're helping at all. I thought Nico was going to be here to give me a hand, but his best friend booked a ticket home, and Nico's gone to pick him up from the airport." Violet blew a curly strand of red hair off her face, her freckled cheeks pink and usually spotless chequered apron covered in an assortment of mystery stains. "Apparently, he's had this trip planned for a while, but conveniently forgot to mention it to us until this morning. He's staying here as well—it was lucky the studio is empty at the moment," she grumbled, though she didn't actually sound that upset.

Violet *loved* to host. It was one of the few hobbies we didn't share. Attending a party was one thing, organising one was an entirely different beast.

"This is the photographer best friend?" I asked, slipping off my cardigan and purse, my eyes drifting over the collection of poster-sized framed photos that formed a gallery down the hallway, from the front door to the kitchen. I'd never met Kit Iyer—the in-demand, always-on-the-road travel photographer who specialised in incredible landscapes—but I'd been admiring his work every time I'd visited this house for the past two years, ever since Violet and I had met at our local yoga class after I'd moved to this part of the city.

"Kit, yeah. He hasn't been home for a couple of years now, and he's going to stay with us for a whole month. Nico is so excited."

"Is he really?" I teased. Nico was as stoic as they came.

"He doesn't *look* excited, but I promise he is on the inside," Violet laughed, wiping flour-stained hands on her apron, reminding me I was here for a reason.

"Put me to work," I instructed with a clap of my hands. "What do you need me to do?"

The next couple of hours passed in a blur as we finished up with the finger foods and stocked the makeshift bar. Even with my snobby upbringing, I thought it was a little over the top, but Violet's family had grown accustomed to her providing them with the finer things in life after she'd mated Nico—who had a fancy oil money job I still didn't understand—and she was a chronic people pleaser.

It was one of the many things we'd bonded over.

While Violet disappeared upstairs to shower and change, I set up fairy lights in the main living areas downstairs and cleaned the beautiful modernised kitchen. The conservatory extension that led into the back garden showed the sky was well and truly dark by now.

At least it kept me busy. If I was at home, I'd be running over the events of the past week in my head a million times, trying to pinpoint the exact moment in time when my brother had become an unredeemable monster and wondering what I could have done to change things.

"Oh, it looks amazing down here," Violet sighed, fussing with her boobs in the little black dress she had put on as she reentered the kitchen-dining space, undoubtedly eager for Nico to get back and ease her discomfort. "I'm so sorry you had to do so much on your own. Nico messaged and said they're on their way back, but traffic is terrible."

"It's really no trouble. You and Nico have practically adopted me since I moved in down the street, this is really the least I can do."

Violet waved off my gratitude as she always did. She and Nico were different from the other friends I had. They were always so conscious of my time and doing things for me, and never expected anything in return, or let me pay them back no matter how much I tried. If I thought about it too much, I got a little weepy.

Not that I minded doing things for other people. I didn't. Really.

Sometimes, it was just nice to not have any expectations of me though.

"I can't wait for you to meet Kit. It just *feels* like you should already know each other, you know? It really hammers home how long he's been away when I think about the fact that the two of you have never crossed paths." Violet shook her head, smiling a little sadly to herself. "Nico has so few friends that he genuinely connects with, it's a shame that Kit is always on the road."

"He's unmated, right?"

It was only with Violet that I would dare to ask that question. Anyone else would have read something into it, but I'd told her about my history, and she understood my stance on mating perfectly. There was no needy, desperate omega within me, slavering over whatever single alpha crossed her path. Those days were long gone.

Besides, we attended the same fuckfests at Bryce and Kane's house each month. Violet knew I was more than comfortable taking what I needed from an alpha then going home and getting on with my life.

"He is. Kit is very happily single by choice." She gave me a significant look. "I really think you guys are going to get on great."

The doorbell rang as the oven timer went off, and I gestured for Violet to go greet her guests while I moved to get the bacon-wrapped asparagus out of the oven.

"You're incredible, Margot. Have I mentioned I'd be lost without you?"

"You'd have been fine," I replied over my shoulder. "You're such a natural hostess, I'm the one who has no idea what they're doing."

Violet had written out cooking instructions for everything on the menu, and I was following them to the letter. If I'd been in charge of food, everyone would be eating crackers straight from the packet with a wheel of brie, elegantly presented on the paper it came wrapped in.

Less cleanup.

"I'm glad you have one weakness or I'd wonder if you were even human," Violet teased, heading down the hall.

It had taken me months to be convinced that Violet wasn't mocking me when she said stuff like that. She was just so genuinely sweet that she didn't seem to notice flaws the way regular people did.

I hung around in the kitchen as more people arrived, saying hello to those I recognised but very much using the excuse of restocking empty platters and filling drink glasses as an excuse to avoid getting pulled into conversations.

Usually, I'd be right in the middle of it, but I just couldn't quite swing it today. I couldn't swing *Accomplished* Margot today. Sociable, organised, charming, put-together Margot who was always on top of her to-do list as well as everyone else's. *Tomorrow.*

"Margot," Nico said, eyebrows raising in surprise as he rounded the kitchen island and leaned in for an air kiss. "What are you doing here?"

Compared to the guests, he looked exceptionally casual in jeans and a polo shirt, his dark hair unstyled and a thick layer of stubble covering his jaw. It was always jarring to see Casual Nico since he usually lived in suits and hair gel.

I blinked at him in confusion, finally registering his question. "Helping Violet. Remember? I offered to help her out in the kitchen a couple of weeks ago at dinner—"

"No, I know—thank you for that, by the way—but I mean *now*. You should be relaxing, enjoying the party. What are you drinking? Go sit down, I'll bring you a glass."

"It's really fine," I assured him with a wry smile. *Bossy alpha*. Nico wasn't much of a talker unless he was speaking to Violet, so he really must be concerned to string that many words together in a row. "I'm not in a super chatty mood if I'm honest. I'm happy right here."

He frowned. "You're always in a chatty mood."

"Did you get your friend from the airport okay?" I asked, hoping he'd let me change the subject.

"I did." Nico glanced out at the back garden, to the small studio they had at the back of the property, a meagre amount of light shining through the front windows. "Kit doesn't much like... these things, but he'll pop in at some point."

"He doesn't much like parties? How are you two friends?" I teased. Nico was quiet and gruff, but he liked being quiet and gruff in the middle of a crowded room.

Nico snorted. "There are a lot of young, unmated omegas here. It can get overwhelming for him, being so popular."

"Ah." No further explanation necessary. Nico and Kit were friends from school, so presumably the same age. Since most alphas and omegas didn't make it past twenty without bonding, the older, established, and successful alphas were a hot commodity. Violet's younger sister and her friends were exactly in the right age range to be interested.

It worked in reverse for omegas. My best breeding years were already behind me, and I was fine with that. Like a bottle of expensive wine being saved for a special occasion that never arrived, I was decidedly on the shelf.

Nico gave me a long look. "You're usually much chattier."

"Long day, nothing to worry about." I waved him off. "Go, socialise. Host. I'll be fine here, I promise." I all but shooed him out of his own kitchen before turning all of my attention to topping up the stacks of napkins that Violet had set out on all the surfaces downstairs, noting which hors d'oeuvres needed replenishing.

It wasn't until my third trip into the living room, carrying a fresh platter of cheese puffs, that I was greeted by a wave of L'Eau d'Unmated Omega strong enough to choke on. There were seven unmated omegas here—myself included—and all six of the others were clustered in one square metre of space in the corner of Nico and Violet's living room, pheromoning away.

I didn't need to see the armchair they were blocking to know why.

Kit Iyer.

If this was a normal response to Kit walking into a room, then Nico really hadn't been exaggerating about it getting overwhelming. I almost felt sorry for Kit for a moment before I remembered literally every alpha I'd ever met. He probably loved the attention.

Not quite able to stifle my curiosity, I shuffled a little closer, peering through the omega blockade for a glimpse of the bulky, muscular example of alpha virility who was undoubtedly preening under their admiration.

I wasn't entirely wrong.

Kit certainly had the typical alpha bulk—tall, broad, definitely virile— but with the added appeal of hot nerd to go with it. Brown skin, black hair that curled up at the ends, fitted dark shirt and jeans, glasses with practical-yet-sexy black frames... Tick, tick, *tick*. No wonder the omegas were rushing for him like he was an end-of-season sale at a designer nest supply store.

There was no preening happening, though.

Despite Kit's impressive size, he seemed to be making himself as small as possible in the armchair, leaning as far to one side as he could. His responses to whatever his crowd of admirers was saying were polite, if not a little clipped, and he wasn't making eye contact with any of them.

I've never met a shy alpha before, I mused, watching as he politely rebuffed a particularly pushy omega. We may not be friends yet, but I hoped we would be through Nico and Violet, and friends didn't let friends stew in discomfort in the corner.

"Kit?" I asked, leaning around a couple of giggling omegas to speak to him. "Could you give me a hand?"

He blinked at me in surprise, and I noticed what a spectacular colour his eyes were. I had brown eyes too, but his were a melting pot of every shade of brown, and mine were dried mud. Another one of life's winners of the genetic jackpot.

"Unless you'd rather stay," I added, giving him an out in case he was secretly enjoying all the attention and just had a really weird way of showing it. "I need to bring in some of the beer boxes from outside."

"No, no, of course. I'm coming." He jumped up, inching around his crowd of admirers, careful not to scentmark any of them with his touch. I hadn't been able to pick up much of his scent over the cloying bouquet of unmated omega before—very much the reason why I doused myself in Om-Guard multiple times a day—but as soon as he broke away from the group, the hints of smoked coffee and whiskey were clear and *delicious*.

After he was so careful not to touch the others, I nearly jumped out of my skin when his large, warm hand landed in the centre of my back for no discernible reason since I was the one ushering him, not the other way around.

"The good ones are always taken," one of the omegas behind us lamented loudly as Kit followed behind me, not correcting the omega's assumption as we headed into the kitchen.

Oh. Perhaps that was his reason. I supposed if he wanted to use me as an omega shield to hide behind, I was fine with that.

Kit dropped his hand the moment we were out of view, and I yanked open the back door, immediately met by a rush of cold air that my slinky top did nothing to protect me from. The dark, still garden and cool night air were refreshing after being in a crowded room filled with scents—those six omegas alone were pumping out enough pheromones to fill a stadium.

"Just here," I said, gesturing at the stack of boxes we'd piled next to the house earlier when we'd run out of fridge space before wrapping my arms around my waist to preserve body heat and hide my nipple beacons.

"Oh." Kit looked briefly surprised before grabbing a box with ease. "There are actually boxes here."

I stared at him for a moment, only a little sidetracked by how put together he looked. Hadn't he just got off a plane?

"Yes, there are actually boxes here. Why would there not be?"

"I thought you were just making up an excuse to, you know."

"To... give you a breather?" I suggested, shuffling around him to pick up two of the lighter packs of sugary vodka that Violet's little sister favoured.

"To get me alone," Kit amended, his expression perfectly serious. Like it was a completely normal, rational thing to stay.

I burst out laughing before I could help myself. Oh, to be an alpha. I couldn't even imagine wandering through life with such unfettered confidence. No wonder my brother had turned into a psychopath.

Chapter Three

"You *are* an unmated omega, right?" Kit asked, sounding less certain now. "Your scent isn't very strong."

"I am," I gasped, still shaking with silent laughter. "Ergo, the only reason I could possibly ask for assistance was to try to get you alone? Why did you even follow me out here?"

Kit squirmed, a very un-alpha response. It was kind of charming. "Well, I figured it'd be easier to shake off one of you than six."

I set down one pack of drinks, swiping beneath my eyes with my knuckle in the hopes that the tears of laughter hadn't done too much damage to my mascara. It wouldn't—I splurged on the good stuff these days. I could go deep-sea diving in this mascara and it wouldn't budge.

"Well, there's certainly good logic in that. I'm sorry, I shouldn't laugh. I don't think it's funny that you're relentlessly pursued by single omegas—that must be exhausting—just that you assumed *I* was pursuing you." I shook my head, bewildered at this whole conversation. "I didn't drag you out here with nefarious intent—the boxes are genuinely heavy, and you looked like you needed a break."

Maybe it was just that the past few days had felt so bleak that I found the idea that Kit thought I was going to jump his bones in my best friend's back garden so ludicrously hilarious. Did I seem that desperate? Was that why Dad had sicced Jimmy on me? That idea was a little grim, but I was plenty used to disregarding alphas' opinions of me.

"Anyway, if you could just put that box down on the counter so I could refill the fridge, that'd be great."

"I shouldn't have assumed," he mumbled, picking up two boxes—*show off*—and heading for the back door. I grabbed the vodkas again, following. "I'm guessing you know Violet and Nico pretty well, since you're so comfortable in their kitchen."

He started so suddenly that I almost ran into his back, twisting to look at me. "You're Margot. Violet's new friend."

"Not that new. You've been gone a while," I pointed out softly.

"Right. Yeah. It's been a while."

Kit wasn't much of a talker either. Did he and Nico just sit together in silence when they hung out?

He took a deep, steadying breath right before he got to the door, as though he was about to march into battle rather than a birthday party hosted by one of his oldest friends.

For all my late nights in my early twenties wishing I was more desirable, I'd never really considered the downsides of being a babe magnet. There was something to be said for being forgettable.

"You know, you could help restock the bottles if you need another minute. People tend to give you more space if you look busy."

Kit glanced back at me over his shoulder. Were those boxes even heavy to him? He didn't look like he was struggling at all. "Is that what you were doing?"

"That *is* what I'm doing, yes. If you want to hang out here a little longer on your own, I won't bother you, but I'm a few seconds away from getting hypothermia, so I might need to squeeze past you if that's—"

Kit yanked open the door before I could finish speaking, stepping back for me to pass him, and I wasted no time in heading back into the cosy house. I'd been exaggerating slightly, it wasn't *that* cold, but I must have accidentally prodded an alpha instinct.

Kit took me up on my offer, occupying himself with opening a box of beers and loading the empty shelves in the fridge before heading outside to grab a third box that I was pretty confident wouldn't fit.

I left him to it, mixing a new jar of the blackcurrant cocktail Violet had come up with especially for tonight and chatting to a few familiar faces as they passed through the kitchen. I'd assumed that Kit would know Violet's family too, but perhaps he'd only spent time with Nico's.

By the time I finished discussing the change in ownership of the local pub with Violet's uncle—bad, we both agreed—Kit was leaning against the counter, staring at me like I'd just kicked his puppy.

"What?"

"You *like* people. People like *you*."

"I can't decide if you're complimenting me or insulting me. Maybe both?"

"You know what I mean." Kit gestured vaguely at the dining table, where two of the omegas from before had migrated to, watching him out of the corner of their eyes while they whispered to each other, occasionally giving me an assessing look. "I thought we were both avoiding social interaction, but you *like* socialising."

He said as though it was a grave insult.

"I see. And you feel betrayed by this?"

Kit's stare turned withering. *Rein it in, Margot.* Just because I had a fun, teasing relationship with Nico and Violet didn't mean Kit would appreciate the same.

"At the risk of sounding obnoxious, I'm usually *great* fun at parties. I'm just having a bad week, that's all. Hence the hiding out in the kitchen."

Kit blinked. "Then why'd you come?"

"I promised Violet weeks ago that I'd help out, and I wasn't about to let her down. I'd given her my word, I couldn't just leave her in the lurch..." I was rambling, I knew I was, but just mentioning my *bad week* had brought a rush of all the feelings I'd been trying to suppress to the fore.

Oh dear. There was a distinct *wobbly* feeling in my lower lip that absolutely would not stand. *No, no crying. Pull yourself together.*

Shit. He'd definitely spotted the wobble.

"You should sit down for a minute."

"You sound like Nico," I replied, shooting for breezy and landing flat. "Alphas are so bossy."

Kit didn't acknowledge that, just herded me into the living room, his fingers just barely brushing my shoulders, touching me as little as possible.

There was a wooden bench in the corner that was more decorative than comfortable, which at least meant it was private, but as soon as we sat down, and our legs angled towards each other, I realised how incredibly *small* it was. Or perhaps just how large Kit was. He leaned towards me, and the movement all but obscured me from the rest of the room.

"Aren't you worried this is some ploy to get you alone?" I teased, because it was feeling sort of awkward being this confined with a stranger.

"Is it?" Kit asked gruffly, raising an eyebrow at me over the rim of his glasses, switching back to Skeptical Mode with apparent ease.

I wasn't sure why he was being nice to me at all—he clearly had a deep-seated mistrust of single omegas.

"Yes. I did all this to get you alone, so I could be the sole recipient of your glares."

He responded with a deeper glare—something new and different—and I used the brief reprieve to take a few steadying breaths, finding that sense of peace within myself and encouraging it to the forefront of my mind.

I didn't even *want* to be sad over Calum. The grief of losing the brother I'd grown up with was something I'd already dealt with years ago, back when he'd presented as an alpha. What I was experiencing now was more akin to guilt, I decided.

Guilt that I somehow hadn't stopped him from turning into the alpha he'd become. Guilt that he was my brother, and I was glad he was dead and couldn't hurt anyone else.

"Are you going to cry? Should I go get Violet?"

"No." I managed a watery laugh. "Please don't. I don't want to put a damper on her night—she's worked really hard planning this party."

Kit nodded. My shoulder was resting against the wall behind us, and he leaned forward to rest his forearm on his thigh. It looked as though we were intimately close, but I was pretty sure he was just giving me some privacy from the rest of the room.

He smelled *really* good. Like an expensive Irish Coffee, if Irish Coffee could *fuck*.

Bad Margot. I really hoped Bryce and Kane were going to host another party soon—I clearly needed to get laid.

"Do you want to talk about it?"

"You don't want to hear about it," I replied drily. "It's not a happy story. And I'm sure you don't want to spend your evening holed up in the corner with me—"

"It's fine. I'd rather sit here and listen to your sad story than be harangued by the other omegas," Kit said absently, glancing over his shoulder at an omega who was shooting him bedroom eyes from the doorway.

What a dick.

I wasn't entirely without an ego, and even Accomplished Margot could be petty from time to time.

"My brother died a few days ago," I said with an extra pitiful dramatic sigh.

Kit made a strangled sound, hit squarely with the force of the awkwardness I'd been aiming at him.

"Oh. Shit. Um. I'm sorry." Kit shifted, twisting to get a better view of my face. "I didn't mean... Do you want to go home? I can borrow Nico's car."

Damn it, he was going to be nice. Now I felt bad for deliberately provoking him.

"I live down the road. I'll walk after I've helped Violet pack up." I flicked my hand dismissively, and he narrowed his eyes at my sudden change in mood. "I'm sorry, I shouldn't have dropped that bomb on you. I usually have much better social skills, I promise. I didn't even like my brother. I'm fine, really."

"Are you?"

The question gave me pause. Perhaps because no one had ever asked me before. I was a practical omega, I got on with things and did what needed to be done. Generally, if I said I was fine, people took me at my word.

"Sure. Why not? Calum wasn't a *good* alpha. It was his own actions that sent him to the grave, and while I miss the sweet boy he used to be, he was *not* a sweet man."

"That doesn't mean you're okay," Kit pointed out, as gently as I thought it was possible for him to be. He didn't strike me as the talk-about-your-feelings type, and we were probably only hiding here because it was convenient for him, but I appreciated the gesture, nonetheless.

"I'm... well, I *will* be okay. My parents aren't taking it well. He was the only alpha out of the six of us. Do you have any siblings?" I asked, desperate to change the subject.

Kit shook his head. "It's just me."

I got the feeling there was a lot more to that statement than he let on, but maybe he wasn't the type to unload his emotional sob story to a stranger at a party for no discernable reason.

Usually, I wasn't either.

It's just the sleep deprivation, I told myself. After a good night's rest, I'd be back to normal.

"Oh, thank fuck, Margot. You're finally sitting down," Nico said, winding through the crowd to join us. Kit and I broke apart hastily—not that there was anywhere to go on the tiny bench—both facing forward as Nico came to a stop in front of us. "I see you two have met, good. I was going to introduce you earlier, but Kit was already surrounded by a flock."

Kit shot him an irritated look. "Which Margot rescued me from, unlike you, leaving me out to dry."

"I would have thought you were an expert at extricating yourself from those situations by now," Nico replied, eyebrows raised.

Kit scoffed. "We're both a little partied out. I was just about to walk Margot home."

He turned and gave me an expectant look while I felt my eyebrows shoot up to my hairline. "Oh. But I'm going to help Violet with cleanup, remember—"

"Absolutely not," Nico interjected. "You've helped us so much today, go and rest. You seem tired."

"Just a busy week," I replied, reflexively justifying why I wasn't on my A game. Kit's eyes burned into the side of my face, but now really wasn't the time to bring up Calum. "If you're sure you don't need me, then maybe I will head off. I can walk on my own though."

Both alphas objected to that because it was dark out and instincts were a hell of a drug. Eventually I agreed with an exasperated sigh that Kit could accompany me down the road.

"I don't want to interrupt her," I told Nico, watching Violet tell a story to a group of her sister's friends that had them all laughing. "Will you tell Violet I said bye and that the party was amazing?"

"Of course," Nico agreed. "Thank you again for everything. We'd be lost without you, Margot."

I waved him off, grabbing my purse and pulling on my cardigan, conscious of Kit shadowing my every step. Generally, I wasn't a fan of strange alphas crowding my space, but he was a close friend of Nico's, and Nico was one of my best friends. I trusted him with my life.

The tightness in my chest relaxed a little more as soon as we were outside, and I at least felt confident that I wasn't about to burst into tears at any moment.

"It was kind of you to help Violet with the party." His voice was filled with suspicion, which I found oddly hilarious. Apparently, satisfied I wasn't on the edge of a breakdown, he was back to seeing me as an enemy omega.

"I'm not a kind person, really. I'm a lawyer—total shark, in fact," I informed him primly. "I just happen to like Nico and Violet."

Kit cut me a side-eye, heading down the street towards my flat at my side.

"Yes. Total shark. Very believable."

"I am," I insisted. "I have quite the fearsome reputation in the world of restructuring and insolvency."

"I find that impossible to believe," Kit said flatly. "I'm struggling to believe you're a lawyer at all."

I tutted. "First the assumption that I only wanted to get you alone, and now this. On behalf of lawyers and omegas everywhere, I am offended by the stereotyping."

Kit opened his mouth to reply before closing it again, his cheeks flushing red.

"I'm joking," I assured him. "Well, I'm kind of joking—you really should work on the whole stereotyping thing. Anyway, here we are. Told you it wasn't far."

Kit grumbled something, rubbing the back of his neck as we approached my house.

"You're very... unexpected," Kit managed eventually, having given it some thought before landing on that word. Perhaps he'd initially been considering a more offensive one?

I was going to reply, to tease him a little more, but a faint scent that absolutely *didn't* belong had the words dying in my throat. Cautiously, I made my way up the short path, freezing when I saw the bouquet of red roses sitting on the stoop. The scent of alpha clung to the front door, as though he'd been leaning against it, but there was no question in my mind that the action had been deliberate. Jimmy had been scentmarking my *home*.

"Friend of yours?" Kit asked quietly, making me jump. I'd forgotten he was even there.

"Friend of my parents actually," I mumbled, silently cursing them again six ways from Sunday for giving Jimmy my address. I grabbed the flowers, hastily shoving them in the bin and slamming the lid down. "Anyway, thanks for walking me home, you really didn't have to."

It was rude, but I was unsettled, and desperately wanted to get into the shower and wash off all the scents of the day before cocooning myself in the safety of my nest. "Nice meeting you, Kit. I hope you enjoy your time at home."

Chapter Four

"I don't know what to do, *Margot. You know what Kev's mother is like—* she hates *my cooking, but now Kev is saying that his mum is right and it's poor form for an omega to insist on having takeout whenever the family come round, and that if I was a* good *omega..."*

I tuned out slightly, Michelle's complaints still coming through my headphones loud and clear as I went through the supermarket aisles, checking items off my list and the Clarksons' list as I added them to the trolley. Mrs Clarkson had bad hips, and Mr Clarkson got overwhelmed by the fluorescent lights and digital payments, so I did most of their shopping for them. It was blessedly early in the morning—my favourite time to run errands since no one was around—but Michelle's family drama never slept.

"I just can't cook a decent meal. No matter what recipes I follow, they don't turn out right. And the kids are a nightmare when I'm in the kitchen—they just want my attention the whole time and it's madness. What would you do, Margot?"

I wouldn't have mated a selfish alpha like Kev, I thought wryly, but there was no benefit in saying that out loud. What was done was done, and Michelle—who'd been the receptionist at the first firm I'd worked at—was stuck with Kev now, for better or for worse.

Kev, whose mother had never cut the umbilical cord, had been waiting outside Michelle's nest once her heat had ended, glaring at the omega who'd dared to snag her precious baby boy. Three grandchildren later, Kev's mother still had a bone to pick with Michelle.

This was why I knew I wasn't the nice person Kit had accused me of being. If I was nice, I wouldn't feel frustrated at having to listen to Michelle repeat the same three problems every few days.

"Why don't I ask Violet for some recipes you can prepare in advance? I think part of it is that you can't relax with Kev's mother breathing down your neck," I replied absently, selecting some different types of nuts off the shelf. My heat was due in the next few weeks, and I knew from experience that it was even more unpleasant if I hadn't upped my protein intake beforehand.

"Oh my gosh, what a great idea! Ooh, I'd love to see the look on Jenny's smug face when I set a delicious meal down on the table that I cooked myself. She'll be kicking herself for all that stuff she said."

I highly doubted that. Even if Michelle was the perfect homemaker who grew her own vegetables and baked her own bread and hand-poured her own scented candles, Jenny would still find reasons to complain about her.

"I'll message Violet now, I'm just going to go pay. I'll talk to you later, okay?"

"You're the best, Margot. I'd be lost without you!"

I shook my head slightly, quickly going through the checkout and packing my things into my rolling bag so I could drag them home. I fired off a quick text to Violet before heading home, the quiet morning streets only just now starting to fill up as more weekend workers headed for the station and kids shouted at each other from across the street.

A wave of something akin to grief hit me as I watched a young alpha teen carefully tearing a pasty to give half to his smaller omega sister. There had been glimpses of Calum's alpha instincts manifesting as protectiveness for his siblings—he'd been the one to half drag, half carry me away from that horrible pool party all those years ago—but they'd been few and far between.

When had he become so twisted? Had the potential for that kind of darkness been within him all along?

I fired off a quick message to check on Asher. I'd managed to delay the art school by letting them know Asher's older brother had died, but I'd need to get back to them with a date for the entry interview soon.

I couldn't even contemplate Dad's ultimatum to invite Jimmy to my nest, but I couldn't contemplate denying Asher the opportunity to attend Sutton-Harris either. He hadn't heard Dad's demand, and I'd never tell him about it. Asher didn't need that pressure on him.

Asher: I'm fine. Jules is practically living with her almost-mate with Mum & Dad's blessing. I'm trying to convince them to let me sign up for more extracurriculars. Get me out of the house more.

I sighed heavily. That sounded like he'd already given up on Sutton-Harris.

Me: Let me message Mum and Dad and see if I can take you and Chels out today. I wish I could do more.

I switched to the chat with my mum, always optimistically messaging her first even though she always let Dad handle replies.

Dad: Not today. We're going to the Nicholson's house for lunch. Their alpha son is Chelsea's age.

I rolled my eyes hard enough to pull a pupil. They were so ridiculous. I couldn't recall the Nicholsons at all, but all of the kids in that community went to the same school. If there was something between Chelsea and their son, they would have undoubtedly discovered before an awkwardly forced family lunch date.

Me: Sorry, kiddo. Apparently, you guys are off playing matchmaker for Chelsea at lunch today.

Asher: Gross. Justin Nicholson smells like feet.

He may not have smelled like feet to Chelsea—what appealed to one omega didn't appeal to another, thankfully, or we'd all be fighting over the same handful of alphas.

I turned off the street up the path to my house, and was so absorbed in my phone, I nearly crashed nose-first into a very solid chest. Only Kit's quick steps saved me from being covered in whatever was in the two cherry blossom-print reusable coffee cups I recognised from Violet's kitchen that he was carrying.

Kit's t-shirt and jeans were rumpled, and his dark hair was damp and curling at the ends. He looked more relaxed, and a little messier, than he had last night, and *oof*. There was no denying that Kit Iyer was Prime Beef Alpha. It was no wonder he had omegas throwing their slick-coated panties at him whenever they were in his presence.

"You've already been to the shops? Violet said you were an early riser, but I didn't know the supermarket was even open at seven in the morning."

He had a really nice morning voice too. All raspy, like he'd just spent the night hoarsely whispering filthy things in his lover's ear while impaling them on his knot.

I blinked, trying to shove that intrusive thought back into the horny box it had come from. *Bad Margot. Stop objectifying your future friend.*

It was probably just my upcoming heat making me view all unmated alphas through slick-tinted glasses.

"It's open twenty-four hours, and I don't like wasting daylight," I replied, eyeing the coffee as I caught a hint of the scent. It *smelled* like one of Violet's Margot Coffees. "You're up early yourself. And hanging around my front door."

Between Kit now and Jimmy last night, my front door had never seen so much alpha attention.

"Jet lag." Kit awkwardly thrust a coffee cup at me. "This is for you."

"That was very sweet and unnecessary of Violet, but thank you." I took a sip of the white chocolate oat milk mocha, savouring the perfect balance of flavours, grateful for the caffeine, and increasingly confused about why Kit was here. "Did you just come by to drop off coffee?"

"No."

Well, alright then. I gave him a few extra seconds to see if any kind of explanation was forthcoming, but apparently not.

"...Do you want to come upstairs?"

"Yes."

I went to pick up the rolling bag of groceries, but Kit beat me to it with a vaguely insulted look. If only scientists could figure out how to bottle alpha pride—there was nothing quite like it.

He hung back as I unlocked the downstairs door that led to a landing, the Clarksons' door to our right and the stairs in front of us that led up to my place.

"Hold on," I instructed, pulling the small cloth bag of items I'd picked up for the elderly beta couple and setting it down in front of their door with a knock so they knew I'd delivered it. I closed the rolling bag, happily letting Kit haul it up the stairs behind me, unlocking the door and holding it for him to follow. If I thought it was small before, the whole place looked like a dollhouse with Kit standing in it.

The kitchen and living area were one open space, and I gestured at the small two-seater cafe table by the window that overlooked the courtyard below since the only other option was the small loveseat.

I loved my teeny flat, though. The bare bones of the place—the paint, the kitchen bench and cupboards that ran along one wall—were all the same shade of inoffensive eggshell, though the polished wood floors warmed it up a little. I'd gone to town on decorating though, favouring bold shades of dark teal, golden mustard and blush pink. Big, statement colours paired with vintage wooden furniture to create the antithesis of the beige and white mansion I'd grown up in.

"Nice place," Kit said, his gaze pausing on the stylised painting of Princess Matilda that hung pride of place over the couch. Asher had eschewed the more stylised version of Princess Matilda that seemed to have gained popularity in recent years, painting her closer to how firsthand sources had described her—a 'plain bluestocking'. Basically, a not particularly beautiful woman of intellectual pursuits.

She was my idol.

She was the idol of unbeautiful omegas the world over.

Kit took a seat, clutching his coffee like a lifeline, and I threw open the window next to the dining table for both of our comforts. Between the air purifiers and the amount of scentshield lotion I used, only my nest really smelled like me, but one could never be too careful.

"So... this is nice," I said, giving him a pointed look as I unloaded the cold items and put them away. "I love spending time with you. Nothing odd about it at all."

Kit gave me a wry look, though it quickly turned nervous. "I'm back in London for an awards thing in a few weeks' time. I'm nominated for something. A photography thing."

"You're nominated for a photography award?" I asked, translating his nervous mumbles. Kit nodded, twisting his cup between his hands. I left the rest of the groceries for later, coming to sit opposite him.

"I don't come home often, so when I do, there are always a lot of invitations to things. People who want to catch up with me." There was another long pause, and I sipped my coffee, giving Kit a moment to gather his thoughts. He was sort of fascinating to watch. Alphas were usually all blustering confidence—talk first, engage brain later. Kit was the total opposite. "My career isn't compatible with having an omega mate. I'm fine with that. Other people in my life aren't fine with that."

I nodded. "I don't know where you're going with this, but sure. That's something I can relate to."

"Violet said as much." Kit glanced up at me before returning his attention to his apparently fascinating coffee cup. "Those roses outside your house last night..."

I paused, mid-sip. "What about them?"

"They were from an alpha. And you didn't seem too happy about them."

"Not particularly. *Where* are you going with this?" Generally, I was pretty good at reading social situations, but this one had me totally stumped.

"I think we could help each other out," Kit said eventually.

"Oh." I watched him for a long moment, feeling myself frown. "*How*?"

Kit blushed, and it was offensively endearing.

"Maybe you could be my plus one to a few events while I'm in town. Some social stuff. The awards night. If my friends and family think I'm pursuing an omega, they won't harangue me about settling down and choosing a mate, and I could actually enjoy going out again. Like last night."

"Last night was enjoyable for you?" I asked doubtfully. Then again, maybe some people enjoyed impromptu breakdowns from strangers.

"After you pulled me away from that group, yeah. Your sad company was preferable to all of... that."

"Stop it, you. I can't take all this flattery."

He winced slightly, perhaps realising his words had been a tad indelicate. "I didn't mean it like... I just mean that I'm always surrounded. And Nico and Violet didn't set me up—they never do—but I know there'll be single omegas with expectations in their heads about me if I visit any other friends or family here, no matter how many times I tell them I'm *not interested*."

Kit looked as surprised by the sudden vehemence of his words as I felt.

I sighed, leaning back in my chair. "I can't relate to the attendant problems of being super popular. I do understand what it's like to have people in your life not accept your answer as final."

Kit suddenly had a look in his eye that reminded me of a hound who'd just latched onto a scent. "Exactly. That's why we should help each other. You said that alpha who left flowers was a friend of your parents'. I could warn him off, alpha to alpha."

A metaphorical pissing contest for possession of me, the hapless omega.

That was basically what he meant, and it annoyed me that a small very omega-y part of me thought that was kind of awesome.

And while scaring off Jimmy would be convenient, I had a far better use for a temporary alpha.

Whatever Kit saw on my face, he must have thought he had me right where he wanted me.

"I'll show up here each day and rub myself over your front door like an oversized cat," he pressed, his mouth flicking up oh-so-slightly at the corners while I snorted at the visual. "And you be my omega shield at social functions for the next few weeks, ending with the awards night. We both win."

"How many social functions are we talking? I can't just drop everything to be your date, you know."

That was a lie—the end of spring was always a quiet time in my social calendar because of my impending heat. I wasn't about to announce that to a near-stranger, though. Kit was Nico's friend and undoubtedly a good guy, but pre-heat was still an omega's prime kidnapping window and we were alone. Better to be safe than ransomed off to the highest alpha bidder.

"Just drinks at the pub with some friends, and the awards night. And a weekend away in Brighton," he added under his breath, mumbling into the lid of his coffee cup.

I raised an eyebrow at him. "A whole weekend away acting like a couple? I'm not sure either of us are good enough actors to pull that off."

Kit grimaced. "It's still a few weeks away. We could hang out in the meantime. Get… used to each other."

"I'm sure we will anyway since you're staying with Nico and Violet." I drummed my nails against the side of the cup. "I have an event of my own that I need a date for."

Kit shrugged. "Fair is fair."

"You don't know what it entails yet."

"I doubt you're asking more of me than an entire weekend away."

"You don't negotiate a lot of contracts, do you?" I asked, shaking my head. "Always clarify terms. That's like… the first rule of negotiating."

"Fine, fine. Tell me about the event, then."

I raised my chin, staring him down until he lost some of the attitude. From my professional life, I knew that alphas were like dogs—it was important to establish dominance right off the bat if you wanted to have a productive working relationship.

"Please," Kit tacked on begrudgingly.

"I need you to come to my Nana's 90th birthday party." Kit nodded, bored. "And I need you to stand by my side and look agreeable while I announce my intention to take you into my nest at my next heat."

Kit's jaw went slack.

"This is why you should always clarify terms," I chided, taking another sip of my coffee. You didn't need my expensive law school education to know that.

"*Why*?" Kit spluttered. "Why? Why do you want to do that?"

"I don't *want* to. I'm perfectly happy living my best single life. But that alpha who left the roses was sent by my dad, and I'm supposed to announce my intention to take *him* into my nest at that party."

Kit looked stricken. "That's really messed up. My mum always throws omegas at me, but it's more in a… maybe-this-will-take-off kind of way."

"They've never been this pushy in the past. They never really expected me to find a mate before now." For reasons that were even more hurtful, and solidly rooted in fact. "But they have something I want."

I glanced up at Asher's painting, blown away by his talent every time I saw it. Of the six of us, he was the only one who had an artistic bone in his body. I wanted him to be free to pursue his dreams, to have all of the opportunities he deserved.

"Obviously, I don't expect you to follow through on the mating part. Once I clear the announcement hurtle, I'll figure out the next steps on my own."

Kit was looking more dark and brooding than ever, so I pasted on my best and brightest smile. The one that screamed 'I'm fine, you can be fine too' in big neon letters.

"So, are we doing this? Or is my asking price too steep?"

"I guess, so long as you aren't expecting me to follow through, it's not too steep," Kit said slowly.

"Don't worry, I won't ruin your reputation when I emerge from my heat alone." I winked, pretending it was just a funny joke and that I hadn't been jilted once before. "I'll take the blame for it all falling apart."

"No, I don't want that. We'll tell everyone it was a mutual decision. It sounds like we've got a deal."

Kit rubbed the back of his neck, and I *almost* didn't look at the way his bicep bulged all prettily underneath his shirt.

Almost.

And that was the real glaring hole in this whole plan. Would people actually believe we were a couple?

I didn't think I was some hideous swamp creature. Maybe I had in the aftermath of The Terrible Thing, when my self-esteem was in the dirt and I was constantly compared to my siblings, but not now.

I was no natural beauty, but I knew how to make myself feel sexy in my own skin, even if it was the kind of sexy that relied heavily on skin treatments, fake tan, make-up, and a positive relationship with my hair stylist.

Kit, on the other hand, looked like a cover model for Sexy Nerd Alphas Weekly, and I was pretty sure he'd rolled out of bed and shoved on the first clothes he'd found before wandering over here.

Had he even washed his face this morning? Did he even moisturise? Did his face just *look* like that?

Life was truly unfair.

"There are drinks at a pub in the city planned for tonight with my school friends," Kit was saying, and I forced myself to stop ogling and pay attention. "It's short notice, and I know that with everything you've had going on—"

"Distractions are always welcome," I cut in quickly. I didn't want to spend my Saturday night stewing at home in the swamp of sadness and anger I'd been in for the past few days. Until last night, really. "Will Nico be there? You know each other from school, right?"

Kit's expression turned thoughtful, which may have been my favourite look on him. "We do, and he does know them, but I doubt he'll be there. Nico doesn't spend as much time around them these days for some reason."

On reflection, I hadn't even heard Nico *mention* any school friends other than Kit, but he also wasn't the most verbose guy.

"Speaking of Nico and Violet," Kit continued, giving me a long look. "Obviously, we won't be pretending in front of them, they know us too well. And you haven't told them about your brother."

"Did you?" It wasn't as though I was *never* going to tell them. I just hadn't got around to it. It wasn't exactly a fun topic of conversation.

"Of course not. It's not my place. They speak really highly of you, though. Violet kept telling me what a great friend you are and singing your praises while she made your coffee this morning—"

"Are you trying to make me feel guilty?"

"No." Kit looked so startled by the notion that I couldn't *not* believe him. "I just… If you needed someone to talk to, or to help you, Violet and Nico would drop everything to be there for you."

That wasn't their job, though. It was mine.

I didn't want to be a burden to the only friends I had who seemed to want to spend time with me purely for the pleasure of my company.

Chapter Five

We'd ended our impromptu relationship brainstorming session on a pretty positive note I'd thought, but by the time Kit swung by my place in the evening to pick me up, he was in such a foul mood that I wondered if I'd imagined our camaraderie over the kitchen table this morning.

It was a ten-minute walk from my place to the station, and we made the entire journey in silence. *It didn't bode well for a good night out,* I thought to myself. Maybe I should have bitten the bullet and asked Violet for a heads-up on this group of friends we were going to meet.

My low-heeled sandals clicked with each step, and I crossed my arms to wrap myself more tightly in my cardigan as the breeze picked up. With zero guidance from Kit, I'd picked a casual navy dress that showed off a decent stretch of legs and shoulders—my two favourite features. It was sexy-ish. Sexy-lite, at most.

Unfortunately, the breeze also meant I'd had to pull my hair back into a low bun to stop it from whipping around my face. Even with a full face of make-up on, I felt incredibly exposed without my hair to hide behind.

Kit stepped aside so I could pass through the turnstile at the station first, following at a rather disconcertingly close clip behind me. It was an odd sensation to have an alpha so close to my back and not be actively trying to get away. There were always weirdos who stood too close on the train, but like any omega, I was proficient at slipping away from them.

The train was pretty quiet, and I led Kit to two empty seats, sliding in next to the window.

Were we just not going to speak for the entire journey? I wanted to know what I was walking into, but there was a part of me—maybe borne of instinct, maybe of experience—that baulked at the idea of provoking a clearly unhappy alpha.

A beautiful omega slipped between the doors right as they were closing, immediately patting her handbag and long black curly hair to check that nothing had got caught before finding her seat. She was tall and elegant, with deep bronze skin and enormous dark eyes, and I wondered if Kit's friends would bring along a beautiful omega like her tonight to try and catch his attention.

"We should probably establish some kind of code word or signal or something," I murmured, half to myself, mulling over options that would be clear between the two of us but not *super* obvious for everyone else. It would have to be something that gave me an excuse to leave. Maybe I could fake a phone call from one of my siblings? I supposed if I was never going to see any of them again, it didn't matter how believable it was.

Kit twisted in his seat to face me, all traces of irritation gone and a serious look on his face. "If you feel uncomfortable at any point, just tell me, Margot. We'll leave right away."

Oh, that was reassuring. Nice, even. Maybe he wasn't in a grumpy mood after all.

Nice Kit made my omega senses go all *aware*, instead of lying politely dormant somewhere in the depths of my being like they were meant to.

"That isn't what I was referring to, but thank you, that's good to know."

"What were you talking about then?"

"I meant we need some kind of signal to get me out of there if they bring someone along you really hit it off with and want to get to know. I could fake a call from my sister and then I'll slip out and call a cab—"

"That's not going to be a problem," Kit interjected, jaw tight.

"You don't *know* that. I mean, you might not want to dive into their nest and make babies with them, but there are levels of intimacy before that. To be super blunt, I don't want to knot-block you," I said wryly.

Kit gave me a withering look. "Aside from the fact that I'd be a total piece of shit to go home with someone when I'd come out with you, the omegas my friends and family set me up with usually have expectations about something permanent. I'd never lead them on like that, even if I did find them attractive."

"Well, if you're sure," I replied, not sounding convinced because I wasn't. Maybe I was a pessimist—almost certainly, in fact—but I found it hard to believe that Kit would still want to continue this charade with me when presented with an omega ten years younger and twice as beautiful.

"I do think we should have a code word though. Just to check in with each other," Kit said thoughtfully. "Something subtle."

"Ask me if I want a wine." Kit twisted slightly in his seat, looking at me with one eyebrow raised. "I don't drink, never liked the taste. I'll know you aren't *really* asking me if I want a glass of wine. 'No' means I'm fine, 'yes' is I'd like to leave, please. Deal?"

He almost smiled, turning to face ahead again. "Deal."

We were quiet for a while, watching as the stops went by and people boarded and left.

"I went to visit my mum. First time I've seen her in a couple of years," Kit said eventually, not looking at me. "She's got this Council job, works really hard, loves her career. She didn't want to fly anywhere to meet me, and I didn't come home, I don't hold it against her."

I didn't say anything, sensing that he needed a moment to gather his thoughts.

"She had to work today, and asked me to head over to where her office is so we could grab something to eat during her lunch break—which I thought was a bit odd, because why not have a longer catch-up over dinner? Anyway, it was because she wanted to bring a single omega from her office along with her."

I winced sympathetically, barely resisting the very omega urge to start stroking the agitated alpha.

"It's fucking *relentless*," Kit grumbled. "She knows how I feel about that shit, and it was just awkward as hell, and I'm not looking forward to tonight. I specifically asked my friends not to try to set me up with anyone, but I'm not optimistic that they'll listen."

Have you considered getting better friends?

I didn't say it aloud because I hadn't met them and maybe I was being too quick to judge, but they sounded incredibly disrespectful already.

"I'm sorry, Kit. That's rubbish—you're entitled to have boundaries and the people you care about should be the first to respect them. And this is why I'm here, right? So you can ignore that crap and have a good night."

I was using my placating omega voice without even realising it, but it did have its intended effect. Kit relaxed ever so slightly in his seat, his arm pressing against mine, scentmarking me, though I wasn't sure if it was a conscious decision or not.

Then again, we wouldn't be a very convincing courting couple if I didn't smell a little like him—alphas were weird about that kind of thing. I leaned into it, letting that delightful coffee and whiskey smell rub off on me while I people-watched.

A beta couple boarded, taking two empty seats farther up the carriage, sitting facing us. I loved being an omega 99% of the time—yes, heat sucked, but it was only once a year and outside of that, I was very fond of my omega vagina and all the perks it entailed. Seeing beta couples always gave me a small pause, though.

Were they married? Planning a future together, unswayed by biological imperative? Or were they just casually seeing each other? Maybe they were just spending the night together, no strings attached, before heading their separate ways, never to be anything more to one another than a fond memory.

"This is our stop," Kit said quietly, bumping my shoulder. I shot him a quick smile, pulling my game face on and headed for the train doors as they swooshed open. I'd never been one to shirk my responsibilities, and this was no different. I was going to uphold my end of our arrangement.

The pub was across the street from the station, the rowdy sounds of patrons standing out front with their pints greeting us before we'd even swiped through the turnstiles.

"Wait," Kit said suddenly, lightly grabbing my forearm before I could cross the street. "Do you think we should kiss now?"

Now? We were standing three feet from a bin that absolutely reeked, the station behind us was blindingly bright, and there were about fifty spectators standing outside the pub on the other side of the road. "Why now?"

"I don't know. In case they expect us to. Isn't that something couples do? I just thought we should get it over with now."

"Well, how could I possibly say no to that?" I deadpanned, throwing my hands up in exasperation. Kit stammered, his face flushing a fantastic shade of red as he realized how begrudging his offer had sounded. "I'm joking. You don't need to woo me."

Kit shoved both hands through his hair, pushing it messily back off his face. "I'm usually better at this," he muttered. "Or I thought I was. You make me nervous, and I say stupid stuff."

"I make you nervous?" I repeated, surprised.

"You're not what I expected. For an omega."

"Well, maybe you should be more open-minded. Come here." He blinked at me. "I thought we were going to kiss? You're very tall," I clarified, gesturing for him to come closer.

"Oh. Right."

Kit leaned in, flexing his hands at his sides like he didn't know where to put them, and I could not, in good conscience, stand here and let myself be led into what was shaping up to be the most mediocre kiss since my first spin-the-bottle experience back in secondary school.

No.

Sometimes, being a good omega meant giving a fumbling alpha a hearty shove in the right direction.

I cupped his face, pulling him the rest of the way to me and pressed my lips against his, kissing him with the kind of confidence that I wanted to be kissed with, in the hopes that it would make him relax.

It certainly made him something.

As Kit took over our movements, one firm hand gripped my hip with the perfect amount of pressure, while his tongue stroked against mine with a sudden obscene level of confidence, I wasn't sure *relaxed* was the best way to describe him.

Danger, the sensible part of my brain piped up, a bright yellow Slippery When Wet sign popping into my head.

"I think that was good," I mumbled, breaking away and stumbling back a step. "Very convincing."

Kit's hand hovered in the air where he'd been holding me, and for a split second, he looked as though he was about to reach for me again.

In all fairness, I was a great kisser.

"Right. Yeah. Very convincing."

"Great." I nodded once. "Good. Should we head in then?"

Why was my heart beating so fast? *Just a kiss. Nothing to lose your head over, Margot.*

Kit exhaled heavily, fingers flexing at his side before he finally nodded.

The moment we were across the street, he headed straight for the doors, holding them open and gesturing for me to enter first. It was an old-fashioned place—with what looked like the original wood panelling on the walls and black-and-white patterned tiles on the floor. With so many people, it was warm and smelled like pheromones and lager, and I quickly shed my cardigan, draping it over my forearm.

"Let's grab a drink first," Kit muttered, resting a heavy hand on the small of my back and leaning down to speak in my ear. I opened my mouth to reassure him that we could go and find his friends right away if he wanted, but one look at his face made me think that the drink was for his benefit, not mine.

Had that kiss shaken him too? I doubted it. Kit didn't look as though he was wanting for great kisses, and I knew for a fact that he'd once been a regular at Bryce and Kane's orgies too, before my time. There were always single and widowed omegas like me there, as well as betas and his fellow alphas.

Weirdly, I didn't like thinking too hard about that.

Kit ordered a pint while I opted for elderflower soda, and as soon as we'd picked up our glasses, Kit slid his hand into mine, guiding me through the crowd towards the back of the pub. While I'd been expecting the contact—it would have looked pretty weird if we *didn't* touch each other—my heart still did a weird skip at the gesture. *I should find a cuddle buddy,* I thought absently. I needed more platonic touch in my life.

A chorus of excited greetings reached us the moment we found their booth, and Kit's grip on my hand tightened ever so slightly.

"There he is! Man of the hour!" A boisterous voice announced, standing up and clapping Kit on the back. "Thought we'd never see you again, ya bastard. It's been *years*!"

"Has it?" Kit said with a grin that didn't look quite natural. "Everyone, this is Margot. Margot, this is Coleman, Beckett, and Rajeev," he said, gesturing at the three alphas before faltering, clearly not knowing the names of their mates. Or the name of the spare, ridiculously beautiful unmated omega who was looking at Kit with a faint frown on her face.

I knew we should have had a codeword.

"Sal, Jocelyn, Lennox," Coleman—the loud one—said, gesturing at each of the mated omegas in turn. "And this is our friend, Sinclair."

Sinclair recovered quickly, shooting both Kit and me a beaming smile as she shuffled over to make room for us on the bench. There really wasn't enough space for two, but Kit set his beer on the table, plucked the glass from my hand to set it down too, and dragged me onto his lap. I perched on one muscular thigh, draping an arm over his shoulders for balance, and attempted to look as though we did this all the time.

"Margot, was it?" Coleman asked reluctantly, apparently unable to dismiss me while I was sat on Kit's lap. Kit banded an arm around my waist, leaning forward to take a sip of his pint.

"That's right. It's so nice to meet you, I've heard so much." *And liked very little.*

Coleman shot me a tight smile, glancing apologetically at Sinclair. "So how did you two meet?"

"Mutual friends," I replied easily, glad we didn't have to lie on this front at least.

"Nico and Violet," Kit clarified.

"They didn't waste any time shackling you," one of the omegas mumbled, as if they were doing any differently by bringing Sinclair along. "How long have you been back in the country anyway?"

"More importantly, how long are you staying?" Coleman boomed obnoxiously. He really did have a very loud voice, and I wasn't just thinking denigrating thoughts about him because he looked at me like I was a particularly gross bug he'd like to squash.

"Maybe a month, maybe longer," Kit replied vaguely. "I got offered a long-term gig in France, I haven't decided whether I'm going to take it or not."

"Where in France?" Sinclair cut in before Coleman could reply, her bright smile unmistakably genuine. "I lived in Caen for a few years—my parents were there for work. It's beautiful."

Sinclair was being nothing but polite, but Kit was stiff as a board, retreating back into that anxious place he'd been in at the party yesterday. I gave him a little squeeze with the arm I had wrapped around his shoulders, shooting him what I hoped was an encouraging smile.

"Paris." Kit cleared his throat.

"You won't take it, though," Coleman said confidently. "You don't like being tied down to one place."

"That must be stressful for you," Coleman's mate—Jocelyn?—said, giving me a look filled with false sympathy. Not that they'd asked a single question about me or what my intentions with their friend were.

Sinclair was nice. The rest of them, I could happily never interact with again.

"No more so than it would be for any other omega, I suppose," I replied, giving her my blandest smile. She did not return the gesture.

"Where were you before you came home?" Rajeev asked.

"The Sonoran Desert in Arizona on an assignment for a few weeks. Then I spent a few days in New York before I flew here."

Kit's voice was so toneless that even his friends looked like they didn't know how to respond. I didn't think he was being intentionally rude, but rather that he was uncomfortable. Or maybe he was just being rude and I was projecting good intentions onto him that weren't there.

"I've always wanted to move to New York," I volunteered, feeling the need to fill the extended silence. "I love the *coolness* of London, but there's something very exciting about the *boldness* of New York, if that makes sense."

"Not really," Coleman said flatly. I could have sworn Kit's arm around my waist tightened a little "Anyway, tell us everything Kit. When are you moving home?"

"I'm really sorry about this," Kit said again, leaning in close so I could hear him over the thudding bass. I wasn't even entirely sure *how* we'd ended up at this painfully loud club, but since the seven of them had all seemed super familiar with it, I assumed it was a regular haunt of theirs.

"It's fine, honestly." I shot him a half smile over the top of my glass of soda, giving the hand I'd been clinging on to a quick squeeze of reassurance. Honestly, I was surprised he hadn't shaken me off—even with the whole fake courtship factor, I was being a little clingy.

I didn't like clubs. Too many scents, too many sounds, too many mystery sticky things on the floor. My omega instincts were going feral in this dark, crowded space that reeked of pheromones.

"Do I smell?" I asked, stepping farther into Kit's space as a group of laughing betas headed for the dance floor behind, bumping into my back.

Kit shook his head, allaying my nerves a little, though not much. I drained my glass, setting it down next to Kit's empty one on the bar leaner.

"Let's dance," I said, steeling myself and holding out a hand for Kit to take. "The whole point of me hanging off you tonight was so you could have a good time."

"Does dancing constitute a good time?" he asked dubiously, resting a hand in mine and pulling me closer. As discreetly as I could, I took a deep whiff of Kit's scent, using it to centre myself. The closer I stood to him, the easier it was to tune the rest of the club out.

"For some people. Shall we give it a try?"

Kit's hands found my hips, and mine came to rest on his chest, my fingers playing with the fabric of his shirt as we swayed to the beat. Each swaying movement brought our bodies closer together, and while I was too on edge to sink into the moment and really *enjoy* it, the closeness was kind of lovely.

He was *safe*. Kit had no interest in screwing me, and that made it very easy to let myself physically relax in his presence.

Kit leaned down, his lips brushing my ear. "Do you want a glass of wine?"

I hid my grin in his shirt. "Not yet."

In all honesty, I'd be more than happy to leave, but the whole point of tonight had been for Kit to have a good time and I wasn't sure we'd succeeded yet.

The others were dancing nearby, occasionally attempting to wave Kit over despite his repeated refusals. Sinclair was animatedly chatting to a cute beta, both of them swaying in time to the beat, and I was glad she hadn't been pushy at least.

No, the pushiness had come from Kit's supposed friends.

Like I'd summoned him with my mind, Coleman broke away from the group, making his way over to us. I could have sworn Kit's grip on my hips grew a little tighter.

"You're being boring," Coleman said loudly, clapping Kit on the back. "Come dance with the rest of us."

He grabbed Kit's arm, attempting to drag him into the throng of gyrating club-goers as though I wasn't right here, physically attached to him. Those pints had really taken hold—while Coleman had been growing increasingly dismissive over the course of the night, this was the most blatantly rude he'd been.

"I'm good, man." Kit twisted his arm out of Coleman's hold, pulling me a little closer to him in the process.

"Oh, come on, Kit. You used to love having a good time, and you're just standing around here all alone." *Ouch.* "Sinclair was so excited to meet you—"

Coleman reached for Kit again, but I stepped between them, pressing my back against Kit's side. He was so much taller and broader than me, but there was a strange sense of calm that washed over my agitated nerves at the feeling of having him at my back.

"It's pretty loud in here, maybe you didn't hear him say no?"

Coleman's cheerful expression contorted into something far less friendly when he looked at me. "Who even are you? I'm Kit's closest friend, and I've never heard of you."

Kit stiffened. "This is *Margot*, and you're being unbelievably rude to her. We're not going to dissect it now, though. Margot and I are leaving."

He didn't pause to say goodbye to his friends, just rested a hand on my hip and insistently steered me away from the dancefloor to the exit.

I stumbled along, the vehemence of his response taking me by surprise. "Are you sure you don't want to say goodbye to the others? I don't mind waiting."

"No."

Okay then.

I pulled on the cardigan I'd had tied around my waist the moment we stepped outside, both Kit and I wrinkling our noses in disdain at the scents that clung to the fabrics we were wearing.

If nothing else, tonight had reminded me that I was ten years too old for clubbing.

"Everything okay?" I hedged, doing up my buttons. The moment I was done, Kit grabbed my hand again, not noticing the look of surprise on my face since he was already heading down the busy street, away from the club. I supposed there was always a chance that his friends had followed us out, which was probably why he wanted to maintain the ruse.

"No."

"Want to grab a kebab?"

Kit paused mid-step. "Yes?"

"Oh good. I'm starving, and a late-night kebab is really the only good thing about being out after ten o'clock."

I tugged on his hand, leading him in the direction of a kebab shop that was all cracked tiles and fluorescent lighting, and absolutely delicious, if my uni student memories served me correctly.

"Shit, it's one am," Kit said quietly. "I didn't mean to keep you out so late."

"It's really fine, it's not like I have work tomorrow. Or today, rather."

Kit grunted, a sound he made a lot, I noticed. It was oddly endearing. "I knew they'd show up with someone—they always do, and they're always kind of pushy—but that was... Fuck, they were so *rude*. I get that they were disappointed, they'd probably told that omega I was single and looking for a mate, but still. We should have left after that first drink."

I privately disagreed that they were rude to me solely for Sinclair's benefit, but whatever. They were Kit's friends, and if he wanted to be friends with obnoxious assholes, that was his call. This was only a temporary thing, I didn't have to get invested.

"It's not a big deal, Kit." I glanced around, making sure none of his friends had followed us. "You don't have to protect my honour. The point of my presence is to make your life easier, not more difficult."

"You did."

He was definitely an alpha of few words, I thought as we queued up at the kebab shop, each ordering our chicken kebabs that he insisted on paying for as an unnecessary apology for how the night had gone.

We managed to crowd onto two stools at the counter, and I valiantly attempted to eat like a lady while sauce ran down to my wrists.

"This was a good idea," Kit said, somewhat begrudgingly.

I hummed in agreement, swallowing my mouthful. "You don't much like omegas, do you?"

Kit made a strangled sound, nearly dropping his kebab.

"It's just an observation, I don't mean anything by it." I carefully pulled the tinfoil wrapping down a little farther, wiping the garlic sauce off my fingers on a napkin. "Based on tonight and last night's party, I'm guessing you've had unmated omegas foisted on you for years. I can see why you're wary."

"Aren't you wary around unmated alphas?" he shot back defensively.

I shrugged. "Jimmy is annoying, sure, but I won't tar all alphas with his brush."

"Not just him," Kit said with a dismissive wave. "The others. Don't you get annoyed having unmated alphas trying to woo you all the time, just because you're an omega and you're available?"

I looked at Kit for a long moment, trying to decide if he was being serious or not. I suppose, with Jimmy hanging around, it may have given off the impression that I had suitors? Or he was joking about alphas wooing me all the time, though if it was a joke, it was kind of a mean-spirited one. Was Kit mean? His friends were, but he'd been protective earlier.

Or had his protectiveness just been instinct?

Trying to figure out alpha intentions was exhausting.

"Or maybe you enjoy it?" Kit suggested, apparently expecting an answer. "The attention. Some people like that."

I shot him a wry smile. "I think you're overestimating the number of alphas banging down my door. In times gone by, I would have been firmly categorised as a spinster by now."

Kit looked like he didn't know how to respond to that, so I took pity on him and changed the subject. "So you've known those alphas since your school days?"

"I have." Kit was quiet for a moment, focused on his meal. "I don't remember them being like that."

"You haven't been home for a long time," I pointed out. "People change. Or maybe they didn't. Maybe it was you."

Kit gave me a long look, while I stared out the window, feeling oddly self-conscious under his penetrating watch. People didn't usually *look* at me so much.

"And what if I have?" he asked eventually. "Changed, I mean."

"Then life changes along with you. Or it doesn't. Only you can decide that."

Chapter Six

Violet: I have been respectfully waiting for you to message me and tell me why Kit wanted to bring you coffee yesterday morning, but I am being respectful no longer. You are coming over for lunch and telling me everything.

I snorted, snuggling further down in the soft linen sheets of my nest, holding my phone up to my nose. I hadn't told Violet about last night—or the scheme we'd concocted—but I wasn't trying to keep it from her either. I didn't think she'd react poorly or anything, but if I was being really honest with myself, I was being hyper-conscious of *not* making a big deal out of this. It was just a temporary arrangement of convenience. There was no need to go around *telling* people. Telling people made it sound like there was something to tell.

I had very realistic ideas about this whole scenario, and I needed everyone else to be on my same realistic level.

Me: I can catch you up on all the gossip tomorrow, at yoga.

Violet: That's a whole day away! Stop delaying the inevitable.

Violet: We're having salmon because it's your favourite and I'm not above bribery.

Damn it. I *loved* salmon, especially when Violet cooked it. I hadn't even got out of bed yet after arriving home sometime after two, and I needed at least half an hour to scrub off the panda eyes.

Kit: Please don't leave me here alone. Violet is like a dog with a bone and you know I'm scared of omegas.

Me: You're scared of *single* omegas.

Kit: I'm considering expanding my parameters.

I caught a glimpse of my reflection in my phone screen, finding myself grinning like a lunatic, and immediately arranged my face into something less... excited.

I wasn't excited.

There was nothing to be excited about.

Me: Fine, fine, for the sake of all omegas everywhere, I'll come over and save you from the big, bad Violet.

Kit: My omega aunties thank you.

Reluctantly, I wriggled out of the soft sheets, taking a moment to remake my nest the way I liked it. I had a full-blown omega-boner for linen which got softer with every wash, and I'd had most of my nesting materials for years. While the walls were painted dark green, with one maximalist floral wallpaper feature wall for impact, everything in the room was pristine white.

I hit the release button to open the electronic sliding door that led to my nest, heading to the bathroom to shower. The door was an eyesore and totally incongruent with the style of the building, but since I lived alone, it was worth the sacrifice to have an auto-locking feature, especially during the haze of my heat.

Cranking the heat up, I didn't linger in the shower, scrubbing myself clean and shaving my legs in record time. I'd planned on finishing up some due diligence for a client I'd been working on today, but I'd been coming up with excuses not to in my head before Violet's message. I enjoyed my job—it didn't light a fire in my soul or anything, but I was good at it and it afforded me a comfortable life—but it had felt draining lately in a way that it never had before. I didn't think it was just because my heat was approaching either, which always made me more physically tired.

It was probably a little early-thirties ennui. A pre-midlife crisis, exacerbated by my impending biological nightmare week and my brother's early demise. Nothing to be alarmed about.

Maybe I should get a tattoo? Something that screamed 'I may be in my thirties, but my life isn't over yet.'

Maybe a giant phoenix rising from the ashes of my wrinkle-free youth.

Still contemplating whether or not I could pull it off, I dried off and covered myself in Om-Guard before blow-drying my hair and putting on my make-up. Shooting Violet a quick message to tell her I was leaving, I yanked on a pale pink sundress and denim jacket before heading downstairs.

Kit was already standing on the pavement waiting for me, though I wasn't shocked to see him since my door smelled like fresh alpha. Vaguely, I wondered if the neighbours across the street had seen him rubbing himself up against it.

"Hello, I wasn't expecting you."

He shot me an impatient look. "You were going to walk over on your own."

"That is how I tend to get around most days," I agreed, checking the lock had clicked into place behind me before joining him. "It's broad daylight and I'm only going five minutes down the road."

Kit harrumphed as though that was the most dissatisfying answer he'd ever heard, and I immediately wanted to needle him again, which was odd because I was, by all accounts, a terminal people pleaser.

"I wanted to check you were okay after last night," he said eventually, concentrating a little harder than strictly necessary on walking in a straight line down a flat pavement.

"It'll take more than some rude comments to upset me, I assure you." Being the ugly duckling child had given me a crash course in rude comments from a young age.

"I mentioned it to Nico and he told me Coleman had been an immature asshole at fourteen and hadn't improved since," Kit said hesitantly, seeming to struggle to find the words he was looking for. "That's why he doesn't bother with them anymore."

The evidence certainly seemed to suggest that Nico was Kit's most tolerable friend so far.

"I don't understand it," Kit continued, more to himself than me. "And you were so polite to them, and conscientious of me. Perfect, really."

I knew better than to read anything into that comment. "Well, Sinclair is a very beautiful omega. Young. Educated. Well-travelled. Giant fertile window remaining." Kit made a strangled sound, and I gave him a moment to recover before I continued. "She's the ideal as far as omegas go; it's hardly surprising they thought she'd be a better fit for you than me. If I charitably overlook their appalling rudeness, I'd say it's nice of them to be looking out for your best interests."

"You and I are closer in age, both established in our careers, have mutual friends, and like chicken kebabs," Kit countered stubbornly.

He was surprisingly worked up about this. Though, I suppose if I'd been matchmade as many times as he had, I'd have some strong opinions about who my friends were foisting on me too.

"It just seems obvious that you would be a better fit for me."

Either Kit was deliberately ignoring the first thing I'd said, or he hadn't registered it.

Sinclair is a very beautiful omega.

Coleman had the worst poker face of the lot, and he'd looked at me like I was a dowdy old maid, leeching on to a successful, attractive alpha that I had no business so much as breathing near.

We'd stopped in front of Nico and Violet's house, and I felt a strange need to offer Kit some kind of reassurance before we went inside, even though I was the one who'd been disrespected all night. I didn't care about their behaviour, but Kit clearly did.

"Look, it's really fine. I'm not upset about how last night went—I was there to be your nice, safe omega buffer and it worked. Awkward rudeness aside, did you have a good night?"

It was genuinely hard to tell with the perma-scowl.

"It was okay. Near the end."

"When we left?" I laughed.

"A little before that." Kit cleared his throat, taking a moment to adjust his glasses.

"Are you two coming inside or what?" Violet called, poking her head out the door and shooting us an inquisitive look.

I shot Kit my most reassuring smile, grabbing his elbow and tugging him towards the house. "Come on. Let's go face the inquiry squad together."

"So," Violet began, passing the bowl of salad across the table to me. "Nico and I have politely been making small talk, waiting for you two to bring it up, but neither of you *are* bringing it up."

"Bringing what up?" I asked, batting my eyelashes innocently at her.

Violet rolled her eyes affectionately. "Don't play coy with me, Margot Bailey."

Nico relaxed back in his seat, one arm draped over the back of Violet's chair, looking between us with a smug smirk. "Whatever it was you're doing, I'm guessing you came up with when you were huddled in the corner together at the party the other night? You did look very cosy..."

"Don't you start," Kit grumbled. "You're the only friend I have who doesn't try to set me up."

Violet frowned, and I shot her a breezy smile to let her know that Kit's surly words hadn't bothered me.

"Relax, Kit." I patted him on the arm. "That isn't what Nico was doing. From what I heard, you used to be their third wheel at Bryce and Kane's parties before I was. These two know better than anyone that we're both capable of enjoying the company of alphas or omegas without any strings attached."

Nico raised his glass to me in agreement while Kit's stare burned into the side of my head. I couldn't imagine why he'd be surprised—just because I wasn't interested in taking a mate didn't mean I didn't want to be knotted until I was bow-legged.

I was a complex, multi-faceted omega that way.

"Not that we're doing *that*," I added hurriedly, catching Violet's raised eyebrows. "I just mean that everyone at this table is aware that both Kit and I are very comfortable in our singleness. You two also know that other people in our lives *aren't*, so we're helping each other out while Kit is in town. Plus one-ing for each other. Nothing to get excited about."

"I don't know about that," Nico replied drily. "It's certainly caused some excitement. Coleman called today to interrogate me about Margot. He was most put out that you didn't fall head over heels for Jocelyn's sister's fellow intern, Kit."

"Is that who she was?" Kit said, sounding bored. Nico grinned.

"What did you tell Coleman?" I asked, not quite able to stop myself even though I wasn't entirely sure I wanted the answer.

"The truth." Nico shrugged, and Kit glanced up at him with a very unreassuring level of alarm. "That Violet and I didn't set you up—the two of you are our closest friends and you just happened to meet at a party we hosted, which led to some follow-up criticisms about us not inviting him and the others. He asked about Margot, and I assured him she was smart, kind, generous with her time and a wonderful friend, and any alpha would be lucky to call her their mate."

"Hear, hear," Violet added cheerfully, smiling at me across the table while I attempted to morph my face into something resembling polite gratitude instead of shock. The flaming cheeks probably gave me away.

"That was very nice of you," I replied cautiously.

"Like I said, I just told the truth." Nico shrugged, digging into his grilled salmon. Kit followed suit, notably silent in response to Nico's words, and I found myself wondering what he was thinking in spite of myself. Did he disagree with Nico's assessment of my character?

Did I care if he did?

Yes, I decided grimly. Even though our scheme was one of mutually beneficial convenience, I still hoped that Kit and I could be friends at the end of it. Partly because we were both close with Nico and Violet, and it would be nice if we could all spend time together. But also because Kit really seemed like he could use more friends. Ones without ulterior motives for him.

"So, when's your next... whatever we're calling it?" Violet asked, gesturing between the two of us with her fork. "Your next not-date?"

"I don't intend to take up too much of Margot's time," Kit said, still looking down at his plate. "I asked if she would accompany me last night, to Brighton for the weekend trip Coleman planned, and to the fundraising dinner I'm in town for. That's all, there's nothing to read into."

"Oh yeah, just an overnight trip where you'll undoubtedly be expected to share a bedroom, and one of the highlights of your professional career where you'll be surrounded by your peers. Nothing to read into," Violet agreed with a bright smile that definitely had her sarcasm whooshing right over Kit's head. "What about you, Margot? Isn't this meant to be a mutually beneficial arrangement?"

I grimaced, realising I'd never got around to telling Violet about Jimmy.

Or Calum, for that matter. That conversation could wait for another day, though.

"My parents have rustled up an alpha they'd like me to invite into my nest—a widowed friend of my dad. He's been... hanging around. Kit has generously volunteered his scent for my front door."

Kit snorted.

"Wait, some alpha has been hanging around your house and you didn't tell us?" Violet asked, looking horrified. "*Margot*. What if he's dangerous? You should've said something!"

"I don't think he's dangerous. Just lonely, and extremely misled about me."

"You are far too cavalier with your own safety," Nico sighed. "I hope you're holding up your side of the agreement, Kit. Margot is the first to volunteer to help anyone, she's constantly rushing around doing things for other people, but she is woefully bad at putting herself first."

"Rude," I mumbled, shoving a forkful of salmon in my mouth.

"Accurate," Nico countered, raising one judgemental eyebrow. I could feel Kit staring at me again. Not for the first time, I wished he wasn't quite so reticent with his emotions.

"Can we talk about literally anything else?" I pleaded. "Jimmy is harmless. Kit and I have this covered."

"You'll tell us if it escalates?" Violet pressed, giving me an imploring look. I hesitated, knowing that I probably wouldn't and not wanting to lie. Nico and Violet had a fairy tale kind of love—if the princess in the tower had a degradation kink and the knight-in-shining-armour had wooed her by telling her what a beautiful slut she was—I didn't want to intrude on their happily ever after with my trivial problems.

"Margot," Violet said in a softer voice, giving me a sympathetic look. "We love you, and we *want* to help. You're never imposing on us, you know that."

"This is all moot," Kit cut in, saving me from lying. "Since this precise scenario is why Margot has me."

"So long as she does have you," Nico replied mildly before smoothly changing the subject into something that had happened at work last week. I focused on eating my lunch and steadying the nerves that were feeling somewhat rocked by Kit's declaration.

It was odd to have someone announce with such conviction that they were on my side. Generally, I was a supporting player on other people's teams, but my bench was pretty empty.

And I was fine with that.

Really.

"So, what happens at Bryce and Kane's next party?" Violet asked suddenly. "I'm sure they'll send a message with the details any day now."

Kit and I shot each other a startled glance. While I logically knew he'd attended the parties before my time, I struggled to picture him in the silk-and-leather den of iniquity that was one of Bryce and Kane's parties. I was fairly confident he was staring at me and thinking the exact same thing.

"We'll go as friends, of course," I replied, meeting Kit's eyes. "Go our separate ways when we get inside, the same as we would with the two of you, and wish each other a pleasant evening. Right, Kit?"

Oof, that *look*. Did he expect me to not go? Tough freaking luck. It would be my last chance to get thoroughly railed before my heat hit, and from experience, that made the eventual heat less painful. Or I'd just convinced myself of that in my head. One of those two options.

We finished eating, and I insisted on doing the dishes because Violet was starting to look uncomfortable, and Nico was starting to look impatient.

They acted like the pinnacle of respectability, but Nico and Violet were two of the horniest people on the planet, I was convinced of it. It was pretty easy to get an omega to lactate during heat, but maintaining it was a twenty-four-seven commitment and a large part of the reason why Violet had given up her job to stay at home after they were mated. It made them both happy, so while I knew I'd *hate* being that tied to a schedule, there was no judgement from me.

Kit cleared the dishes off the table, bringing them over to me while I loaded the dishwasher and filled the sink to scrub the pots.

"They really care about you," he murmured, setting the empty salad bowl down on the counter and watching me from the other side of the kitchen island.

"The feeling is very mutual. Violet was so welcoming when I moved into the neighbourhood, introducing me to everyone and checking in on me because she was worried about me living alone. I'm lucky to have them in my life."

"I wouldn't say *lucky*," Kit replied, using that disgruntled voice he seemed to fall into when he was unwillingly dragged into having a real-life conversation with actual human words. "They enjoy your company. Care about you. That's not luck."

"Why Kit Iyer, if I didn't know any better, I'd think you were giving me a compliment."

"I'm making an observation." Kit fussed with his glasses, careful not to make eye contact with me.

"A very flattering observation."

"If you want to take it that way, take it that way," he grumbled, moving back to the table to clear the condiments while I laughed. He really was a fascinating mix of grouchy and conscientious.

"Tell me what your life is like when you're travelling." Kit startled at the question. "My life here is very… structured. Routine, I suppose. I'm so intrigued by what your life must be like on the road."

"It's probably less glamorous than you think. I shoot at sunrise and sunset for the light, which often means very early starts and very late finishes, depending on the time of year and where I am. During the day, I hole up in whatever hotel room I'm staying in to edit. And nap," he added, pursing his lips. "And I'll scout locations, either for the assignment I'm on or any future trips."

"That sounds pretty glamorous to me. Naps? Travelling to far-flung places? Wandering around new locations and finding interesting things to take pictures of? Seeing the sun rise and set each day? *Naps?*"

"You said naps twice."

"I can't even remember the last time I took a nap," I said with a dramatic sigh.

"Is there some particular reason why lawyers can't take naps?" Kit asked drily.

"The general workload? Peer pressure? Our naturally competitive natures?"

Kit's lips twitched, and I silently swore to myself that I'd get a full-blown smile out of him in the next few weeks.

"Do you like your job?" he asked, grabbing a tea towel to dry the pots.

"I do," I replied after a short pause. "I used to work in the office until a few years ago. Obviously, by my age, most omegas are mated and transition into working from home. I didn't *need* that, but I guess HR didn't know what to do with me, so they pushed me in that direction."

"You don't like working from home?"

"Omegas are social creatures," I pointed out with a soft smile. Actually, we were needy little hornballs, but we liked regular, non-sexual socialising too. Sometimes. "That being said, the oddness of my situation can make people uncomfortable sometimes, even colleagues who have known me for years."

He hadn't asked me yet *why* I didn't have a mate. He'd accepted it as fact without question—a rarity I appreciated—but I could see the wheels turning in his head now.

Fortunately, Violet reappeared before Kit could put those thoughts into words, the buttons on the front of her dress skewed and her cheeks flushed, offering the perfect excuse to change the subject.

"So," I began. "Shall we get out the board games?"

Chapter Seven

There was nothing more mortifying as an omega than submitting the same five-day leave request each year.

Nothing.

I would rather go into a real-life, in-person sex-toy store—something I had never done—and buy ten Colossal Cock dildos, the ones with the silicone knot as big as a tennis ball and a ridge of piercing simulations around the crown, than submit this fucking form again.

If I had an alpha of my own, my heats would only be a couple of days long and easily chalked up to a sick day, and so routine that HR wouldn't blink an eye.

But no.

I was monestrous, going into heat once a year as I had done every year since I was eighteen. It was my body waving a sad little pick-me flag for alphas, and I resented the inconvenience immensely.

With a heavy sigh, I clicked the 'submit' button, giving HR a heads up that they absolutely didn't need that I'd be taking a few days off in the foreseeable future.

Smug Lora, the HR Manager and my nemesis, probably had a bet going with her underlings about when my leave request would arrive.

With a heavy sigh, I pulled off the headphones that had been blasting classical focus music in my ears and rubbed my temple. I still had a few weeks to go before the big bang-my-dildo-collection event arrived, but my back was achy, and I was bloated, hungry, and extremely irritable.

Tea, I decided. A cup of tea would help the achiness.

And a pack of biscuits would help my mood.

My phone buzzed and I glanced down, expecting to either see an eight-minute voice note from Michelle about her mother-in-law, or another weird meme I was too old to understand from Asher.

Kit: I'm downstairs.

Well, that I hadn't expected.

I pushed out of my uncomfortable office chair and grabbed my keys so I could head down and let him in. It had been a couple of days since I'd seen him at Nico and Violet's for lunch, and we definitely hadn't made plans to meet up again.

Kit's hair was wet from the faint drizzle that had been falling all morning, his glasses speckled with water and skin all damp and glowing. A light drizzle made me look like a rat who'd just climbed out of a particularly objectionable drainpipe. Some people had all the luck.

"Come in, come in, let's get you out of the rain."

I led Kit upstairs, and he set down a paper bag on the table before taking off his wet jacket and drying his glasses.

"I bought you lunch," he said gruffly, gesturing at the bag on the table. "Well, us. I bought us lunch. Rice bowls. Violet said you like them."

"I do." I fetched us some proper cutlery and some water, wishing I had some other drinks here to offer him. I was good at many things, but hosting wasn't one of them. "This is an unexpected surprise. I wasn't sure I'd see you before Brighton."

Kit made a noncommittal sound, pulling out two containers and sliding the chicken one towards me. Violet had briefed him well. I definitely wasn't going to object to his company when there were rice bowls involved.

"I've been scentmarking as I go past each day," Kit said eventually. "I thought this would be more thorough. Stick around more. With the rain and stuff."

"I imagine so," I agreed mildly. Kit's coffee and whiskey scent was truly going to linger now. I didn't know how I felt about that.

It was close enough to my heat for me to question whether having Kit's scent constantly around my house was making *my* life more difficult, rather than Jimmy's.

"Where is your scent? Even your flat smells like… nothing," Kit said suddenly, glancing up at me.

"Om-Guard." I gestured at the family-sized pump bottle on the other side of the table—one of many I kept scattered throughout the house. While the white bottle was pretty inoffensive, the flower-clitoris-inspired logo was an abomination. Om-Guard Max—the blue-and-black version marketed to male omegas—didn't have have an artsy-looking dick scrawled on the side of it.

While I was always liberal with my Om-Guard application, I went extra hard in the lead-up to my heat. Everything about my scent screamed 'fuck me', and I just didn't need to go around projecting that while I was trying to get my groceries, or getting a cheese and bean pasty for breakfast.

"I didn't realise scentshield lotion was that effective," Kit replied cautiously, clearly fishing for a better explanation.

"You tricked me."

Those three damning words had lived in my mind for over a decade now, and apparently I wasn't going to shake them any time soon. I wasn't about to tell Kit that story though. That was one I was taking to my grave.

"Well, there's also an air purifier in each room that runs all day and night," I added with a tight smile, pointing out the white cylindrical machine on the top of the bookshelf with a nod. It was probably the most expensive thing I owned. "I'm very diligent about it."

Kit gave me a long look. "I can see that. Though I imagine it's impossible to cover up at Bryce and Kane's house."

I paused, my spork midway to my mouth. "Well, no. I don't bother with it there."

There was no scentshield product on earth that could stand up to omega slick. I mean, the pre-heat industrial knickers were pretty effective, but I didn't go to those parties to keep my knickers on.

"So I guess I'll get a good whiff then." Kit shrugged as though that was an entirely normal thing to say.

"You do know you are sitting in front of me, eating your lunch, bold as brass, talking about getting 'a good whiff' of my slick, right? I'm worried you don't know."

Kit's lips twitched. "I know. Though I appreciate you clarifying the terms of the conversation. Very lawyerly of you."

I narrowed my eyes, contemplating throwing an edamame bean at him. Then again, he was teasing me which was kind of lovely? Kit was so serious all the time, I hadn't even seen him tease his friends the other night and he'd known them for years.

"I hope I didn't interrupt a busy day?" Kit asked after we'd eaten in companionable silence for a while.

"No, it's not too bad. I wind down this time of year in preparation for my heat."

Kit froze. "Your heat is approaching?"

I frowned. "Didn't I mention that?"

"No, you absolutely did not mention that." He set his spork down as though he'd lost his appetite, giving me a look that definitely bordered on *alarmed*.

"Oh. Well, it'll be here in a few weeks." I shrugged, shooting him my best client-facing smile. "You don't need to worry, Kit. I'm thirty-two, this is not a brand-new event for me. I'm more than capable of functioning right up until the last minute when I go into my nest *alone*. I'll be fine to accompany you to Brighton and your dinner."

Kit didn't look reassured. I stood up, taking my empty bowl over to the counter to give him a moment.

"Did you know your heat was approaching when you spoke to me at the party?"

Usually, I was pretty even-tempered, but the doubtfulness in his voice really got my back up.

"It's an annual event, Kit. If I'm not currently in heat, then it's approaching."

"Soon. Did you know it was approaching *soon*?"

I turned, leaning back against the bench with my arms crossed and giving him an assessing look. "As I said, I'm thirty-two. It comes in late spring every year. I've never been caught unawares by it."

"If you don't want a mate, shouldn't you stay at home this time of year?"

"Are you suggesting a voluntary house arrest for a couple of months each year in anticipation of a five-day event? I'd tread carefully if I was you." My voice was mild, but there was no mistaking the edge of impatience in it.

"No, I'm not suggesting house arrest. It's just... don't you ever worry that you'll trick an alpha into claiming you if they get a hint of your pre-heat scent?"

Trick.

"You tricked me."

They really were all the same, these alphas. I really didn't *want* Kit to be the same as Fraser, but they'd both used that same, awful word. That cursed word that implied that I was the problem just by existing and having an appealing scent that I had no control over.

Kit hadn't even *smelled* it.

"Were you not just marvelling at my ability to mask my scent?"

Kit had the grace to blush, suddenly looking very interested in a scratch on the wooden tabletop. "It only takes one slip. And you said yourself that you have no intention of hiding it at Bryce and Kane's place."

"Among a thoroughly vetted group of people who are familiar with me as a person and an omega approaching heat. I'm hardly the only one who goes there to get their rocks off." He was dancing around what he wanted to say, and it was making me surprisingly furious. Why did I care? Did his good opinion mean that much to me? Clearly, it shouldn't. "Just come out and say it, Kit. What's on your mind?"

"I guess I'm wondering if it was all a ruse. If you masked your scent deliberately, knowing I'd be at Nico and Violet's party, to lull me into a false sense of security."

"That sounds like an awfully elaborate scheme. To what end did I concoct this nefarious plan?" I asked sharply.

"I don't know. To entrap me into claiming you when my guard is down?" Kit replied with an almost breathtaking level of insensitivity.

Truly, there was nothing quite like alpha confidence.

"Are you seriously suggesting," I said slowly. "That I came up with an elaborate plot to ensnare you with alpha-bait pre-heat scent before I'd even *met* you—because, obviously, you're just that wonderful? Not only that, I somehow hypnotised *you* into showing up at *my* scent-free flat to propose a plus-one-relationship-of-convenience as, what, a ruse to spend time with you? Am I missing anything? It was a real evil mastermind move for me to accompany you to the pub with your friends and politely allow myself to be totally disrespected by them, no? What a genius I am. Perhaps I'll write a book for other single omegas: How To Ensnare an Alpha in a Thousand Degrading Steps or More."

I paused my increasingly snarky rant to catch my breath, my face thoroughly on fire at this point from a mixture of rage and humiliation.

"Margot—" Kit began, pushing up from the table to stand.

"Because I couldn't possibly *want* to be single, right? That would be absurd. It's *much* more logical that I'd be desperate to throw away the comfortable life I've built for myself for an alpha I hadn't even *met* yet."

"*Margot—*"

"The absolute nerve of you to complain that the people in your life don't respect your choice not to take a mate and then come to my house, and sit at my kitchen table, and tell me that not only must I *actually* want an alpha—despite my assertions to the contrary—but also that in my desperation, I must also be a morally bankrupt person who *lulls alphas into a false sense of security* in order to *trick them* into claiming me." My stomach churned, and I briefly wondered if my rice bowl was going to make a reappearance.

It was one thing to be accused of being a sad, desperate, on-the-shelf singleton, but it was wholly another thing to imply what Kit had implied.

"Margot, I'm sorry," Kit rushed out quickly before I could open my mouth to resume ranting. "I'm *sorry*. I didn't mean that, I wasn't thinking—"

"Yes, you were. You *were* thinking. You were thinking that all single omegas are untrustworthy snakes, out to sink their teeth into you the first chance they get. You're full of ideas about omegas that run well into offensive territory, Kit, did you know that? Sinclair wasn't the problem the other night, your asshole friends were. How often is that the case?"

To think, I'd thought we would become friends. I'd thought I would help him review some of those offensive notions he had and show him the error of his ways. Then again, why should I? I'd spent half my career correcting outdated assumptions at work and being the default go-to for such questions as the highest-ranking omega in the firm. Sometimes, I just wanted to be seen for myself, not as an endless fount of information.

There was a faint, dull ache in my chest, the echoes of an old wound that like to pop up occasionally and remind me that the only way any alpha would ever be interested in me was if I tricked them into it, but I was long beyond the days of letting that pain rule me. There was more than enough going on in my life to fulfil me, I didn't need an alpha to make up the difference.

But I still had my pride, and that pride was stung by the implication that I wouldn't be able to stop myself from begging at Kit's feet for scraps of his blessed alpha attention.

He still looked as though he was scrambling for an answer, but I wasn't interested in hearing it. Actually, what I wanted to do was rail against him some more, maybe throw something to make myself feel better, but it was an irrational reaction and very unlike me. With every ounce of calm I possessed, I forced a mask of perfect civility back into place, looking at the alpha standing across the kitchen from me as the stranger he felt like.

"Thank you for lunch. I have to get back to work," I said, proud of how natural my voice sounded when my throat felt so tight.

Kit looked briefly startled, glancing around the room like he was flailing for some kind of lifeline. "I don't want to leave things like this, Margot, with everything unresolved. I was bang out of order for what I said, and I thoroughly regret it—"

"I have to get back to work," I reiterated, tipping my chin up stubbornly to hide the brief frisson of panic. At the end of the day, Kit was an alpha, and we were alone. It would be nothing for him to physically overpower me or even to manipulate me into compliance using his purr if he so desired. When it came to alpha and omega, the scales were always tipped in their favour.

"Okay," he said quietly, seeing something in my expression and backing towards the door. "We can talk later. Whenever you want."

"Sure," I lied, having zero intention to ever speak to him again, deal be damned. "See you around, Kit."

With an agonised look, he let himself out, and I listened to his footsteps retreat down the stairs, not releasing the breath I was holding until the front door lock clicked shut.

Then, and only then, did I let the full weight of the *hurt* settle into place.

Here I'd been, thinking of Kit as some kind of victim in his friendship with his awful friends, but we were all the company we kept, and Kit was no exception. I'd been feeling *sorry* for him.

Apparently, I wasn't as immune to soulful eyes and broad shoulders as I thought I was.

Somewhere inside of me, that sad little omega who *wanted* still existed, and I was going to make an extra effort to cauterise her now before I made the same mistake a third time.

Chapter Eight

"Oh, you are a dear," Mrs Clarkson said gratefully, accepting the package of meat I'd picked up for her from the butcher. "Lawrence and I would be quite lost without you, you know? We'd have to move up north to my son's town, and his girlfriend wouldn't like that. She thinks I'm quite the interfering old biddy."

I laughed at Mrs Clarkson's mischievous wink. Since she was all but technology illiterate and never visited Manchester, where her son had moved for work, I couldn't imagine how she'd be in any way interfering. She almost never spoke to her son.

"That alpha of yours was back today," she added with a conspiratorial look, leaning against the door frame. "He and Lawrence had quite the chat out the front of the house. I invited him in for tea of course, but he insisted he couldn't stay. Handsome one, that."

My smile turned brittle. Kit had annoyingly been upholding his end of our agreement for the past three days, no matter how assiduously I ignored him. Did he expect me to uphold *my* end of the deal after what he said? I had less than zero interest in going away with him and his awful friends after what he'd said to me.

"He's not my alpha," I corrected as politely as I could. "He's just an alpha I know, doing a bit of scentmarking to discourage the riff-raff."

"Come now, Margot, you can't think me that wet around the ears! I'm an old woman, I know what a wooing male looks like."

Mrs Clarkson had terrible cataracts, I doubt she was even certain what *I* looked like.

"He spoke very highly of you, you know, young Kit."

"Did he now?" I deadpanned. That he'd managed to turn on the charm for Mrs Clarkson after being so insultingly rude to my face was salt in the wound.

"Oh yes. He had a lot to say about you, and your kindness in particular—that really stuck out to me since you are so lovely and helpful to your batty neighbours when you don't have to be."

"You're not batty," I laughed. "And you're my friends. Of course if I can help out with anything, I'm more than happy to."

Mrs Clarkson gave me a long look. "Says a lot about your character that, for all you try to downplay it. And it's a credit to young Kit that he noticed it, I thought. Lawrence agrees and all, I'd pull him out here to tell you himself, but he's nodded off in the chair in front of the telly. Anyway, I won't keep you, I know you're a busy wee thing with your important job. But I just wanted you to know that I like Kit, and I'd heartily approve if you decided to knock boots with such a fine alpha."

I shook my head, laughing to myself as I hefted my own bag of shopping up the stairs. "Thank you. You know I value your opinion, Mrs Clarkson."

"Always happy to screen any of your prospective bedmates!" she called after me. "Oh, Lawrence! You've woken up!"

I was still chuckling to myself by the time I got upstairs and put the shopping away. It was mostly bottles of electrolyte replacement drinks that I carefully stacked in the mini-fridge next to my nest.

Orgasming every few minutes for days really made a girl sweat.

Violet: Want to come over for a movie night? I'm making fancy nachos.

I groaned, staring down at my phone. Avoiding Kit meant avoiding Nico and Violet—at least for the next few weeks—and I was feeling a little starved for company.

Not starved enough to put myself through that, though.

Me: I think I'm going to have a quiet night in. Raincheck?

Violet: Are you sure? Is everything okay?

Me: Just a long week. Have a good night!

That wasn't a lie. It had felt like a *very* long week, mostly spent stuck inside my own head, which was a fairly awful place to be at the moment.

I headed back to the kitchen and opened the fridge, looking at the neat stack of containers filled with perfectly balanced, nutritious meals I'd prepped earlier in the week, not feeling particularly inspired by anything.

Maybe I should make a cottage pie and drop it around to Michelle? The baby hadn't been sleeping well recently, and I was sure she could use some meals in the fridge.

My phone buzzed again, and I pulled it out of my pocket, steeling myself to assure Violet again that I really was fine hanging out alone tonight.

Asher: What are you doing? Taytum and Jules are going to this food festival thing in the city, and me and Chelsea blackmailed them into bringing us along too!

"Little shit," I muttered, shutting the fridge door with my hip while I tapped out a reply.

Me: What do you mean you blackmailed them? Why do you sound so proud of this? What festival?

Asher: Spring Food Fest, I think it's near your house?

I quickly looked it up, noting it was being hosted at a park two train stops away.

Me: I'm heading over now to take you two hellions off Jules and Taytum's hands. You can explain the blackmail in person.

Asher: They ditched us as soon as we got here. Yes, come join us!

I groaned, not bothering to check my face or hair, just pulling on a cardigan and grabbing my purse and shoes. They were both far too confident for their own good. Usually, my parents kept a closer eye on them—or at least Chelsea—but I was guessing they were distracted after Calum.

They probably also assumed that Chelsea and Asher were careful, obedient teenagers the way all their other children had been. Even Calum had been mostly cooperative at that age, but his challenges to authority were seen as a rite of passage anyway.

Chelsea and Asher were a different breed of kid, though, made of whatever fearless substance youngest siblings were constructed out of.

I was at the park within half an hour, tucking my purse close to my body so I didn't bump into anyone and weaving my way through the crowd. It was busier than I expected, though the afternoon was a warm, sunny one and there were still plenty of hours of daylight left, so I supposed I shouldn't have been surprised. Fortunately, the delicious scents of food coming from the various trucks and food stalls made the smell of the crowd tolerable at least as I hunted through people for my wayward siblings.

I spotted Jules' dark curly hair first, finding her sitting on a fence with Taytum standing between her legs, feeding my sister a churro. Fortunately, Taytum had quick reflexes, since Jules nearly fell off the fence when she saw me.

"Where are they?" I asked by way of greeting.

Jules had the grace to look sheepish, her pretty face flushing pale pink—not the splotchy shade of magenta I went when I got embarrassed. "They're around here somewhere. I said they weren't allowed to leave the park."

I gave her my best disapproving big sister face before heading back into the crowd, shooting Asher a message to meet me at the taco truck near the centre.

"Oh hey sis," Asher said cheerfully, scaring the life out of me as he popped up behind me with some pink candy floss on a stick as big as his head in one hand, and a can of lemonade in the other. "You got here quick."

Chelsea clutched her drink in front of her, looking slightly less brazen about her shenanigans. Asher was the baby of the two of them, but absolutely the lead troublemaker.

"You two are in my bad books," I told them sternly, not actually that upset now I saw them safe and sound in front of me. "At least next time message me *before* you go out. And use some scentshield, you both reek of baby omega," I grumbled, fishing a tube of Om-Guard out of my purse and handing it to them. Aside from the general risks associated with being an omega, pubescent alphas and omegas had a particularly pungent scent that was incredibly unpleasant for those who had reached maturity. It was a smell that really shouldn't be inflicted on anyone.

It was the same scent that could also make them trafficking targets.

"For sure, we'll message you next time," Asher agreed solemnly, the lying little shit. "Can I borrow some money? I ran out and Chels won't share."

Chelsea rolled her eyes, applying the lotion. "I already bought you lemonade."

"I'll go buy us all some real food," I interjected. "Candy floss does not a balanced meal make. Let's look around and find what we want to eat."

"Mmk," Asher replied cheerfully, falling into step next to me while Chelsea appeared on my other side. "You know, you really shouldn't be cross with us. What were we supposed to do when Jules said she was coming out? Stay at *home*?"

"Yes? They're on a *date*, Asher."

"Well, they should go on dates to less interesting places." He shrugged, totally unbothered, and I shook my head, laughing silently to myself.

I'd never intentionally annoyed Layla at that age, and for the most part, she'd never intentionally annoyed me. I'd been entirely confident in the perfect trust between us.

Until I wasn't.

"How did you blackmail her?"

"Jules has been climbing out the window at night to go hook up with Taytum by the pond," Chelsea replied, still working lotion around her neck. "We said we'd tell Mum and Dad if she didn't bring us along today."

"There's that sibling solidarity," I deadpanned.

"We wouldn't have *actually* told," Asher clarified around a mouthful of candy floss. "We were just threatening her, so it's really not that bad."

"You're a little sociopath, you know that?" I bumped him with my shoulder. "Did Mum and Dad not have anything to say about you two tagging along? With only one alpha between you? An alpha who probably has very little interest in keeping an eye on the two of you, at that?"

"They were kind of distracted." Chelsea leaned in close, her voice barely above a whisper. "They've got some seedy private investigator beta over to talk about Calum. He's been by the house a few times, and Mum and Dad always just want us out the way when he shows up."

"Is that so," I muttered. "Any idea what his name is?"

Chelsea shook her head.

"We can find out," Asher replied breezily, not bothering to keep his voice down.

"Don't do anything stupid," I warned. "You can be so reckless you know—"

I froze mid-step as we rounded a corner, finding a collection of standing tables made out of old barrels, and an alpha I really wasn't in the mood to make small talk with at the closest one, staring right at me, his mouth parted in surprise.

"Holy shit," Asher whispered. "Who is that guy? He's staring right at you, Margot. Is he a friend of yours? Alpha bang buddy?"

"Shut up," I hissed, elbowing him in the gut. I, for sure, was not this disrespectful as a teenager.

I swallowed thickly as Kit ignored the other two people at his table, coming straight for me. Being the sole focus of all that alpha intensity was heady, even if I was still mad at him and didn't want it.

"Margot."

Oof. Screw him and his stupid gruff voice, and hot nerd glasses and fitted t-shirt that showcased his even stupider biceps and perfect chest.

"Kit," I replied, absolutely nailing the cool, calm, collected tone. *Look at me, totally unbothered, going about my day with my heat approaching, not tricking anyone into lifelong commitments.*

I mentally sat down on a throne and started filing my nails. Un. Bothered.

"I'm Asher," my brother announced loudly, smiling cheerfully and not picking up the fuck-off vibes I was projecting at all. Probably on purpose. "Margot's baby brother. And this is one of our other sisters, Chelsea."

Poor Chels didn't do well with strangers. She'd gone as red as a tomato, and was attempting to subtly angle herself behind me.

"It's a pleasure to meet you," Kit replied gallantly, not looking as cripplingly uncomfortable as I'd seen him at other social functions. Maybe he was one of the rare people who found teenagers less terrifying than adults.

"Well, we won't interrupt—" I began.

"I wish you would," Kit cut in smoothly. "Only I've been telling my aunt and her *friend* about you for the past hour and a half. I'm sure they'd love to meet you."

There was definitely a note of pleading in his gaze, and I hated that it affected me. I *didn't* like to see him uncomfortable, but me and my saviour complex needed to learn boundaries.

"I'm a little busy with my siblings," I gritted out. No matter how good his puppy dog eyes were, I wasn't about to drag Chelsea and Asher into my lies.

"That's okay," Asher said hurriedly. "We'll just grab that table right there so you can see us. We won't go anywhere. Well, except to get dumplings. Right, Chels?"

Chelsea nodded vigorously, happy with any plan that didn't involve making small talk with strangers.

For one stupid moment, I actually considered it. Kit looked miserable, and I *did* have a saviour complex.

But then I remembered that he'd suggested with a straight face that every interaction we'd had was some kind of nefarious plot to trap him, and all my sympathy evaporated.

"I'm here to keep an eye on my siblings. Enjoy your meal." I grabbed Chelsea and Asher by an arm each, steering them towards the dumpling stall before Kit could answer, though I could feel his eyes on me the entire way.

"He's very handsome," Chelsea murmured, glancing back over her shoulder, not a shred of sisterly loyalty to be found.

"Seriously," Asher agreed. "Where'd you find him?"

"Mutual friends. Can you please make it a smidge less obvious that you're talking about him?"

"Sure. So, what's the story? He obviously likes you," Asher pressed, acting more obvious if anything. "He said he's been talking about you all night. Are you playing hard to get? Is this, like, a dating strategy or something?"

"No," I gritted out. "Stay here, I'm ordering us dumplings. Feel free to talk about literally anything else."

They were still whispering loudly when I returned with two trays of dumplings for us to share, setting them down on the table and distributing chopsticks.

"We were just saying that we should go find Jules and Taytum and ditch you with Mr Still-Staring Alpha," Asher said conversationally. "But I'm hungry, so we're going to eat first and then ditch you."

"You are not ditching me. I'm going to put you two little menaces in an omega car service and send you home," I corrected, helping myself to a chicken and shiitake mushroom dumpling.

"What about Jules?" Asher asked, affronted. "Why doesn't she have to go home?"

"Jules is nearly an adult, and she's with an alpha. I know it's unfair," I added in a rush when Asher opened his mouth to argue. "But honestly, even if you two were alphas, you're in the city miles from home and you're only fourteen and sixteen. Have a little self-preservation, would you? For my stress levels, if nothing else."

"We'll go home like good, obedient little omegas *if* you promise to go hang out with Mr Definitely-Still-Staring Alpha," Asher said stubbornly, tipping his chin up.

"Kit," Chelsea added helpfully. "She said his name is Kit."

"I will promise just about anything to get you two to eat your food then go quietly to the car," I grumbled before shoving another dumpling in my mouth.

"Okay, okay," Chelsea agreed, the more conflict-averse out of the two. For a while, we were able to enjoy the *delicious* gingery, garlicky dumplings in relative peace, even if I could still occasionally sense a pair of eyes burning into the back of my head. Well, whatever, Kit could stare all he wanted, I still wasn't going over there.

"Who's the omega at his table? Ow!" Asher asked, leaning around me to get a better look until I pinched him in the side. "You're my least favourite sister, you know."

I slid the tray of dumplings out of Asher's reach, raising an eyebrow at him.

"Fine, fine. Layla is still my least favourite, gimme."

I snorted, pushing the rest of the food towards him and Chelsea.

To my enormous relief, Chelsea and Asher got into the cab I called for them without protest. Unfortunately, I wasn't the only one who'd made their way out to the street to see them off.

"Your brother is very energetic," Kit commented quietly, standing a few feet back. He'd shoved his hands in his pockets and was rocking slightly on the balls of his feet, trying to make himself smaller and less intimidating despite his size.

"He is." I turned away, heading for the train station, not entirely surprised when Kit followed me.

"I kind of hoped you were going to come and see me, since you didn't leave with your siblings."

"Logistics. I'm only two stops away, they're heading in a different direction."

"Well, we can head back together then. I'm leaving now anyway."

"Grand."

Think aloof thoughts. Think aloof thoughts.

"That was my dad's sister who was in town for the night with an unmated omega who goes to her gym. She didn't want to be there as much as I didn't," Kit added, giving me a sideways look. Ah, so he'd been paying attention during my thorough dress-down.

"Okay."

I didn't ask and I don't care, I told myself firmly. Except I had been a *little* curious, wondering if Kit was looking for a replacement fake omega for his social engagements.

Kit looked like he wanted to say more, but I slipped easily into the crowd at the station, attempting to shake him off as I headed down the stairs to the platform. I weaved through the waiting passengers, tying my hair in a low bun in case Kit was looking for my blonde waves, before ducking onto the farthest carriage the moment the train pulled up. Maybe I was being immature—it wasn't like it was going to do me any harm to stand next to him on the train for five minutes—but the accusations he'd made against me had been weighing heavily on my mind for the past three days, and the deadline Dad had set for me was still looming.

I'd been so careful for *years* in my interactions with alphas. The ones I spent any degree of time with were mated and, therefore, more interested in *who* I was rather than *what* I was. The unmated ones who attended Bryce and Kane's parties were there to fuck, not talk, and so long as I had all the requisite omega parts they were interested in, that was all that mattered. So long as they had functioning knots and kept their teeth to themselves, that was all that mattered to *me*.

Kit didn't fit neatly into either of those boxes, and spending time with him had reminded me why I strictly kept to those parameters.

Not keeping to those boundaries only led to trouble.

I wasn't entirely surprised to find Kit waiting at the top of the stairs when I disembarked, a surly look on his face. Alphas didn't like to be given the slip.

"Can I apologise, Margot?" he asked, keeping up with me easily as I made my way out of the station.

"If it'll make you feel better."

"I don't want to make *me* feel better. I want to make *you* feel better."

"And you think an apology will do that?"

Kit made a strangled sound, weaving around a small crowd of women chatting on the pavement before catching up to me again.

"You can stop scentmarking my house, by the way," I told him over my shoulder. "I don't intend to honour my side of the deal, you don't need to bother with yours."

"I disagree."

"That's very on-brand for you."

I'd rather show up at Nana's party with Jimmy and figure out a way to get rid of him afterwards than sacrifice my pride for Kit's help.

The crowd thinned out as we moved farther away from the shops along the high street. Kit all but plastered himself to my side, just a hair's breadth of space between our arms.

"The moment I said all that stuff, I realised it was ridiculous. Some of the matchmaking stuff in the past... It's been a little more insidious than what you saw the other night. But you're not like that—most people aren't like that—it was wrong of me to project that on you."

"It was," I agreed, though his admission did soften me up a little.

"Can we start over?" Kit asked, gently pulling me to a stop. The puppy dog eyes were working a little harder now. "Hi, I'm Kit Iyer. Travel photographer, alpha, idiot who puts his foot in his mouth sometimes."

I gave him a long look. "Hi Kit. I'm Margot Bailey, omega going into heat soon who has no interest in being claimed by an alpha."

He winced. "Good to know."

"Let's just... leave it there for now, okay?" I sighed.

Kit nodded, looking dejected. "For now."

Chapter Nine

"You sure you won't come for dinner?" Violet asked, already dressed and drying her hair from the shower after our particularly intense yoga class. Or maybe I just found it intense because it was getting to the pre-heat point where I really needed to ease off the exercise.

"I'm sure," I replied with my most dazzling smile, still wrapped in just a towel as I doused my limbs in Om-Guard. "I promised Michelle I'd come by and help out with the kids; her mother-in-law's car broke down and Michelle is at her wit's end having to chauffeur her everywhere."

"Oh. I'm sorry to hear that." Violet wasn't as good a liar as I was, she couldn't quite keep the hurt out of her voice and I felt terrible about it. While we'd never explicitly stated it, my going to her place after yoga every Monday was sort of a tradition at this point. "It's just that you didn't come last week either," Violet hedged after a moment's silence, looking away as I pulled on my clothes, dressing for comfort rather than style to go to be clambered on by Michelle's children.

"I know, I'm sorry. Work has been—"

"Busy, yeah you said. Though you usually wind down this time of year with your heat approaching. Not that you've mentioned that, but Kit did say it was coming soon," she interjected, faintly accusatory.

Did he now? I thought wryly. Of course he got all chatty now.

Then again, Violet hadn't mentioned the food festival, so Kit hadn't been *that* chatty.

"I had a call with a client in Belize last week." Which I'd scheduled deliberately, because I hated saying no to people without having a legitimate reason.

Violet made a grumbling noise of assent, hanging back while I finished dressing and carefully reapplied my make-up. As always, she looked cherubic without a stitch of make-up on, her freckled cheeks flushed red from exercise and the steam-filled changing rooms. The wispy red baby hairs around her face had curled up with the humidity, and she smoothed them back irritably, though they just added to the general halo effect.

Meanwhile, my entire face was tomato red and somehow pallid at the same time, my hair more thin and limp than ever after a heavy dose of Om-Guard shampoo, and where Violet's green eyes sparkled after exertion, it only seemed to make the shadows under mine more pronounced.

I hated how sorry for myself I was feeling. With a little more force than necessary, I liberally applied my concealer, blaming my stupid hormones for my morose mood. Stupid heat. Stupid alphas. Stupid everything.

"I know you're very independent, but I hope you know that if something is bothering you that you can always talk to me," Violet said quietly. "And if Kit is being an asshole, you can totally tell me and Nico and we'll happily tell him to pull his head on. We're friends with both of you, but we're both very aware that Kit can be a bit of a grouchy bastard when he wants to be."

I snorted, sponging away all the redness in my cheeks. Her words were reassuring in a way I hadn't expected them to be. After all, Kit had been their friend first.

My phone buzzed and I shot Violet an apologetic look as I pulled it out.

Layla: I need you to look after the kids tonight. I'll drop them at your flat.

How thoughtful, I thought uncharitably.

Me: I can't, sorry. I have plans.

Layla: Cancel them. This is family, Margot. You have responsibilities.

Me: Maybe next time.

It wasn't what I *wanted* to reply with, but I still struggled with the idea of upsetting my sister, even though she'd never shown me the same courtesy.

"Who's put that look on your face?" Violet asked with a sympathetic frown. "Your parents? Layla? Calum?"

Ah. Kit had been true to his word and not told them about Calum. Unfortunately, I hadn't told them either.

"Margot? What is it?" Violet asked, her scent souring with the distinct scent of omega distress at whatever she saw on my face.

Hearing his name mentioned so casually was jarring. Like for a moment, he was still alive, still occasionally sending me offensive messages demanding either my help or money.

"Calum... Well, he sort of died." I winced. That had sounded a lot better in my head.

"Calum... *what*? When? How— No, you don't have to answer that, I'm sorry. I'm just... I'm so sorry, Margot."

We were drawing a little more attention than I was comfortable with. I quickly shoved the rest of my stuff in my duffel bag, linking my arm through Violet's and pulling her towards the exit, cursing silently to find Nico standing outside, waiting for her.

It wasn't as though either of them had ever met Calum—I'd deliberately had as little to do with my brother as possible after I left home, but they'd heard my complaints over the years.

"What happened?" Nico asked, looking alarmed as he pulled Violet into his arms, a low, soothing purr rumbling from his chest immediately in response to her distress.

Of all the intimate moments I'd witnessed between the two of them, hearing Nico purr for Violet was the only one that felt kind of intrusive. The only one that felt like a moment they would choose *not* to share.

"I'm fine," Violet gasped, pushing out of his embrace before his purr had her melting into a puddle on the floor. "Stop, I need to focus. Margot, tell us what happened."

Nico's purr came to an abrupt halt, his hand resting reassuringly on Violet's back as he gave me his full attention. For all my cynicism, Nico was a reminder that there *were* good alphas in the world.

Alphas who listened to omegas, cherished them, and respected them.

Calum hadn't been one of those alphas.

"Calum died," I repeated flatly, not allowing one single tendril of emotion to bleed into my voice. "He attacked an omega who wasn't in heat and sent himself into rut. The toxin caused heart failure."

Nico's eyes widened a fraction while Violet clapped her hands over her mouth in horror.

"The omega?" Nico asked gruffly.

"Long gone by the time Calum was found in some seedy back alleyway. My parents are trying to track them down." I swallowed thickly as Violet's eyes flashed dangerously. "I'll protect them. Somehow."

I hadn't worked out precisely how I was going to do that, but I'd come up with something.

"When did all this happen?" Violet whispered.

"A couple of weeks ago."

"That explains why you were so reserved at the party," Nico observed.

Violet grabbed my hands, giving them a squeeze, her eyes shining with tears. "You're so independent, Margot. So brave, so fiercely determined to face life on your own terms, and I admire you for that so much. But this is a big burden for you to carry on your own, and you don't have to. You never have to."

I nodded, giving her hands a quick squeeze. The close, loving, supportive relationship I had with Violet was what I'd envisioned myself having with Layla back when we were teenagers. I didn't mourn the loss of it anymore. Violet was the sister I'd *chosen*.

"I wasn't carrying it entirely alone," I admitted. "Kit knows. I told him that night we met. I'm not even entirely sure why."

And I could begrudgingly admire the fact that he hadn't immediately told Nico and Violet after I'd asked him not to. Whatever faults he had, he'd kept my secret until I was ready to share it on my own terms.

Nico blew out a long breath. "That's what you were talking about that night? I kind of thought that you two were hitting it off. That maybe there was something *there*."

"Nico," I chastised. "You know that neither Kit nor I is interested in mating."

"What I know is that you're two of the most stubborn people I've ever met," he replied with a pointed look.

"Sounds like the makings of a terrible, dysfunctional relationship," I shot back with a syrupy sweet smile. Nico snorted.

"You're sure you won't join us for dinner?" Violet asked. In all honesty, I was a little tempted now—Nico and Violet were comforting company when I felt down, but I'd already made plans.

"Michelle is really relying on me to help with the kids tonight—"

Violet sighed. "You're always there for everyone else, Margot. When is it your turn? When are you going to put yourself first?"

"Hey Margot," Luna whispered in my ear, pressing a sticky hand to the side of my face to hide our conversation. Why were kids always so sticky? She'd only just come out of the shower, surely she should manage to stay unsticky for longer than five minutes.

"Yes, Luna?"

"Remember when Archie threw a bean at me at dinner?"

"Half an hour ago? Yes, I do remember."

"*Well*," Luna began conspiratorially. "I peed on his dinosaur loofah."

"You *what*?" I choked out, keeping my voice low so I didn't wake the sleeping baby in my arms. "He's in the shower right now, Luna!" I whisper-shouted.

"I know." I'd never seen a six-year-old look so smug. I'd mostly come to terms with the fact that children weren't in my future, and I didn't mourn the life I thought I'd have in the way I used to, but sometimes being around children could make that old wound ache a little.

And then they went and told me that they peed on their brother's shower loofah in an act of diabolical vengeance, and I wondered if maybe the universe knew what it was doing.

"Kid, that is super gross. Go tell your mum so she can... I don't know. Dispose of the loofah, at least." Maybe set it on fire.

Luna groaned, throwing her arms up dramatically before stomping towards the kitchen. I guessed she confessed, since there were some muffled raised voices from the kitchen before Michelle thundered up the stairs.

Little Freya let out an adorable baby snore, cradled in the crook of my elbow with her mouth wide open. She was a terror when she was awake—one year old and already an accomplished escape artist who had an aversion to wearing any kind of clothing no matter how cold it was—but asleep, she was a perfect little angel, and I was more than a little impressed that I'd managed to rock her to sleep on my own.

My phone buzzed, and I quickly silenced it before Freya woke up and started taking her clothes off again.

Kit: Are you avoiding Violet because of me? This is the second Monday night dinner you've missed.

I tapped my thumbnail against the screen, debating whether or not to reply. It would be a lot easier to stay mad if Kit didn't appear to be genuinely contrite. He'd also won over Asher in their five-minute interaction, and now I had my brother pestering me about Kit as well.

Ugh, plus he was still showing up to scentmark my house. And he'd been nice to the Clarksons downstairs. *And* he hadn't told Nico and Violet about my brother when I'd asked him not to.

He also hadn't mentioned the looming deadline of my nana's birthday party and Dad's stupid ultimatum.

It was really rude of Kit to be so considerate after he'd basically called me a scheming omega to my face.

Me: You think awfully highly of yourself.

Kit: I'll take that as a yes.

I scoffed silently, locking my phone screen. *Stupid, cocky alpha.*

"Kev said he's running late," Michelle said in apology, heading back into the room with her eyes glued to her phone, a still sniffling Luna trailing behind her. "He said he can still give you a lift home but it might not be for a couple of hours."

"Oh, tell him not to worry." I unlocked my phone again, debating whether or not to take the train or call a cab. It really wasn't *that* late, and it was all one train line to my place...

Kit: Don't avoid Violet because of me. Preferably, don't avoid me either, though I get why you are. I'll go out next Monday so you can be assured of a Kit-free evening at Nico and Violet's.

"I'll take the train," I said decisively, suddenly eager for some fresh air.

"Oh, are you sure?" Michelle twisted her fingers nervously. "It's so dark out—"

"It's really fine. You're only five minutes from the station."

"Yes, but it's at least double that walk on your end," she pointed out, lips pursed in disapproval. "I'll call Kev, see if I can hurry him along."

"No, no, I insist. I can always get a cab up the road from the station."

I wouldn't, but Michelle didn't need to be stressing about me when she was already at the end of her rope looking after the three kids alone.

She hurried over, easily plucking Freya from my arms without much effort to avoid waking her, though Freya didn't stir. I headed for the entryway, grabbing my denim jacket off the stand and shrugging it on before slipping my feet into my flats.

Michelle exhaled. "You'll message me when you get home, won't you?"

"Absolutely."

I bent down, giving Luna an apology hug for not supporting her evil revenge plans, before giving Michelle a quick air kiss. Shouldering my purse, I let myself out into the surprisingly warm night air.

Michelle's neighbourhood looked much like mine—rows upon rows of Victorian terrace houses—though she was a little closer to one of the forests, and there was more greenery around here.

I pulled my phone out of my bag to check the time, finding Kit's name flashing across the screen.

"Impatient, aren't you?" I said by way of greeting. "I was going to reply."

"You were taking too long. I don't have much in the way of alpha instincts—" That was a lie, though I didn't think it was a conscious one. He was just out of touch with them *"—but between you and Violet—who was sad all through dinner—I'm feeling like I need to urgently... I don't know. Fix things. Make things better, somehow."*

"It's really fine, Kit. There's nothing to fix. Violet is sad because I told her about my brother. And I'm not sad. I'm not anything—" A car sped past, and I paused for a moment before I continued so he'd be able to hear me. "We put this whole thing to rest the other day—"

"What was that?" he interrupted. *"That sound."*

"What sound?"

"It sounded like a car."

"Oh. A car. We can continue this conversation later—I guess? I don't really think we need to—I just got to the station—"

"You're getting on the train? Now? Where are you?"

I snorted. "There are those instincts flaring again. When it rains it pours, huh? I'm nearly home, nothing to worry about. Thanks for unnecessarily calling, I'll be sure to join Violet for dinner next week."

I shoved my phone away as I hung up, scanning my card and merging into the crowd going down the stairs to the platform.

That explained why he'd been rushing after me the other day when I'd left the festival. *Instincts.* For all Kit's incorrect and offensive assumptions about omegas, the powerful pull of *alpha* instincts was nothing to be sniffed at. I could just ignore him, ignore any alpha I wasn't mated to, so long as they weren't purring or growling in my face, attempting to exert control over me.

But without doing anything at all, I was stuck in Kit's brain like an annoying ad jingle. I'd entered his orbit as an omega that he gave somewhat of a shit about—whether he wanted to or not—and therefore he was stuck caring about my safety.

Not for all the money and no heats in the world would I want to be an alpha.

Kit looked like an avenging god, standing at the station entrance when I disembarked, muscles tight with tension and dark eyes flashing furiously.

I wasn't surprised to see him, but I didn't ask for his instincts to single me out. Contrary to his claim that I'd tried to trick him, Kit had been the one to show up at *my* house the day after the party. He'd sought *me* out. His instincts weren't my job to cater to.

I straightened my shoulders and strolled right past him.

With a satisfyingly incredulous sound, he scrambled to follow.

"Don't," I clipped as Kit fell into step next to me, tension rolling off him in waves. "Save the whole overprotective alpha routine for an omega who wants it."

"It's *dark*, Margot. And you're—"

"Do not finish that sentence," I cut in, flashing him a warning look. If he announced to all and sundry that my heat was approaching, I'd slice open my finger and poison him myself.

Kit checked himself, taking a deep breath and pressing his lips tightly together, but he was still clearly in a bear of a mood. Well, that was fine by me. I hadn't asked him to swoop in and save me. I didn't need saving.

"Margot," he began in an infinitely reasonable tone that annoyed me even more. "Don't be stubborn—"

"Or, hear me out, you could not tell me what to do," I cut in.

He threw up his hands in exasperation. "I don't know why I'm telling you what to do. I'm not one of those alphas. I'm acting like a total asshole."

"Better," I conceded, tipping my chin. "You may continue telling me all the reasons why you're terrible."

Kit snorted. "No. Tell me you won't traipse around the streets alone in the dark any more."

"Also no."

"Then it seems we're at an impasse." He was clearly agitated, being ridden hard by instincts he didn't really understand, and I found myself taking pity on him.

Damn it.

In spite of everything, that reaction was *my* instincts, rearing their ugly head. Alphas grumped and sulked and beat their chests. Omegas whined and stomped their feet and *soothed*. It was that soothing urge that was riding me hard now, watching Kit struggle, which was some serious horse shit since Kit wasn't *my* alpha.

Why was I getting saddled with these emotions? What deity had I offended for this to be my fate?

With a heavy sigh, I stepped to the side of the path so the crowd could pass us, Kit dogging my every step. Not letting myself question it too much, I reached up and wrapped my arms around his neck. He only froze for the briefest second before he was hugging me back, arms banded tightly around my waist.

"What exactly are we doing?" Kit murmured, his lips a hair's breadth away from my ear.

"Hugging."

He hummed. "It's nice. Why are we hugging?"

"Alpha nonsense, with a generous side of omega nonsense. Stop questioning it, it's already awkward enough."

Kit shook with silent laughter, the tension bleeding out of him as though I'd snuggled it all away. I could begrudgingly admit that it was a powerful feeling to be able to *tame* an alpha who was probably four times stronger than me.

"I'm not accustomed to alpha nonsense. I can't help but question it. I sort of feel like I'm losing my mind."

"If it helps, from what I know about alphas, that seems normal."

Satisfied that he was calm, I pulled away, though Kit immediately grabbed my hand, keeping me close to his side as we headed past the closed shops to my quiet street.

"I'm still annoyed with you," I said conversationally.

"I know."

"Good."

Kit followed me as I turned onto the path leading up to my freshly scentmarked stoop, maintaining his hold on my hand which made unlocking the door difficult, but he was clearly feeling edgy, so I let it slide. *I was too accommodating for my own good*, I thought to myself.

"I'm guessing that alpha hasn't been back?" Kit asked gruffly, following me into the entryway, his hand still superglued to mine.

"You're coming in, are you?" I asked wryly.

He didn't answer, just closed the door behind him and kept holding on to me. I dragged him up the stairs, letting us into my flat where he finally released his hold on me, the lock clicking into place behind us while I flicked on the lights.

"The alpha," Kit prompted, crossing his arms over his chest. "I've been by most days and haven't picked up his scent. Has he been back?"

"Not yet." I busied myself taking off my jacket and shoes, giving Kit plenty of opportunity to excuse himself now that I was back behind my own four walls and he'd done his perceived duty. "He did send a message, but I ignored it."

"What kind of message?"

"Something about dinner, I don't know. I blocked him."

Much to my dad's chagrin. I was going to get it in the neck from him at Nana's birthday party.

Kit paced the few steps between the front door and the dining table, not looking as though he was in a rush to leave.

"Do you want a cup of tea?"

"No, I don't want a cup of tea, Margot. I want to have a fucking word with this alpha who keeps bothering you."

I filled up the kettle, flicking it on and pulling out two cups.

"I'll make you a cup of tea."

Kit made a grumbling sound. "I actually do want a cup of tea. And I want to talk to that alpha. Why don't you give me his number? I'll tell him to fuck off."

"That might make it seem like I was actually bothered about it."

"Well, *I'm* actually bothered about it."

"Yes, I see that. And I suppose, if Jimmy has stopped by since his first visit, he'd have picked up your scent here and your irritation wouldn't be totally unwarranted in his eyes," I mused. "That is the kind of thing alphas read into."

Kit perked up. "So you will let me have a word with him?"

"No, I deleted the message, so I don't have his number. And even if I did... still no."

Kit immediately deflated, resuming his pacing.

"I don't know why this is bothering you," I pointed out, giving the tea a moment to steep. "I'm a nefarious trickster omega, out to ensnare you with my gold-star vagina."

"You know I regret saying that," Kit groused, finally ceasing wearing a path into my floorboards to sit down at the table as I set down the tea and grabbed the milk for him to add his own. "I know you're not trying to entrap me. I think we both know that you'd be the one getting a raw deal if you were. Of the two of us, you're the catch."

Kit added an ungodly amount of milk, turning his tea a pale shade of tan at best. *I guess nobody's perfect.*

"Let's not get carried away." There was no world in which I was a better catch than Kit, as evidenced by the fact that he had a queue of omegas lining up for him wherever he went, and I'd only been in one courtship back when I was a horny teenager, and it was with an equally horny teenager. "Have you seen your friends since our night out at the pub?"

"Didn't want to. I said I'd see them in Brighton. I was hoping maybe you'd change your mind and come along." I raised an eyebrow over my teacup. "I know I'm being selfish, but that night at the pub was a lot more fun because you were there."

"You didn't look like you were having fun."

"I spend a lot of time in my own company," Kit said eventually. "More and more each year. I'm not very good at socialising anymore."

"You won't improve unless you practice," I replied wryly, giving him a small smile.

Kit hummed, falling silent for a long moment before speaking again.

"My mum wants me to meet her at a pub in Greenwich tomorrow night." I waited for Kit to continue, sipping my tea. He didn't strike me as the type to volunteer information so freely very often, and I supposed I was the sucker that it had piqued my curiosity. "I doubt she'll be alone. But I also want to see her? Even though I know it'll probably just piss me off."

"Don't be hard on yourself. It's natural to still crave those familial connections even when the relationships themselves aren't necessarily *good*. You also don't see her very often, I'm sure that impacts how you view things."

Kit nodded, though he still seemed annoyed with himself.

Ugh. Omega instincts.

"Want to binge-watch some home reno shows?"

Kit tilted his head to the side. "Not really, but also yes...?"

"Just go with it," I advised, setting my cup down and dragging a chair in front of the sofa to put my laptop on since I didn't have enough space for a TV. "I promise, sometimes the best medicine for a restless mind is watching other people pick tile patterns. You'll see."

I'd just got my favourite show up—it was set in New York and was basically apartment porn—when my phone buzzed between us on the couch.

"What the fuck," I whispered, staring at the image I'd just received in revulsion.

"What is it?" Kit asked, clearly fighting the urge to lean over and look at my phone screen.

"It's a *dick pic*. An out-of-nowhere, entirely unwelcome *penis* picture. From a grown man! Is that a thing that grown men do? I assumed unsolicited genitalia pictures was the kind of thing people grew out of."

"If you're the kind of person that sends unsolicited... whatever you called them, then maybe not," Kit muttered, glaring at my phone. "This is from Jimmy?"

"I mean, I can't say for certain. I *assume* so, but I didn't save his number last time, and I've never seen his penis for identification purposes—"

I fell silent as Kit abruptly got up and started pacing again. He appeared to be taking this new development worse than I was, but I supposed it wasn't surprising. After scentmarking my door so consistently, Kit was probably taking Jimmy's disrespect personally.

"Send him a picture of my dick," Kit said suddenly, spinning around mid-stride to face me, his expression deadly serious.

"Send him a picture of... wait, what did you say?"

"My dick. Send him a picture of my dick."

I blinked up at him. "Why?"

"Because! I'm your alpha. I mean, he's supposed to think I'm your alpha. That's why I've been scentmarking your door."

Kit gestured at the door as he spoke, his cheeks slightly pinker than usual. He was *flustered*.

So was I.

I didn't want to think about Kit's dick. It made me feel... some kind of way. *Specifics: TBD.* Not curious or anything, though, of course. Obviously not.

That would be inappropriate, at the very least.

"That's, uh, very generous of you," I replied slowly, thinking about his dick just a little bit, in spite of myself. *I bet it's impressive.* "But totally unnecessary."

"I disagree."

I raised an eyebrow. "Are you even, you know, photo-ready? I'm not an expert on these things, but based on Jimmy's sample, the flag is meant to be at full mast."

"If you stop talking about Jimmy's *flag*, then maybe I could hoist my own," Kit muttered grumpily, his cheeks now a vivid enough shade of red to rival mine without make-up.

"Or I could just take a picture of the actual dick that takes care of me," I pointed out, already unfolding myself from the corner of the couch I'd been tucked into. Kit glanced around alarmed, like I'd been stashing an alpha in the linen cupboard for just such an occasion.

"It's a sex toy," I clarified, taking pity on him.

Kit's brow furrowed. "You have a dildo?"

We had veered into very inappropriate territory, and neither of us were making much headway at getting out of it.

"I have a hoard of dildos. An abundance of dildos. A *trove* of dildos. I'm a single omega, what did you expect?" I asked, laughing as I walked towards my nest, leaving Kit standing slack-jawed in the living room.

Now, which dildo would annoy Jimmy the most before I block him?

Chapter Ten

The words were blurring together on the screen in front of me by the time I finished the section of the agreement I'd been drafting and closed my laptop.

I checked the time on my silent phone, chewing my lower lip. *Six pm.*

I wasn't going to do it.

We'd reached a truce last night, bonding over tea and a mutual dislike for grey floors. But that was all it was.

Just a truce.

And if my door was freshly scentmarked this morning, smelling like coffee and whiskey and supportive friendship? Well, that was Kit's decision. I hadn't asked him to do that.

I drummed my nails on the desk, locking my phone and unlocking it again.

I didn't *owe* him anything.

Maybe I'd just see if he'd left yet. Except instead of pulling up his name, I found myself opening my message thread with Violet instead.

Me: Has Kit left for dinner with his mum?

Three little dots popped up immediately, before suddenly disappearing. Had she forgotten to hit send?

Before I could message again to ask, Nico's name started flashing across my screen.

"Hello?"

"Hello, Margot. Need a ride to Greenwich?"

I really hope I don't live to regret this, I thought to myself, smoothing down my mum-friendly navy dress and stepping into the pub Nico had just dropped me in front of.

It was a historic building that had been stripped of all its charm on the inside, leaving it grey, white, and soulless, but I'd searched it on my phone on the way over, and I knew the beer garden was the crown jewel of this place.

The moment I got outside, I paused for a moment to take in the lush green space before following the white pavers that led past wooden bench tables shaded by umbrellas.

My heeled sandals clicked along the path as I scanned the after-work crowd, looking for Kit's wavy black hair.

If he took one look at me and sent me on my way, I was going to die of embarrassment right here on the pavers.

"Margot!"

I turned at the sound of my name to find Kit already striding away from the table towards me. He looked extra nice in a pale cotton button-down shirt, having obviously made an effort for his mama, and I felt my mouth go dry in spite of my best intentions to ignore his physical appeal.

"Please tell me I can kiss you," he murmured, his body blocking whoever he'd been sitting with from view.

"You can kiss me?"

I had no idea why I said it. Masochism, perhaps. Before I could take it back, Kit was on me. One hand cupped the back of my head, the other banded around my waist, and I just held on for the ride as his lips crashed into mine with an intensity that made my legs shake.

Good thing I'd worn the super absorbent, slick-suppressant granny panties.

At some point, I'd started shamelessly squeezing his biceps, meeting his tongue stroke-for-sinful-stroke.

I didn't like the taste of lager as a general rule, but Kit-flavoured lager was freaking *delicious,* I decided, all but sucking it off his tongue.

There was a sudden burst of clinking glasses and laughter from a table nearby, startling Kit and me apart. We were both breathing heavily, limbs tangled around each other in a way that bordered the line of decency in public.

"You kissed me," I rasped, blinking up at him. His lips were swollen from my attention, and it took everything in me not to give them a little bite.

"You said I could."

"I did." We stared at each other for another long moment, vaguely aware of the world around us, but both lingering in this strange, emotionally heavy in-between. "But why did you want to?"

If he'd been set up with another omega and was slaking his lust for *them* on *me*, I was going to claw his face off. I'd never been a violent person in my life, but I could feel the borderline feral reaction in my bones.

"Because I'm so fucking happy to see you."

Oh.

"So, you're happy I'm crashing your dinner?"

"So very fucking happy," Kit muttered, draping an arm around my shoulder and leading me to the table where two women sat.

One of them was very clearly his mother—aside from the fact that she was an alpha, Kit had definitely inherited his dark eyes, curly hair, and sharp cheekbones from her.

She was also an alpha, which I hadn't expected.

The pretty omega next to her awkwardly pushed her long brown hair out of her face, staring into her glass of rosé as though it held the answers to every question in the universe.

The kissing was probably a little much.

"And who is this?" Kit's mum asked politely, clasping her hands together on the table and looking up at us.

"This is my Margot," Kit replied, gesturing for me to sit down before climbing onto the bench next to me,

My Margot.

Don't read into it, don't read into it, don't read into it.

"Margot, this is my mother, Seniya. And her colleague, Thea."

"It's a pleasure to meet you both," I said, giving them my best and brightest smile as though I hadn't interrupted a matchmaking session. Poor Thea was as red as a tomato, and I didn't want to make her more uncomfortable.

"Kit has told me about you," Seniya said, making my cheeks red enough to rival Thea's. She had a faint accent, though I couldn't place where it was from. "I didn't realise it was so... Anyway, I'm happy to meet you. Tell me about yourself."

It was a very different experience from Kit's asshole school friends, that was for sure. Seniya wasn't overly friendly either, but it was more in an assessing way, like she was getting my measure and seeing if I was right for her baby boy.

There were clearly bonus points for being a lawyer. She warmed up to me a lot more after that.

"I'm from Singapore," Seniya was explaining to me, shooting Kit a look that was *almost* affectionate but not quite. Like she *wanted* to be maternal with him, but wasn't sure how to be. "But my mate and I agreed that we wanted to raise Kit in the UK around his paternal family."

Her not-quite-warm expression faltered entirely at that, and Kit shifted uncomfortably next to me. It hadn't escaped my notice that Kit's father wasn't here, though I hadn't read anything into it. Seniya was an alpha, and they went wherever they pleased, though I was curious about Kit's dad. Was he an omega? A beta? Another alpha? That was the least likely option since Seniya had called him her mate, and alphas made for dysfunctional, combative pairs.

Then again, maybe that was why he wasn't here.

"I'm going to get us drinks," Kit said quietly, leaning in close. "Are you alright here for a minute?"

I nodded, shooting him what was meant to be a quick smile but stumbling ass over tit into a lingering glance.

There was something in the air tonight, there was no other explanation for it.

"Okay. I'll be back soon."

The moment he left, Seniya excused herself to use the bathroom, and my cautiously optimistic opinion of her dropped dramatically.

Thea drained her wine glass, her hand trembling slightly as she set it back down.

"I'm sorry if I'm making things awkward by being here," Thea mumbled, staring at the table. "I said after last time that I wasn't interested in Kit—he very clearly wanted nothing to do with me—but Seniya is sort of my work mum, and I think she got a little fixated on the idea of having me as a daughter-in-law, you know?"

"There's no need to apologise," I assured her with what I hoped was a soothing smile. From Thea's scent, she had definitely reached maturity, but she didn't look *much* older than eighteen, and there was never more pressure on an omega than at this time of their life.

"You guys seem really well-suited," Thea offered, hesitantly returning my grin. "You're so in-sync with each other."

"Thank you," I said after a small pause, a little thrown by her words. Maybe we were better actors than I thought.

"Were you waiting for him?"

"Waiting?"

Thea cleared her throat, seeming to struggle for a moment to find the words she was looking for. "Seniya talks a lot about Kit's job, and how he travels all over the world. You two seem so close, I assumed you've known each other a long time. That you were... holding out for him or whatever."

"Oh. *Oh*. No." I laughed, partly at the general awkwardness, and partly at the idea of pining after an alpha. Been there, done that, zero desire to repeat the experience. "I only met Kit a few weeks ago."

Thea frowned. "Would it be, um, rude to ask why you're unmated then? It's just you look a bit older—in a good way, I mean."

Don't be offended. She's a teenager, and teenagers think anyone over thirty has one foot in the grave.

Asher and Chelsea regularly made me feel like the crypt keeper, intentionally or otherwise.

Thea was blushing at her own question, stammering as she attempted to explain herself. "Also you have a proper job and stuff, which is cool. But isn't it really hard? Like the heats and stuff? I've only had one, and it was *horrible*. But I also feel all like... hot and panicky around alphas, and I don't know what to say, and they get annoyed with me not making eye contact, so maybe I'll just be single forever."

I hummed in agreement, feeling something of a kinship with this young, overwhelmed omega. "I've met plenty of alphas like that—ones who wear their dominance like a crown. Trust me, they're not worth your time. A *good* alpha doesn't need to lord their dominant nature over you, they're secure enough in themselves that they don't need to *command* respect. And it's not respect, not really. Not if it isn't freely given. That's just fear."

"Is that why you never bothered finding a mate? Before now, I mean," she added hurriedly, glancing at the door that Kit had disappeared through. Right. Because she thought we were a real couple and actually going to go into my nest side-by-side when my heat hit.

It didn't feel good to lie to Thea. Especially since she seemed like she could use an omega friend. She reminded me of how lost Michelle had been when I first met her. How lost *I'd* been at that age, though for slightly different reasons.

"Not finding the right alpha was definitely a big part of it. Not being someone's first choice was another," I added, infusing a little more honesty into the conversation than I usually did when I gave my reasons for being single. "If I'm tying myself to someone for life, I want to be confident that it's because they genuinely want *me*, not because I was there at the right place and the right time, that my heat struck and they found me convenient enough."

Thea nodded earnestly, easily managing to make eye contact with me now. She had a very pretty, angelic face, and it was no surprise that alphas wanted her for themselves.

"As to whether it was hard being unmated..." I looked around, surrounded by laughing groups of friends and loved-up couples. Logically, I knew that all those people probably had their own struggles too, but in theory, loneliness wasn't one of them. "Sometimes. Without the default companionship of a partner, I had to work really hard to build and maintain friendships. I was able to prioritise my career in a way that I'd struggle to do if I was in a relationship."

"And the heats?" Thea asked in a small voice.

"Are never pleasant, but they do get easier. Each time, once it ended, I wrote down things that I thought would make it easier and more comfortable next time around. It's a manageable sort of pain."

"It *was*," Thea amended. "You have an alpha now."

Maybe it was that ickiness about lying that prompted me to keep speaking. Or maybe it was that I'd once been naïve and hopeful, and the world had burned that out of me in one perfectly-timed hit, and I didn't want Thea to go through that.

"I've been in a courtship once before." My voice was barely above a murmur, noticing Kit and Seniya making their way back to the table. "We'd talked about my heat, he bought me blankets and pillows for my nest, we were serious. I was only eighteen, but I fully expected that we were going to go into my nest together when the time came, and that would be that."

Thea stared at me wide-eyed, and though my face was already starting to burn with decade-old embarrassment, I took a steadying breath and kept going. "He changed his mind the day before my heat set in proper, and I went into my nest alone. He found someone else. Anyway, sorry to be a downer. The point was just that I don't count my chickens before they've hatched."

Thea nodded, a grim look of determination on her face. "That's a good thing to bear in mind. I'd really like to talk to you more if you're open to it. My mum is an omega, but she's not very... helpful."

"That, I can relate to. Maybe we can swap numbers—" I pulled out my phone, intending to pull up a new contact for Thea, but a message appeared, stealing my attention. Judging by the way Kit froze behind me, he'd just received the same one.

Bryce: Party at our place, 10 pm tonight. You know the drill—get yourself drilled!

On a *Tuesday*? While they did randomise the dates since these gatherings weren't a hundred per cent legal, I'd never been to one on a Tuesday before.

I turned back slowly to look at Kit, finding his expression unreadable but his eyes blazing.

"We'll go as friends, of course. Go our separate ways when we get inside."

That's what I'd said. And he'd agreed, hadn't he? The conversation was a little fuzzy now.

Except Kit wasn't looking at me like we were friends, and we hadn't been *kissing* like we were friends.

So where did that leave us?

Chapter Eleven

Kit and I had returned to our respective lodgings after we said goodbye to Seniya and Thea, the air between us taut with tension.

It's going to be fine. Either you're friends, and you'll go your separate ways, or...

Or what?

There was no denying that I was incredibly attracted to Kit, but if something happened between us and he accused me again of trying to entrap him...

I shook off the thought. We'd moved past that, hadn't we? He'd been different since then.

There was nothing to worry about.

After verifying that Nico and Violet's car was idling outside my flat, I belted the shin-length black coat I was wearing over my outfit and grabbed my clutch and change of clothes, my gold heels clicking down the stairs with each step.

I was way more nervous than I usually was for one of Bryce and Kane's parties, which were usually the highlight of my month.

Kit unfolded his enormous frame from the cramped backseat, running an appraising eye over my curled hair and red lips, down the coat that covered everything, to my exposed ankles and sexiest heels.

His eyebrows pulled down in a faint frown, and I did my best to squash my reaction. We weren't a real couple, and we were even *less* real tonight on our hiatus from the arrangement I'd already called off.

Tonight, I was just Margot, the single omega who was here for no-strings-attached orgasms among trusted friends.

I probably shouldn't have muddied the waters by going to meet his mum.

"Hello." I paused, leaning in for a quick cheek kiss before sliding past Kit into the backseat. I was absolutely not going to overthink any part of tonight.

"You look lovely," Violet said, twisting in her seat to look back at me. "Love the red lippy."

"Thank you. You look stunning, as always." I didn't need Violet to take her coat off to know what she was wearing underneath—she basically had a uniform for these things.

Kit climbed into the seat behind Violet, his knees practically touching his chin in the small space, pulling the door shut a little harder than necessary. He didn't look nearly as enthusiastic about tonight as I'd expected him to look.

If anything, he looked a little surly.

"Are you looking forward to tonight?" Violet asked me, though I didn't think I imagined the flash of a glance at Kit.

"Of course." I shrugged, buckling myself in while Kit did the same. "Bryce and Kane always throw the best parties."

They *were* the best parties—everyone was fucking, safety was paramount, there was always a great range of alcoholic and non-alcoholic drinks to keep the participants hydrated, and they always ordered the greasiest cheese pizzas in the early hours of the morning.

Nico mentioned an old school friend he'd run into, and he and Kit fell into a one-sided conversation, where the usually quiet Nico was doing most of the talking as we headed away from the city. Eventually, Nico gave up and turned on some music, and I stared out the window as the houses grew larger and farther apart. Out of habit, I undid the clasp on my purse, pulling out the travel tube of Om-Guard and rubbing some into the pulse points on my neck out of habit, feeling Kit's eyes follow every movement. It was ultimately pointless—there was no way to hide my scent when the slick got going, and I absolutely intended for the slick to get going tonight.

"Here we are," Nico said, pulling up to the enormous wrought-iron gate and speaking to whoever was on the other end of the intercom until it slid open. From the outside, Bryce and Kane's grey stone mansion was the height of old money respectability.

On the inside, it looked like a sex shop and a particularly tacky circus had given birth to their interior design scheme. Everything was jewel-toned silks, interspersed with the occasional gold-painted sculpture that was always at least a little bit phallic-looking. I loved it.

We climbed out in front of the front steps, and Nico handed the keys to the valet to go and park the car.

Usually, Violet would be half all over Nico by now in anticipation, but she linked her arm through mine, shooting me a reassuring smile as we went up the steps to the front door.

"We can leave whenever you want," Violet whispered. "Just say the word. You're always bending yourself around our plans, tonight is about you."

Thank you, I mouthed, giving her arm a squeeze. I wasn't entirely sure where this weird mood had come from—was it having Kit here? Or was it because I was close to my heat and worried? Safety-wise, I couldn't be more protected here, but instincts were instincts.

"You look remarkably reserved," Nico was saying to Kit right behind us. "You used to get really excited about these nights."

I held my breath waiting for his reply, but Kit only grunted.

Kane was there to greet us at the door, his bushy beard twitching as he shot us a beaming smile, ushering us inside.

"Kit! Is that you? It's been forever, how are you?"

Kit gave him a half-smile, looking more relaxed than he had all evening and giving Kane a one-armed hug, careful to keep some distance between them. Probably because Kane already reeked of Bryce's arousal, and Kit was being careful not to pick up the scent.

"I'm good, man. You? You smell like you're already having a good night."

"I told Bryce he'd regret being so greedy so early in the night, but he whined, and I couldn't help myself." Kane grinned. "He's sprawled out on the couch, trying to find the energy to move."

I snorted, undoing the belt on my coat. Bryce was a delightfully, willingly, gratefully spoiled omega. He had his whine down to an art form, and Kane was helpless against it.

"Is that Margot?" A familiar voice rang out. "Oh, it is!"

I gave her a little wave as Nora approached, blue eyes raking down my body from the swell of my breasts to my exposed thighs, visible under the silky emerald slip dress I was wearing, skipping over my face entirely.

There were no games, no artifice with Nora. She was an alpha with cum for brains, a particular appetite for my slick, and gave me orgasms until I begged her to stop. After that, we went our separate ways with a smile and no expectations. It was usually the perfect level of superficiality but tonight, the idea had me feeling a little hollow.

Suddenly, I found myself being dragged backwards, my back hitting Kit's chest while his forearm wrapped tightly around my waist. Vaguely, I was aware that Nico was saying something, but was too surprised by the sudden show of possessiveness to register what it was.

"Don't tell me you're spoken for this evening." Nora shot Kit a sullen look over my shoulder, undoubtedly mad he'd spoiled her plans.

Spoken for.

I wasn't *meant* to be spoken for. That wasn't our original agreement. But based on how tense Kit was behind me, how surly he'd been since we got the message from Bryce, and how uncharacteristically touchy he was being…

"I am." I rested my hands on Kit's forearm, stroking his skin with my thumbs, trying to soothe whatever alpha urges that had him suddenly feeling so territorial, knowing he'd be mortified later. "Though I'm sure you'll have plenty of willing participants to spend your night with, Nora."

"Yes, but now that you're here, I want *you,* Margot."

I wished I could permanently kill with fire the stupid omega part of my brain that perked up at being told by an alpha—any alpha—that they wanted *me.* It was an embarrassing physiological reaction that I should have long since outgrown.

Kane opened his mouth, clearly ready to intercede and tell Nora to back off, but he didn't need to. A deep, rumbling growl emanated from Kit's chest, travelling through every inch of my body where we were connected and making everyone take a healthy step away from the two of us.

He was growling… for me? No alpha had ever growled for me before.

Don't read into it! The warning bells in my head were now blaring sirens, practically screaming *danger ahead.* Control of this situation, of this night, of the whole relationship in general was rapidly slipping between my fingers, and while part of me was worried, another part was happy to stand by and watch the chaos unfold because I was enjoying Kit's company too much to be sensible.

"Message received," Nora said with a light laugh, her mood immediately shifting from sulky to gleeful at this turn of events. She was unpredictable like that. "I hope you know what a lucky alpha you are. The *taste* of her… I'll never forget it."

She flounced off with one last wistful look at my thighs, and I was all but petting Kit's arm to keep him calm, his hold around my waist bordering on uncomfortably tight.

"Your slick should come with a warning label," Violet teased, handing her coat to the staff member waiting for it, revealing the fitted grey jersey dress she wore underneath with the explicit purpose of leaking through. "May contain addictive properties."

Kane and I laughed while Kit adjusted his stance behind me, putting a little more distance between our hips. There was a burgeoning bubble of disappointment in my chest, ready to rise, but I refused to let it out. Maybe instinct had demanded he monopolise my attention tonight, but he wasn't actually interested in anything more than that.

That was fine. We could still have a good night.

"Hush you. Come on, let's grab a drink before you two disappear."

Kit let me go, and the bubble attempted to inflate again, but he didn't go far—just pulled my coat down my arms to give it to the waiting staff member. A shiver ran down my spine as I *felt* Kit's gaze on my back, where the silk fabric dipped low, the whole scrap of a dress held up by delicate spaghetti straps. He wasn't quite growling, but I immediately turned to face him, reacting to the pheromones he was inadvertently pumping into the air.

The ones that called and demanded and claimed. They were dangerous and intoxicating, and I grabbed his forearms, letting him know that everything was fine, that I was here, that I wasn't going anywhere.

Not for tonight, at least.

"Do you want a glass of wine?" I asked, meeting his eyes, surprised at the ferocious look I found there. He shook his head stiffly. "Everything is fine, there's nothing to stress about. We're going to go get a drink with Nico and Vi, then we'll find a spot to sit down and chill. Sound good?"

"You're managing me."

"You need to be managed," I replied wryly, trying to wrangle Sensible Margot back into the driver's seat. "I'm not mad or anything, but it does appear that your alpha instincts have chosen to rear their head. I know you don't want me hanging all over you—"

"It's fine," he interrupted. Well, okay then.

I slipped my hand into his, following Nico and Violet farther into the mansion, heading straight for the sitting room where the bar was always set up. Bryce was sprawled out on one of the couches, giving us a lazy salute, a glass of whiskey dangling from between his fingers.

It was early enough in the evening that people were mostly still milling around, flirting and feeling each other out. Nico went to grab us drinks, and despite the relaxed ambience, Kit seemed to be tensing up again in the more crowded room.

Deciding to take Kit's gruff "it's fine" as permission, I led him to a sofa on the edge of the room, gently pushing him into the corner seat before perching myself daintily on his lap sideways, crossing my legs so I didn't inadvertently give Violet a show as she took the seat next to him, looking far too amused at this turn of events.

I'd never really dealt with alpha possessiveness before, but I knew scentmarking helped. Not that I had a lot to work with since I'd slathered myself in lotion, but I draped my arm over his shoulders and played with the ends of his hair, hoping it would soothe him a little. It seemed to work, if only mentally since Kit's posture relaxed slightly. His arm wrapped around my back, his enormous hand covering half my thigh, one thumb at my hip. I swallowed thickly. I was going to be giving off plenty of scent soon if he kept that up.

Nico returned with bottled drinks for all of us, and I gratefully accepted my soda while Kit cracked open his beer.

"I wonder if Marissa is here tonight," Violet mused, scanning the room. "She's so fun. Remember last time? When she was paddling that *enormous* alpha? I don't think I've ever seen a man come so hard."

Nico growled—an entirely playful sound, nothing like the full-blown chainsaw rumble that Kit had let out earlier.

"Oh please," Violet giggled, twisting to drape her legs over his thigh. "You said as much at the time, don't play coy now."

Their pheromones were already growing cloying, and I found myself leaning into Kit a little more, wanting desperately to bury my face in his neck and breathe only him but having just enough presence of mind to remember that it was a terrible, humiliating idea.

Except, Kit's fingers were brushing the hem of my dress, his hand skating farther away from my knee with each pass.

"I'm sorry," Violet said, turning to face me with an apologetic look. "My tits are aching, we're going to go play. Remember what I said, though. Tonight is your night."

I nodded, sipping my soda while the two of them moved into the centre of the room, Nico on a chair and Violet on the floor between his feet, ready to perform.

Kit nosed at my shoulder, startling me into returning my attention to him.

"What did that alpha mean about the taste of you?" Kit rasped. He shifted slightly beneath me, drawing my attention to a *very* alert part of his anatomy.

My face heated, both at the question and at the blooming ache between my thighs that could only lead to one thing.

I was old enough and experienced enough to control my reactions to a certain extent—I didn't *want* to walk around smelling like a horny mess all the time, so I'd practised taking my brain to a place of perfect peace and calm where my body would follow suit.

All of that discipline, that honed control, that *desire* for control, seemed to have gone out the window.

Horny Margot had entered the building.

"I'm told that my scent is very enticing, and my slick is particularly, er, flavourful," I replied eventually, my cheeks burning. It was like the omega gods had given me a consolation prize for my lack of looks—a particularly delicious pussy.

Lucky me.

Kit blinked at me. "How the fuck are you single?"

"You're cute." I laughed because I'd cry if I didn't. Because being a good fuck with more-ish slick didn't make up for my lack of looks, and everyone knew it.

Violet's back was to Nico, and he leaned over her to cup her breasts through her dress, kneading and squeezing until twin wet spots appeared, turning the pale grey fabric a charcoal colour. As always, they'd attracted a crowd, and Violet was panting as she performed for them, mouth open and eyes unfocused.

"Do you like watching them?" Kit's voice was a soft murmur in my ear but with the faintest hint of danger to it. Like a loving caress from the blade of a knife.

Was he jealous?

"I don't like or dislike it. I don't get off on it, if that's what you're asking."

He hummed, the hem of my dress inching a little higher, and with a mild cramp, I felt the gusset of my impractical lace knickers grow wet.

Kit stiffened, his hand freezing in place and his nostrils flaring. I attempted to stand, not entirely sure how to read his reaction, but his hand pinned me in place, fingers now splayed over my thigh, his thumb *almost* close enough to feel the damp fabric for himself.

It wasn't helping with the horniness, that was for fucking sure. I was barely stopping myself from begging him to shift his hand higher, to cup my pussy beneath my dress like he fucking owned me.

Instincts. Just instincts.

"I thought you didn't get off on watching them," he growled, inhaling deeply. "Fuck, you smell *incredible*."

"I promise, this has everything to do with you and nothing to do with them." I was breathing like I'd run a marathon, locking my muscles so that I didn't languish all over him with my thighs spread and ready, a willing omega, desperate for a knot.

Kit used his grip on my thigh to roughly pull me up against him, his hard cock digging into my ass cheek. "And *this* has everything to do with you. So what are we going to do about it?"

Kit could have yanked my knickers aside and sat me on his cock, and I'd have moaned in gratitude, not questioning anything about it until I was well and truly sated. That he was forcing us both to talk about it first was very level-headed and deeply attractive.

On the other hand, why did we need to discuss it? My vagina was in the driver's seat, and my vagina was ready now.

"Margot," he chided, giving my thigh a quick squeeze. I was pretty sure my eyes rolled back in my head. "What are we going to do about it?"

"Our regular arrangement is on hold for the night," I rasped. "We can do whatever we want to do."

Kit hummed, pressing his mouth to my shoulder. "A lazy answer, and we both know it. You cancelled our arrangement."

Omegas didn't growl like alphas. Mostly we whined to get what we wanted, but we certainly *could* growl, especially if someone we cared about was being threatened or our territory wasn't being respected. Neither of those things was true at that moment, but I growled anyway, as fierce as a furious kitten.

Kit shook with silent laughter, his thumb resuming those circles that perhaps he thought were soothing but were actually maddening.

"I'm sorry, omega. I didn't mean to tease. Will you let me take care of you? Will you let me tend to this sweet, needy cunt?" The question was a sweet plea and a growled command all at once.

I choked on my own saliva. "Yes, please."

"Such a sweet omega." Kit dropped a featherlight kiss on my shoulder before pushing his skewed glasses back up his nose. "As much as I don't want to think about what you usually do at these parties, you need to tell me what your comfort levels are. Do you like to perform like Nico and Violet?"

"I keep all the important bits covered if I'm in one of the shared spaces. If you want to... you know, under my dress, I wouldn't mind."

"But then everyone will smell that delicious slick of yours."

I managed a nod. "Well, yes. It's usually people's favourite thing about me at these parties."

"I don't care about them." Kit stood, easily taking me with him and setting me on my feet, an arm around my waist to keep me steady. "Let's go somewhere private, I want you to take the dress off."

I nodded, my mouth suddenly too dry to form words. There was a muted sort of warning bell doing its valiant best somewhere in the back of my mind, a vague this-is-a-bad-idea-Margot type of alarm that wanted me to consider things like consequences and future awkwardness.

I hit snooze on that bad boy. Those were Future Margot's problems. Present Margot was more focused on having her brains knotted out of her skull.

Bryce and Kane's house was a ten-bedroom Georgian, and we didn't even attempt the first four doors because of the sounds we could hear from the corridor.

Kit led me towards the stairs, but I hesitated, tugging him to a stop. The upstairs rooms were bigger, tending to attract group activities.

"Those rooms will be full."

"I know," he growled, glancing at a semi-private nook in the hallway. I could do a little better than that.

I took the lead this time, pulling Kit through the kitchen—where some highly unsanitary things were happening on the counter—and through a discreet side door that led down a couple of steps.

"A laundry room?" Kit asked doubtfully, hand tightening around mine ever so slightly.

"It's a very nice laundry room," I pointed out. "It's got custom cabinets and everything."

Kit gave me a withering look, his free hand moving to his waistband to adjust himself.

"You deserve better than a laundry fuck, Margot."

I paused, frowning. "What if I want a laundry fuck?"

I wasn't twenty anymore, and I'd definitely be feeling it in my lower back tomorrow, but there was something *very* sexy about fucking in such a mundane, semi-uncomfortable setting. Like the sex was just so *worth it* that the location didn't matter.

It was the total opposite of my nest, too, which helped me keep things straight in my head that I couldn't afford to get confused.

Kit groaned, glancing between me and the stretch of granite counter that covered the washer and dryer, far more conflicted than I expected any alpha presented with a wet and willing omega to be.

Had I given him the impression that I was precious? If I needed soft blankets and gentle words every time I wanted to get railed, I'd visit one of the dens and hire a professional alpha to coo in my ear while he tended my cunt.

I pulled my hand free of Kit's, putting a little extra swing in my hips as I strutted over to the counter and made eye contact with him as I turned and boosted myself up. My heels immediately clicked against the plastic window of the washing machine, and I made a show of adjusting the top of my dress, fussing with my cleavage as Kit's breathing grew increasingly heavy.

There was no bigger threat to me than an alpha on the edge of control, and yet there was also no bigger turn-on. Being an omega was like being a fragile fluffy bunny with a hard-on for slavering wolves.

With an exaggerated sigh, I parted my thighs and slipped my hand between my legs. "I guess I'll just finish what you started then."

Kit was on me within seconds, a growl echoing in the small tiled space. "*Fuck*, Margot. Tell me you want a nice comfy bed and some mood lighting. Somewhere you're not leaning up against a cold, hard splashback."

I gave him a wicked smile, shifting my dress a little higher. "I'm an omega. I could always benefit from a splashback."

Kit's eyes darkened, his hands sliding beneath my dress, knocking mine out of the way in the process. He found the sides of my knickers instantly, giving them a hard enough tug that I would have slid off the machine if he wasn't standing between my thighs.

His position also meant he couldn't get the fabric all the way down, and it was creating a lace prison just above my knees that he was in no hurry to free me from.

"Your *scent*," Kit groaned, leaning in to nip at my lower lip. "Like the richest vanilla cake and great sex, wrapped into one. It seems a crime to cover this up, Margot. A fucking cruelty."

I hummed, letting my fingers trace the bulging muscles of his biceps before drifting down to his veiny exposed forearms. "It's distracting. Better for everyone if I only break out the cake-fucking smells on special occasions."

I wasn't even sure he was listening. Kit nosed at my neck and shoulders, grumbling with displeasure even as he pushed my dress up to my waist. *Alpha nonsense*. The scentshield lotion on my skin would be bothering him.

Too bad.

There was no hiding the scent of slick, and I refused to live without sex, but other than that, my scent had been banished to the dungeon of expensive de-scenters, never to be whiffed again.

Kit took a small step back, finally dragging my knickers off and stuffing them in his pocket, the move startling a full-blown *gulp* out of me, frog-style.

His gaze dropped, a smug smirk transforming his features.

"You've made a mess, Margot." I whimpered—just a little—my pussy clenching around nothing. Slick *was* pooling on the counter beneath me at an embarrassingly fast rate, my body primed and ready for a knot.

"Why have you chosen *now* to be talkative?" I rasped, squirming as Kit's thumbs languidly slid up my inner thighs. "You hate talking."

"I like talking to you."

That was unexpectedly sweet.

"And I fucking *love* talking about your perfect, slick cunt. Your face goes such a pretty shade of pink."

That was unexpectedly *filthy*, made even more so by the way he casually removed his glasses while he spoke, gently setting them down on the counter next to me.

"Give a girl some warning, would you?" I choked out, the rest of my complaints dying on my lips as he shoved his perfect fingers in my perfect cunt.

The *squelch* was obscene, a veritable puddle of slick spreading underneath my ass and thighs as Kit leisurely explored my pussy with two fingers, slowing down every time I rocked against him.

I'd never been so ready so quickly in my life. The usual flutter of nerves and crush of self-consciousness was totally absent when Kit was staring down at me like I was a total revelation.

"Why are you torturing me?" I panted as he slowed his movements, taking me right to the edge before backing off again. "Is this punishment?"

"Yes. This is punishment for thinking a laundry room is any way adequate for our first time. This counter is completely the wrong height to eat your cunt."

Our first time?

Stop it. Don't read into it.

"Do you know what would be a real punishment? Fucking my brains out and stuffing me full of your knot," I suggested sweetly, sucking in a sharp breath when he pushed in a third finger, stretching me in the most perfect way. "That would be awful. Super punishing. I'd really learn my lesson."

Kit picked up his pace, fingering me roughly, sending a spray of slick everywhere. "I'm not knotting you on top of a washing machine, Margot."

That wasn't a no to the fucking my brains out, at least. I was about to point out us much, but Kit's talented fingers shoved me over the edge into an orgasm that had all of my faculties going briefly offline. I attempted to dig into the smooth stone surface with my nails for purchase before slumping back against the tile while Kit continued fucking me with his hand, dragging one orgasm into another.

One-handed, he flicked open the button of his jeans, unzipping them and pulling his cock free.

And what a cock it was.

Granted, I was in a lust haze, but if I had a single musical bone in my body, I'd have composed a ballad dedicated to such an exemplary appendage.

Maybe a full-blown opera.

Respect had to be paid.

"You're going to make my ego swell if you keep looking at me like that."

"I hope that won't be the only thing swelling," I murmured, greedily eyeing the slightly flared base of his cock where his knot would form.

"Flatter me all you like, you're not getting my knot tonight."

Kit yanked his fingers free of my still-fluttering pussy, pulling me right to the edge of the counter and rubbing the fat tip of his cock over my clit.

"Will you stop teasing?" I hissed, wrapping my legs around his hips and digging my stilettos into his ass. "Never met an alpha in my life who played hard to get with his knot, and I've got to say, I'm not a fan."

"Liar," Kit purred, impaling me in one rough thrust.

Every thought—logical or otherwise—fled my brain as Kit's fingers dug into my hips, pinning me in place while he fucked me senseless, shaking the appliances below.

The puddle of slick expanded, seeping under my palms, and I clapped my arousal-soaked hands down on Kit's shoulders, scentmarking his shirt as I held onto him for dear life.

"Fuck, Margot," Kit grunted, fingertips digging into my ass cheeks hard enough to bruise. "You feel... indescribable."

I made an undignified sound of agreement, a noise I'd never heard myself make in my life, throwing my head back and letting the wave of pleasure consume me. My pussy contracted around Kit's cock, and he let out a low alpha growl that had all my nerves tingling, his entire body stiffening. With an effort so agonising, I could see it in his face, Kit pulled almost the full way out, just the tip buried in my pussy as he came, his knot swelling in his hand.

Don't growl, I told myself, trying to ignore the visceral reaction I was having to *not* being knotted. The fact that Kit looked like he was suffering more than I did—roughly massaging his knot while he bit down hard on his lower lip—made me feel somewhat placated.

I released his shirt, pushing his hand out of the way so I could wrap mine around his knot, squeezing it in a poor imitation of what my pussy would feel like.

Kit watched me work before lifting hooded eyes to meet my gaze, and I almost came again from that look alone. When his fingers traced my inner thigh, I gladly took the excuse to break eye contact, looking down as he oh-so-slowly pushed the cum I was leaking back inside me.

Oh, Margot. You are in so much trouble.

Chapter Twelve

Kit reluctantly disappeared to grab my bag and some towels from the communal pile—omega problems—and I did my best to calm my breathing and get my wild emotions under control—not an easy feat in a confined space that reeked of our coupling.

I'd had sex with Kit.

Great sex.

Sex that I very much wanted to have again.

Shit.

Obviously, it didn't mean anything. That went without saying. This was clearly a one-off.

Best if I just forgot about this entire thing.

Kit slipped through the laundry door, laden down with supplies. "The downstairs shower is free if you want to make a run for it?"

I pasted on my most unbothered smile and gestured at the puddle I was sitting in. He snorted, setting a towel down on a clean patch of counter and then lifting me around the waist like I weighed nothing and plonking me down on it.

Blushing something fierce, I did my best to discreetly clean myself up while he tackled the counter, grabbing a lemon-scented bleach cleaner from the shelf and hiding the evidence of what we'd been up to in here. Bryce and Kane always had a cleaning crew through the house the next day, but all of us guests tried to be as considerate as possible with our bodily fluids. That was just basic decency.

The moment he was done, Kit shouldered my bag and scooped me up bridal-style—towel still in place—ignoring my protests as he carried me through the blessedly empty kitchen to the downstairs guest bathroom.

"Okay, well, thanks," I mumbled as he put me down in the tiled walk-in shower. I hurriedly turned the water on, careful to avoid the cold spray. "I'll just meet you out there?"

Kit frowned, standing at the edge of the glass partition.

"Unless you want to shower too," I tacked on, realisation suddenly hitting me. "Of course you do, you reek of me."

The night was young, and the party was just getting started. No other omega out there was going to touch him with a barge pole while he smelled so strongly of my slick.

I dropped the towel and peeled off my silk dress, handing both of them to Kit when he held his hand out, before stepping into the shower and angling the spray of water down so I didn't ruin my hair and make-up.

"I don't want to wash off your scent," Kit muttered, still standing at the edge of the shower, watching as I pumped a generous dollop of unscented body wash into the palm of my hand. "I *really* don't want to. Why is that?"

I blinked at him before turning away to wash between my thighs with some modicum of privacy. "I'm not sure, Kit. Maybe it's just been a while? Don't answer that, I'll start growling, and it's embarrassing."

That wiped the confusion off his face, a smug smirk replacing it.

"Or maybe you just like my scent." I shrugged, finishing my rapid-fire wash before someone else needed the bathroom. "As you've pointed out, I smell glorious."

Like a vanilla-scented cock sleeve, custom-made for an alpha's knot.

I'd been joking, but Kit growled out a sound of approval. "Yes, you do."

I snatched up the clean towel he was holding out, my face so hot I was probably melting off my make-up, drying my body and moving around him to get clean clothes out of my bag.

Usually, I didn't get to the shower-and-change point until the early hours of the morning when I was ready to get home. The comfy grey track pants and slouchy black knit sweater weren't party clothes, they were leaving clothes.

Then again, I could always take a cab home. It wasn't as though I had any interest in pursuing anything with anyone else tonight.

Kit watched silently as I reapplied my Om-Guard and got dressed, sealing my silk dress in an airtight bag for laundering and switching out my heels for black slides.

"Where are my knickers?" I asked, pausing in the middle of stuffing everything back in the duffle bag.

Kit glanced shiftily at the door, his cheeks blooming scarlet. "Shall we go then?"

"Kit Iyer, are my knickers still in your pocket?"

"Nico and Violet are probably wondering where we got to." He pushed his glasses up his nose, still looking slightly sheepish.

I narrowed my eyes at him, zipping up my bag and stalking towards the door. They probably *were* looking for us, which was the only reason why I was letting this slide. Usually, I gave them a heads-up before I went off with someone.

"We'll discuss my missing underwear later," I told Kit, giving him my best schoolteacher face before leading him down the hallway, back to the living room where we'd last seen Nico and Violet.

I half expected them to be either fornicating on the sofa or in another room completely, so it was a shock to find them making small talk with Bryce, both completely clean and dressed in their spare clothes.

"Ah, there you are," Violet said with a beaming smile, ushering me over. "Are you two ready to go?"

"Yes," Kit replied instantly, before I had a chance to formulate an answer. None of them looked surprised—probably because Kit was strutting around stinking of my slick, which I felt kind of bad about.

I was the one omega Nico and Violet trusted *not* to be trying to get into Kit's pants, and I felt a little bit as though I'd betrayed them.

"Oh good," Violet sighed, leaning against Nico and staring up at him dreamily. "I'm starving."

I'd heard milk production had that effect.

We all said our goodbyes to Bryce and Kane, slipping out the front door before we had to make small talk with anyone else. Kit carried my bag for me, opened every door, fussed over my seatbelt when we climbed into the backseat of Nico's car. In the frontseat, Nico was doing the same for Violet, and it all felt very... double date-ish.

Which was not what it was.

At all.

Even though I'd thoroughly coated myself with Om-Guard after my shower, smelling myself on Kit in the small confines of the car was messing with my head. I pulled out the travel-sized tube and began slathering over all the exposed skin I could reach.

"So," Violet began brightly. I braced myself in anticipation. "Do you want to talk about it, or do you want to listen to music?"

"Music," I replied instantly.

If she was disappointed, she didn't let on, and I'd never appreciated her more.

The soothing sounds of sixties soul music—Violet's go-to—filled the car, and I tipped my head back against the seat, letting my eyes drift shut so I could pretend not to notice Kit's stare burning into the side of my head.

Within the hour, we were pulling onto our street. My house was first, but Nico wasn't slowing down yet.

"Aren't you dropping me home?" I asked, sitting up in my seat.

He glanced at me in the rearview mirror. "I don't know, am I?"

Somehow, even with the music playing, the car felt oppressively silent.

"Yes, please."

"Of course," Nico murmured, flicking on the indicator. I made a show of reorganising my purse, using it as an excuse to keep avoiding Kit's gaze.

He couldn't come up with me, and we all knew it. In my tiny flat, the only sleeping space was the nest, and Kit wasn't my mate. My nest was off-limits.

"I'll walk you to the door," Kit said in a low voice the moment the car pulled to a stop. He grabbed my duffel bag and climbed out before I could protest. *Bossy alpha.*

"Thanks for the ride," I said awkwardly, having never once felt awkward around Nico and Violet before.

Violet twisted in her seat, giving me one of those radiant smiles that felt like a warm hug. "We love you, Margot. You can stop looking at us like we're about to bring a guillotine down on your neck at any moment."

Nico snorted. "We're also not at all surprised, just so you know. It was pretty obvious to anyone with functioning eyeballs or olfactory senses that this was going to happen, it was only a matter of time."

"If you're trying to make me feel better, it's not working," I told him tartly, blowing Violet a kiss before getting out of the car.

Had I been making moon eyes at Kit this whole time? What a mortifying thought.

Kit was waiting on the stoop, the automatic light that hadn't worked for months suddenly functioning again. Huh. Maybe Lawrence had fixed it? The Clarksons never left the house after six pm, I'd be surprised if they even noticed it wasn't working.

"Are you okay?" Kit asked, giving me a slightly unnerving stare as he handed me my bag.

"Of course. Why wouldn't I be? I'm fine. Better than fine, even. That's what a few good orgasms do to you." I was babbling. No, I'd gone right past babbling into some heretofore-unknown stage of humiliating chitchat. "Anyway, thanks for, you know. All the orgasms. And I'll see you... later. We still have to talk about my underwear. Okay, never mind, bye."

My fingers fumbled with the keys, and Kit made a quick rescue before they fell to the ground.

"Here," he said softly, leaning into my personal space to unlock the door, smelling unfairly tempting. He brushed the faintest hint of a kiss over my cheek as he pulled back, so light I wondered if I'd imagined it. "Goodnight, Margot."

Kit was looking at me like he couldn't decide whether he wanted to stay or go, but he seemed torn about it. As though he *wanted* to know what the right choice was, but felt ill-equipped to make it.

It made something in my chest tighten.

Get your shit together, Margot. You have come too far to lose your head over an alpha.

I twisted to face him, giving him a breezy smile as I hooked my finger in the pocket of his jeans, snagging the lace of my knickers and pulling them free, feeling a flash of victory at the slightly crestfallen look he tried valiantly to cover up.

"'Night, Kit."

By the morning, I felt like myself again. After coffee, I got in the shower and all but boiled my skin off before slathering a borderline uncomfortably thick layer of Om-Guard on every inch of my body that I could reach.

The reason I went to Bryce and Kane's parties was because sex made all the omega parts of me relaxed and happy. I was never feeling the potent impact of fucking an alpha more than I was at this exact moment. Kit hadn't even *knotted* me. He probably had magic jizz. Why not? He was a freaking catch in every other way, why not have super powerful relaxant cum too?

I tipped my head forward to wrap it in a drying cloth, twisting the material into place before grabbing my buzzing phone off the bed.

Kit: Good morning.

...A good morning message? He'd sent me a *good morning* message?

Was he trying to make sure there was no awkwardness after last night?

Was it *flirty*? He had mentioned last night being our *first* time, which would imply *more* times...

What did it *mean*?

For the first time in my life, I was thrown back to the early days of exchanging flirty messages with the cute alpha boy who'd just moved in next door. The vaguest flutter of a butterfly wing attempted to get off the ground in my belly, and I sent as many murderous thoughts towards it as I could.

That's not what this is. This isn't the start of something. There is no need for butterflies here, thank you very much.

Me: Good morning.

There. Done.

There was no lingering awkwardness now. We'd messaged each other, we'd made contact, and now our relationship could return to what it had been before last night.

Kit: What are you doing today?

What the fuck was he playing at? If Kit was trying to act normally, he was failing miserably. I twisted from side to side, trying to work out the kinks in my spine while I typed, deleted, then retyped a reply.

Me: I'm meant to be working, but I haven't got that far yet. Maybe I'll book a massage first.

My phone rang instantly, and I was so surprised that I nearly dropped it.

"Hello?" I said hesitantly. Surely, he'd hit the call icon by accident.

"Are you at home?"

"...Yes?"

"I'm on my way."

The call clicked off, and I stared down at my phone in shock. And then the panic set in because I was fresh out of the shower, with my hair in a drying wrap and my skin pink from exfoliating, and I definitely hadn't drawn my eyebrows on yet.

Shit.

I ripped out the hair wrap, tossing it somewhere in the vicinity of the bathroom as I rushed to my room, yanking a pair of loose shorts and a black tank top out of the drawer and dropping my robe so I could put a bra on. There was a slouchy cardigan around here somewhere that I could pull over the top of my casual loungewear. That would look semi put-together, right? Very effortless comfort, I just happened to have this very flattering, matching outfit lying around.

Maybe I should dry my hair first? Yes, that was the priority. I didn't have time to fix my whole face, but I could at least hide behind a fluffy mane of hair—

I froze at the knock on the door. *My* door, not the main door downstairs that led to both flats.

"Kit?" I called hesitantly, heading back into the living area and pulling the wet strands of hair over one shoulder.

"It's me." Kit's voice rumbled through the door, rough with impatience in a way that I probably shouldn't have found so attractive. "Mrs Clarkson let me in."

Good of her, I thought wryly. Most of the time, it was a boon having beta neighbours—their scents were inoffensively mild, and they didn't fuck like feral beasts at all hours of the day—but the fact that they thought it was totally fine to let some rando alpha off the street in wasn't ideal.

Then again, Kit wasn't quite a rando alpha. He'd already charmed them by the sounds of it.

Since I could hardly leave him out there while I spent half an hour drying my hair, I conceded defeat and pulled the door open, bracing myself for him to recoil in disgust or at the very least, do a double take before schooling his expression into something polite.

Except, I doubted he got a look at my face at all since he was on me before the lock on the door even clicked into place. I found myself scrambling to grab his shoulders, cursing the straps of his backpack that were in the way, my legs wrapping automatically around his hips to get myself upright as he turned us, pressing me against the door and plunging his tongue between my parted lips.

"Need you," Kit mumbled against my lips, gripping my ass and rocking his erection against the growing damp patch in the gusset of my shorts. "Fuck, can't stop thinking about you. Been losing my mind."

He was tugging at the waistband, annoyed that they weren't coming off despite the fact that he'd been the one to haul me off the ground and encourage my legs up around his waist.

With a growl of frustration that morphed into an approving groan, Kit's hand slid up one leg of my shorts, instantly finding the slick that was seeping through my underwear.

Thanks, vagina. Way to play it cool.

"You need me too, omega?" he rasped, delivering a gentle nip to my lower lip, careful not to break the skin.

It was a sex question. A heat-of-the-moment, throwaway, this-means-nothing question. And yet...

And yet.

"Put me down so I can take my shorts off," I demanded breathlessly, avoiding his terrifying question.

Shit, we were going to have to do this out here on my tiny two-person loveseat. There was no way I was inviting Kit into my nest. I didn't want to, and he'd probably expire from panic if I did.

I panted with a mortifying level of enthusiasm as Kit leaned his weight harder against me, rubbing my clit at just the right speed with just the right pressure through my thin cotton knickers. Furiously bucking and writhing, the door banging loudly in its frame behind me, I came with a shudder and a gush of slick, slumping forward against Kit's chest.

"Such a good, sweet omega." Kit's voice started out a sinuous purr, though his sentences grew more broken and his tone more raspy with each passing moment. "You come so pretty. Fucking love the way you soak my fingers. Going to soak my knot now, aren't you?"

Knot. Yes. Knot.

I made a breathy noise of agreement, burrowing my face further against him as he moved to the sofa, deftly undoing his trousers and kicking them off as he walked. The moment he set me on my feet, I was shoving down my shorts and knickers, desperate to get the sticky, wet fabric off my skin, before spinning around and kneeling on the sofa, propping my elbows on the back and shielding my face with my hair.

Out of the corner of my eye, I saw him put down his backpack and remove his glasses with care before discarding his t-shirt with much less caution.

"You want me like this?" Kit murmured, his hand ghosting over the curve of my hip before giving my ass a firm squeeze. Fortunately, that appeared to be the full extent of his questioning when presented with an eager omega positioned as though she was in heat. With a firm hand in the centre of my back, pushing me forward, Kit thrust into me in one smooth motion, knocking the air from my lungs and every logical thought I had out of my brain.

There was nothing but us, but this. But a strong, confident alpha and a needy, willing omega. We were safe within the walls of my apartment, there was no risk of being interrupted.

His knot was mine for the taking, and we both knew it.

"Margot," Kit groaned, shifting his grip to my hips, his fingers digging possessively into my skin. "You feel so good, so perfect."

I threw my hips back against him, using him to get myself off before I did something embarrassingly stupid like *cry*. Why did he have to compliment me so much?

"That's it," Kit encouraged, his voice a low growl. "So eager, my omega."

My movements faltered at the endearment, but he blessedly took over, slamming me back against him, fucking me the way that any good omega wanted to be fucked—in a way that pleased their alpha. Unlike last night's clandestine tryst in the laundry room, this time Kit was *loud*. Every masculine groan of satisfaction seemed to travel down my spine, sending consistent jolts of pleasure to my clit.

I bit down on the top of the sofa cushion as I found my release, clenching tightly around Kit's cock as he surged forward, his knot rapidly expanding, stretching me to the point of discomfort. Right as it became too much and I wondered if I could actually bear it, he shifted forward, locking us together, and suddenly that thick bulge was in *exactly* the right place.

With a mewling gasp, I was shuddering my way through another orgasm, this one slightly more soul-shattering than the last. Whatever that magical spot he was pressing against—one that none of my knot-shaped toys had ever reached—it seemed to have the added side-effect of destroying the wall I was valiantly trying to keep up between us. There were no barriers when we were connected like this.

Thank all the high powers in the universe that I'd turned around. I hated to think what he'd see in my eyes right now—I was barely holding back a strange and very unwanted bout of tears.

"I didn't think this through," Kit said regretfully, sounding winded. "Hold on, I'm going to move us."

I braced myself as he banded his arms around my middle, gently guiding us backwards so he was lying on the sofa, and I was sprawled on top of him, staring up at the ceiling as a steady wave of orgasms dragged me under, making my vision waver.

With the knot in place, only a small trickle of slick escaped, but I could feel how much my body was producing with each rush of pleasure. I was going to need to drink several litres of water after this.

"You're incredible, Margot," Kit rasped, planting his feet flat on the sofa so I was cradled by his bent knees, taking some of the strain off my spine. "Give me another one," he demanded, his middle finger finding my clit with perfect accuracy, circling my hypersensitive nerves with just the right amount of pressure.

I grabbed his forearm, nails digging hard into his skin, not entirely sure if I was holding him in place or pulling him away. There wasn't anywhere to really brace myself, and I ended up squirming all over him like a worm, using his body to ground me when I felt like I was going to float away.

"Shh, it's okay," Kit murmured, smoothing my hair back off my forehead with his free hand and pressing a kiss to my temple. "You're doing so good. So good. Relax, I have you."

I didn't realise I'd been tensing until he told me to relax. I slumped over top of him like an omega blanket, catching my breath as my pussy continued to occasionally spasm around Kit's knot, wringing a few more gentle orgasms out of me as my eyes drifted shut. His scent had thoroughly blended with mine, drenching every inch of the room. I was going to have to air out the flat for days or risk turning into a horny, emotional mess each time I stepped foot in the door.

"Are you still with me?" Kit murmured eventually, one hand resting just below my belly button, the other still playing absently with my hair.

"Hm? Yes, of course." Where else could I be? Our bodies were literally stuck together.

"Sorry for the, uh, abrupt visit." *Now? He wanted to chat now?* "I didn't sleep. I think my instincts were rebelling at the idea of leaving you alone after... last night."

"Oh. You needn't have worried," I assured him, awkwardly patting his arm.

"You were fine on your own?" I didn't think I imagined the hint of sharpness in his voice. Did he not *want* me to be fine on my own? Maybe it was an ego thing.

Before I could respond—and I had absolutely no idea what to say since it seemed to be a sensitive subject—his knot softened. I squeaked in dismay as his cock slipped free, a waterfall of our combined fluids accompanying it.

I don't have high hopes for the future of this sofa, I thought in dismay. Clearing his scent from the air was one thing. Fluids on fabric were an altogether different beast.

Kit scooped me up in his arms bridal-style, and with a muffled shriek of alarm, I threw my arms around his neck, clinging on tightly.

"You really don't have to carry me, you know."

Did he think this was a requirement? Kit had carried me to the shower last night as well, and while I appreciated the reduced slick trail it left on the floors, it was by no means expected.

"I want to," Kit replied easily, quickly crossing the small space and turning sideways to fit us both in the bathroom door. Kit set me down in the stall so I could finish undressing while slick ran freely down my legs, and I yanked on the lever the moment I was naked, stepping under the spray the moment was somewhat lukewarm.

I watched out of the corner of my eye as Kit took off the remainders of his clothing with more care, his hands briefly rising as though to remove his glasses before realising he'd left them next to the sofa.

I'd always thought I'd had a perfectly adequately-sized shower, but that illusion was shattered as Kit squeezed into the tight, enclosed space behind me, his front pressing to my back. I shivered despite the warmth of his skin on mine, tucking my chin down so my now-soaked again hair formed a curtain around my face.

I wasn't surprised when Kit's hands landed on my shoulders, gently encouraging me around to face him, but I was slightly more surprised that I let him. There was no raging lust clouding his judgment now, he was going to get an unvarnished look at my bare face without an erection to distract him.

Kit gently cupped my jaw, encouraging me to meet his eyes, before stroking his thumb over my cheek, a small smile playing around his mouth. "You have such a pretty blush."

I swallowed thickly, squashing the wobbly emotion that was trying to sink its claws into my chest. "I probably need some water. I'll grab a drink after I wash up."

Kit grimaced, releasing my face and turning his attention to the row of bottles on the shelf before picking out my unscented body wash. "I'm not very good at this alpha thing, am I? Dropping you home after last night, knotting you from behind on the sofa, and now my abysmal aftercare..."

"It's really fine," I assured him, quickly pumping some soap into my hands so I could wash myself because he looked like he was about to try to rectify all that lacking aftercare right here in the shower, and my shields weren't strong enough to withstand that kind of tenderness right now. "You don't have to do all that stuff with me, remember? That's the point of this whole... arrangement."

I wasn't entirely sure what he expected to have done differently, in all honesty. It wasn't like he could have come upstairs last night anyway—there was no way a fake boyfriend was sleeping in my real nest. And I'd been the one to turn away from him on the couch.

Kit was silent for a long moment. "You cancelled our arrangement."

"For all the good it did, you've been upholding your side of the deal anyway," I pointed out drily.

"So have you when you came to meet my mother," Kit pointed out looking rather pleased with himself. "You've gone above and beyond our deal, actually."

"Don't read into it," I mumbled, keeping my head bowed and focusing a little harder than necessary on washing away the slick coating my inner thighs.

"Too late." He was almost cheerful by Kit's standards. "Our arrangement was briefly on hold, but now it's back in full effect, with an amendment for sex, of course."

"An amendment for sex?!" I sputtered.

"Absolutely. The amendment being: I think we should keep having sex. And whatever pretending we do when we're in public doesn't extend to what we do when it's just the two of us. I'm not faking this."

How was he so being so infuriatingly calm and logical about this? As though we were discussing the train schedule or something?

"Do you think you can let me look after you, Margot? Just occasionally? The way I should have insisted on last night?"

Do you think you're capable of looking after me? I almost shot back, though it was impossible to voice that snarky thought when he sounded so contrite. Kit's track record suggested no, he wouldn't be capable of looking after me, but he was clearly wrestling with these new urges, and I didn't have it in me to hold it over his head.

"If it's important to you, sure," I replied carefully, steeling myself to peek up at him through my lashes. "But you were probably only feeling so driven today because you didn't knot me last night. Now that you have, do you think there's a very great risk of this happening again?"

Somehow, Kit's eyes seemed to darken. Something within me, some primal, purely omega part of my soul responded almost instantly, the word *alpha* looping around on repeat.

"Oh, yes. This will most definitely be happening again."

Chapter Thirteen

Since he didn't seem in any rush to leave, I set Kit up in the armchair in the corner of my office to edit photos on his laptop—a task he'd been on his way to do at a cafe when he'd decided to come and see me instead.

Once he was situated, I escaped into my room to dress—in slightly more presentable clothes than I'd intended on wearing today—and to do a full face of make-up and fix my hair.

Kit did a double take as I re-entered the office, a look on his face that I couldn't quite read.

"Everything okay?" I asked, unscrewing the lid of my glass water bottle to chug some more. Orgasms were so dehydrating. "Do *you* need a glass of wine?"

"No, no wine," Kit replied a little too quickly. "I want to make you dinner tonight."

"You can cook?" I winced. "Sorry, that came out more judgemental than I intended."

Kit snorted. "When I'm on the road, there's no Violet around to prepare a three-course meal with wine pairings each night, so yes, I can cook. Usually, it's simple stuff I can make in my hotel room on a hot plate, but I wanted to make something a little more complex today. A comfort food from my childhood."

"I certainly won't say no to that." I sat down at my desk, shaking the mouse to wake up my computer. "I usually do meal prep one week at a time. There's not a ton of variety."

Kit wrinkled his nose, and I laughed quietly to myself, logging on to my computer. There was no motivation to cook each day when it was just me, and besides, I liked to have the flexibility to eat whenever since I was often out and about.

For a while, we worked in silence—me writing an article on some recent new legislation for my firm's website, while Kit edited some sunrise photos he'd taken at Epping Forest. Eventually, he excused himself to pop to the shops to get ingredients for whatever it was he was planning on making, while I continued on my draft.

There was a level of comfort to having Kit in my space that I didn't want to analyse too closely. Omegas were territorial beasts for the most part, and while my office wasn't nearly as sacred as my nest, I still hadn't ever invited anyone else into it.

You're just feeling extra relaxed from all the orgasms. It doesn't mean anything.

Except my heat was approaching, so that was a total lie. I should be *more* tense, *more* territorial, and *far* more selective about having an alpha anywhere near me for more than the time it took for his knot to go down.

I shook my head slightly. *Don't think about it.* Was I in denial? Absolutely. But sometimes denial was a necessary self-preservation tool, so I wasn't going to be too hard on myself.

Kit let himself in with the key I'd lent him—*swoosh* went my idiot belly at the casualness of it all—and started moving around the kitchen while I hid out in my office, using work as my shield.

I finished the article, sending it off to a colleague to review, before answering a few emails until the delicious scents coming from the kitchen enticed me out of hiding.

"Ah, she lives," Kit said drily, stirring something at the stove. "I wondered if you'd climbed out the window and done a runner."

"How ungallant of you not to check and follow me."

"I figure you'd come back and omega-hiss me out of your space if you didn't want me here."

"That sounds about right, though I'm surprised you know that. No offence, but I didn't think you knew much about omega instincts."

"I don't," Kit agreed easily. "I've been doing some long overdue reading up on them, though."

"Oh. Well, uh, good for you," I replied awkwardly, not entirely sure how to respond to that. I didn't want to give him too much credit—if Kit had paid more attention in the mandatory sex ed classes we all had in secondary school, he'd know most of this stuff.

"What are you making?" I asked, coming to stand next to him as he pulled a whole chicken out of a stock pot and transferred it to a casserole dish filled with ice and water.

"Hainanese chicken rice. After my mum got really busy at work, she didn't have time for us to cook together like she did when I was little. But this is one recipe she made sure to pass on. I wanted to make it for you."

There was more to that statement beneath the surface, but frankly, I wasn't sure if either of us wanted to dive down and look.

"Thank you. I can't wait, it smells so good."

A smell that was only slightly ruined by the fabric-cleaning foam I'd sprayed all over the sofa. While Kit finished cooking, I grabbed a damp cloth and started scrubbing, ignoring his guilty expression.

Honestly, the cleaning solution smelled *much* worse than the evidence Kit and I had left behind, but it also wouldn't turn me into a useless puddle of arousal every time I caught a whiff of it.

Or maybe it would, since I would forever remember why I'd needed to bust out the fabric cleaner in the first place.

"How are your siblings?" Kit asked, taking the lid off the pan the rice had been cooking in. *What sorcery was this?* I thought, washing my hands at the sink next to him. Rice never smelled like that when I made it.

"They're fine." I grabbed some cutlery from the drawer, setting it out on the table. "It hasn't been easy on Asher, presenting as an omega. Our parents haven't been the most supportive about it."

"Why? Because he's a boy?" Kit asked, sounding genuinely baffled in a way that I found incredibly gratifying. That was the way it *should* be—a total non-issue.

"Exactly. Home isn't the happiest place for Asher right now, which is why I'm trying to get him into the Sutton-Harris School." I gestured at the painting on the wall. "He's a really talented artist, and the school has an omega-only dorm. I already asked—he wouldn't be the only male omega there."

"He's very good," Kit murmured, looking up at the painting. "Your parents said no?"

"There's an interview stage. I was grinding them down to let Asher at *least* interview, but then Calum died, and they won't even acknowledge when I ask about the possibility now. That's what my parents have that I want, the reason why I went along with this whole scheme in the first place. "

"Ah. I might have known your reasons were selfless."

I frowned. "I don't know about that. You're so determined to believe I'm nicer than I am."

Kit hummed, giving me a knowing look as he carried two plates over to the table, setting them down before returning for condiments.

"I'm at your disposal for whatever help you might need in getting Asher into that school, though I'm sure you'd figure it out without me anyway."

"Well... yes," I conceded. "I mean, I'm not giving up. It's important to Asher."

"Of course. I get the impression that you're very determined when you want something."

We took our seats at the table opposite each other, my mouth almost watering at the scent of the meal.

"What makes you think that?"

"All of this." Kit gestured at my tiny flat with its now-unusable sofa "I definitely didn't appreciate it at first, but there's a lot of odds to go up against to make this life happen as a single omega. You're quite remarkable, Margot."

Kit gave me more compliments than anyone I'd ever met in my life, and they threw me off-balance every single time.

"Thank you," I murmured, awkwardly shoving a spoonful of rice in my mouth to avoid having to say anything else. And then pausing mid-chew because *what. The. Hell.*

Was this rice made by angels?

I didn't even know rice *could* taste like this. I mean, I cooked it all the time, but it was a rather bland accompaniment to go with the rest of my bland meal prep.

This rice was so flavourful, it tasted like a whole meal all on its own.

"This is so good, Kit. I hope you're not expecting me to reciprocate with a comfort meal from my childhood. Beans on toast with a side of fish fingers doesn't hold a candle to this."

I could have sworn he looked a little embarrassed. "I'm glad you like it."

I tried the super soft, perfectly cooked chicken next, hyper aware of Kit watching my every bite.

He watched a lot too. Lots of watching, lots of compliments. Both of which were disconcerting in the amount of pleasure they gave me.

"Tell me about your other siblings," Kit said suddenly, surprising me with his interest. "You don't talk about them much, except Asher."

"I don't have much to do with any of them except for Chelsea and Asher. Not just my siblings—my entire family, though I'm very fond of my Nana—she was quite the rebellious omega back in her heyday, and she seemed to relate to me more than her other grandchildren."

"Does that bother you that you're not close with them?"

I liked the non-judgemental way he'd asked. Sometimes people didn't *get* it. They put the *concept* of family above everything, but the reality of family wasn't always so straightforward.

"I've made my own family. When I had the flu, Mrs Clarkson downstairs made me soup and homemade bread for a week straight—far more nurturing than my own mother ever was for me. Violet and Nico are everything to me. I'm closer to my friend Michelle's kids than I am to my biological nieces and nephews."

Not to mention all the friends I'd made at uni and through the various firms I'd worked at over the years. As we all got older and their lives got busier with kids, we didn't see each other as much, but I knew they were lifelong friendships.

Kit glanced at me, shooting me a half-smile. "That doesn't surprise me at all. You're very good at making yourself important to people."

"Am I?" No one had ever said that to me before. "That's surprising, considering what a shark I am."

Kit snorted. "You're the nicest person I've ever met, Margot. That's why it's so surprising that you're unmated. I'm not sure we've ever discussed why you're so averse to it?"

His tone was light and conversational, and I didn't buy it for a second. "My, my, Kit. Are you prying?"

He had the good grace to blush. "A little."

I let him sweat for a moment, taking a bite of the impossibly tender chicken. It was plain white and looked like it *should* be bland. What was this magical dish?

"It's sort of a snowballing collection of reasons," I told Kit eventually, finding it easier to look at my plate than make eye contact with him for this conversation. "It just... didn't happen. And so I threw myself into my education, and then into my career, and before I met Bryce and Kane, I used to go to the paid clubs whenever I needed an alpha fix."

Kit scooped some chilli onto his plate with a little more force than necessary, and I hurriedly moved the subject along.

"The longer I was alone, the more comfortable I got with it, I suppose. I liked that I could work late and didn't have to apologise for it. I liked that I could prioritise my friends and my younger siblings without feeling like I was letting someone down. I liked that I could choose the flat I wanted to buy and I could decorate it the way I wanted, and there was no one to tell me otherwise."

Kit gave me a long look. "You could have all those things with the right alpha. The way Nico and Violet do."

"Yes, well, with the benefit of hindsight, they're the exception rather than the rule." I thought of Michelle, constantly scrambling to keep the alpha she'd mated and his family happy. "For a lot of the omegas I knew, it seems more as though their heat was approaching, and they were at a point where they were ready to settle down, and whichever alpha they were seeing, they invited into their nest. It was more right place, right time than right *person*."

"I don't think you'd ever be at risk of making that mistake. You know exactly what you want and would never settle for less," Kit said with quiet, steady confidence, never breaking eye contact.

"You have too much faith in me," I murmured, my mind flashing back to being that wildly naïve eighteen-year-old who'd thought there was nothing more important than locking down an alpha. Who was so flattered to be the centre of someone's attention.

"Not too much, I don't think." Kit glanced at me through ridiculously thick black eyelashes before returning his focus to his meal.

Oof.

Between the showering with me and the cooking for me, and the *looks*, I desperately needed to steer this ship back to safer waters.

"Obviously, I don't need to ask you why you're single," I teased. "Your lifestyle doesn't suit it."

"I'm pretty sure I never said that," Kit said, a touch defensive.

"*My career isn't compatible with having an omega mate*," I recited, dropping my voice lower in an attempt to sound more like him.

"I don't think I said those *exact* words—"

"You did. That first time you came over with coffee and propositioned me." I winked. "I went to law school. I have excellent recall."

Kit shifted in his seat. "The travelling around, never having a base, a nest... That's not exactly omega-friendly."

"No," I agreed, a little more sadly than I'd intended. There was no need to pity Kit. I didn't like when people pitied me.

"But I won't travel around forever. Alphas like having a home base, too, it's just not as necessary for us."

"Oh. I guess I thought... well, you're a *travel* photographer."

Kit's lips curved ever so slightly. "So I am. Tell me more about this school Asher is trying to get into."

We finished dinner, and I insisted on washing up because it really seemed like the least I could do after Kit had cooked.

It had taken me an embarrassingly long moment to remember that the stockpot he'd used to cook the chicken was mine. It had been one of those optimistic, I-will-definitely-use-this purchases that had lived at the back of the cupboard since I'd bought it.

"Sorry there's nowhere else for you to sit," I told Kit apologetically over my shoulder. The dining chairs weren't exactly comfortable, but the sofa was soaking wet.

"I'm pretty sure I should be the one apologising for that," he deadpanned, his phone buzzing before he could say anything else.

"Hey," Kit said, seemingly more interested in watching me wash up than his phone call.

"Did I catch you mid-fuck?" Coleman laughed, his booming voice coming through loud and clear despite the fact that he wasn't on speakerphone. *"Oh no, I forget you're tied down these days. Or did you kick her to the curb already?"*

This guy was the *worst*. If I was looking for an alpha to mate—which I wasn't—Kit would truly have been the perfect candidate if not for his giant-red-flag taste in friends.

"No, of course not." Kit looked immediately annoyed, which was somewhat gratifying. "Surely, being tied down, you'd be more likely to catch me mid-fuck, if anything?"

"I suppose," Coleman agreed, not sounding particularly convinced. Probably because he didn't see me as an attractive prospect, though there was always the possibility that he and his omega hadn't slept together during the courtship. Some omegas preferred for the first time to happen during heat. *"Anyway, I'm calling to see if you're still coming to Brighton this weekend."*

Ah, the infamous Brighton trip.

"You don't need to worry about accommodation—Beckett's mate, Sal, inherited a fancy house there. We thought we'd head down on Friday night after work, back on Sunday. There's plenty of room. I've even messaged Nico, asking if he and his omega want to come with. He usually says no, but he might deign to join us if you're going."

There was that grating snideness again. Did Kit not hear it? He might be used to it, I supposed. Maybe Coleman was like a worn-out pair of socks that weren't actually that comfortable to wear, but he'd just never got around to disposing of.

"Margot would be coming with me, of course."

My hands hovered above the sink, pausing mid-motion. That was what we'd agreed on. *Before.* Before I'd called the whole thing off, then we'd semi-called it back on again. And before we'd started fucking.

If I went, we'd definitely have to keep it in our pants for the weekend, or Kit would be constantly doused in the scent of omega-nearly-in-heat, and that wasn't fair on him. His instincts would be unbearable.

"Would she?" Coleman asked eventually.

"I'm courting her, and her heat is drawing closer. I'm hardly going anywhere without her."

I spun around to stare at Kit, giving him my best *what-the-fuck* look. There was no way of misinterpreting that—keeping an omega close while their heat approached was a solid declaration of intent. He was only making life more difficult for both of us when we had to part ways.

"Right. Well, plenty of room, like I said."

"I'll check with Margot and get back to you."

They exchanged quick goodbyes while I continued to lecture Kit with the force of my stare, waiting for him to offer up some explanation of why he'd said that.

His phone buzzed. "Nico said that he and Violet will go if we're going." Kit finally looked up, startling slightly, when he caught the look on my face. "No? You don't want to go anymore? I guess things have changed since we first discussed the idea—"

"Kit!" I sighed, exasperated.

"What?"

"You told Coleman I was close to my heat?"

He blinked at me. "You are close to your heat."

"Well, yes, but you *told* him."

"Was I not supposed to?" Kit tilted his head to the side, reminding me of a curious puppy, cuteness and all.

I groaned, exasperated with both him and myself. "Call Nico. Put him on speakerphone."

I was being extremely bossy, on reflection, which wasn't something alphas always responded well to, but Kit didn't seem to mind.

"Hi," Nico said in a distracted voice, the clacking of a keyboard audible in the background. *"Yes or no to Brighton?"*

"We need you to settle something for us first, you're on speaker phone," Kit said, staring intently at me as he spoke.

The typing sounds stopped.

"Go on," Nico replied, curious.

"I told Coleman that Margot was close to her heat, and I obviously wouldn't be leaving her on her own—"

"You said what?" Nico asked in a strangled voice.

"Thank you," I muttered, throwing my hands up in exasperation.

"Kit, my friend, that is basically an official announcement that you're taking Margot as a mate. That your courtship was successful, and she's invited you into her nest. There's no other way of reading that."

I waited for Kit's dawning look of horror, but it never came. Such was the downside of dealing with an alpha who knew nothing about omegas, I supposed. The magnitude of his actions was lost on him because he'd never bothered to learn the significance of them in the first place.

"Well, that's what I said." Kit shrugged, unbothered, uneducated, or both. "Are you guys going to come with?"

"If you'd like us there," Nico replied cautiously. *"More specifically, if Margot would like us there."*

"You're not even pretending to hide the favouritism any more," Kit joked. Maybe he'd been body-snatched at some point?

"Margot is absolutely our favourite. Margot? Do you want us to come to Brighton?"

I hesitated, very much wanting to have friendly faces in the viper's den but also not wanting to impose on Nico and Violet's kindness. Nico didn't bother spending time with Coleman and his crew for good reason.

"She does, but she's too polite to say so," Kit replied, staring at me.

"Alright, we'll be there. If Coleman pisses me off, I'm going to punch him in the mouth." With that reassuring proclamation, Nico hung up.

"He's kidding," Kit said quickly, catching my wide-eyed look. "Well, he's mostly kidding. Or I think he is, at least. Nico has become a little more brash in the two years I've been away, and Coleman has become a little more obnoxious, so I guess we'll see."

"Comforting," I muttered, turning back to the bench to dry a pot. "It feels like this weekend is going to be a disaster."

"It'll be fine. You never know, we might even have fun."

He'd definitely been body snatched. There was no other explanation.

Chapter Fourteen

Even with Kit's hasty declaration to Coleman about my heat, I'd still half expected there to be a single omega waiting at the house when the four of us showed up—the last to arrive at Sal and Beckett's Brighton mansion. Okay, maybe mansion was an exaggeration, but compared to the surrounding houses, the ten-bedroom white-washed historic home was an imposing building.

Fortunately, as we all converged on the front hall to make our greetings, it appeared that only the six of them were there—Coleman and Jocelyn, Beckett and Sal, Rajeev and Lennox.

"I can't believe you actually showed up," Coleman said in that incredibly loud voice of his, clapping an already irate-looking Nico on the shoulder. "I was beginning to think you'd forgotten all about us."

"Have you met you? You're not an easy guy to forget," Nico deadpanned.

They all laughed, though I was pretty sure Nico hadn't been joking.

"Well, come in, come in," Sal said. "I'll show you up to your rooms, and then we'll figure out dinner. We did a big shop, but none of us are particularly good in the kitchen. We *could* always get a takeaway, of course..."

Ugh. Everyone knew Violet was an amazing cook. There wasn't even an ounce of subtlety there.

"Well, I'd be happy to make dinner," Violet volunteered. Nico sighed heavily, carrying both of their bags and following Sal up the stairs.

"I'll help," I added, giving Violet a smile that verged slightly on pleading. *Don't leave me alone with these people.*

Not that anyone had acknowledged me so far. I couldn't decide whether it was a blessing or a curse.

Kit grabbed my bag, giving me a small half-smile that boosted my confidence somehow, and I fell into step beside him as we climbed up the stairs. Our room was right at the end of the hall, next to Nico and Violet's.

It was small but pretty—all painted white with the cornices and a small golden chandelier hanging from the ceiling.

And it contained two single beds, separated by an antique wooden vanity that looked heavier than me.

"Well, this is you," Sal said hurriedly, already walking away. "I'll meet you downstairs in a bit."

I listened to his footsteps retreat down the hallway, wondering if that vein in Kit's forehead was about to explode.

The second he looked at me, outrage written all over his face, I bent double, shaking with silent laughter.

"Stop it," Kit grumbled, chucking the bags down on one of the beds with a look of utter disdain. "This is a piss-take. I bet no one else has single beds."

"They probably ran out of double bedrooms," I managed to reply, still trying to get my giggles under control. "And since we're unmated, I guess we're the logical choice for the single beds."

"I'm pushing them together."

"The dresser looks as though it weighs a ton. Besides, you can't move around other people's furniture." I shook my head, checking my reflection in the mirror on the vanity and swiping away the tears of amusement with the heel of my hand so as not to disturb my mascara.

"Is that so, Ms Lawyer?" Kit asked, finally losing some of his agitation.

"I mean, it's been a while since I did my Laws of Being A Guest In Someone's Home paper at university, but yes, I'm pretty sure that was covered."

"I'll take the risk," Kit replied in a low voice. His eyes raked over me, lingering on my denim jeans and half-tucked white shirt like it was lingerie. That look was *potent*. Already, my body was primed to respond even though my brain very much disliked the idea of showcasing my heat-tinged scent in front of these people.

"Single beds?" Nico asked, striding into the room behind me and breaking the spell. As discreetly as I could, I gulped down a lungful of air to clear my head.

This weekend would be testing in more ways than one.

"Oh my," Violet murmured, looking around disapprovingly. "And they know your heat is approaching. That was... uncharitable of them."

I snorted. Maybe Kit's friends knew we weren't *actually* going into my nest together when the time came. If we were in a real courtship, I'd be feeling extra needy right now and demanding as much closeness as possible, but we weren't, and I didn't feel that way.

Mostly.

At least, I didn't *want* to feel that way.

"It's only two nights, it's not a big deal," I assured them because Kit looked like he was getting ready to bust out the forehead vein again. "Shall we head downstairs? See what's in the fridge for Violet to cook?"

"Don't even get me started on that," Nico muttered, falling into step with Kit as Violet linked her arm through mine. "We're only here for you guys."

Violet gave my arm a squeeze, shooting me a reassuring smile. "It's no hardship, we love Brighton."

The others were waiting in the kitchen when we got downstairs, pouring glasses of bubbly for everyone.

Sal tensed ever so slightly when he saw Kit, but he must have decided he was safe when Kit didn't immediately bring up the sleeping arrangements.

"Well, we're all here!" Coleman announced. "Shall we toast?"

I accepted the glass of bubbles Beckett passed me, waiting as Coleman dramatically cleared his throat.

"To Kit! Our favourite wandering friend. It's good to have you home, brother. Long may you stay and actually spend time with us for a change. Cheers to Kit!"

"To Kit," I murmured, less enthusiastically than some of the others present.

Kit gently tugged me back with an arm around the waist as conversation broke out around us, plucking the glass from my hand and setting it down.

"I'll find you something else to drink, what do you want?"

"I'm fine with water, honestly."

"Don't tell me you don't drink," Coleman said, wrinkling his nose and looking at me like he'd just made another mental strike against my name. "Let your hair down a bit, this is meant to be a fun weekend."

"Good thing I'm plenty of fun without alcohol," I replied easily, accepting the glass of water Nico handed me. Coleman's answering smile didn't meet his eyes, and the disapproval fairly radiated from the rest of his crew, but it was hardly the first time someone had called me boring for not drinking, so I ignored it.

"I could make fettuccine alfredo," Violet announced. "But I'd need to get double cream. There's a shop round the corner, isn't there?"

Sal groaned. "Let's just get a takeaway, that's too much effort."

"I'll go to the shop," Kit volunteered. "I want to get Margot some sodas anyway."

Strange that the force of all the disdain hadn't made me blush, but Kit's offhand comment about wanting to get something that he thought I needed *did*.

Well, maybe it wasn't strange. Maybe I was just in far more danger of growing attached to Kit than I thought.

No, I was fine. I understood the parameters of the arrangement. There were no risks here.

Kit rested a hand on my hip, leaning around to brush a kiss against my cheek before excusing himself, and my heart started beating a little faster than I was entirely comfortable with for a gesture that was meant to mean nothing.

"Let's head outside," Beckett suggested, already throwing open the French doors that led from the kitchen to the sun-drenched courtyard. "Grab a bag of crisps, yeah, Sal?"

Violet looked as though she was dying inside, probably doing her best to push away visions of elaborate charcuterie boards as Sal ripped open a bag of crisps and tossed it into the middle of the long outdoor table.

Nico and Violet sat either side of me at one end of the table, stalwart pillars of support, and I'd never appreciated them more.

Rajeev was at the head of the table, his mate on one side and Beckett on the other, leaving Coleman and Jocelyn to take the seats opposite me. Without Kit there, Coleman's expression reflected the obvious dislike he felt for me—no veneer of politeness in sight.

I imagined it was my dad sitting there instead, eyes full of disappointment, and found it was quite easy to sink into that place of disassociated ambivalence. I wasn't going to let myself care about Coleman's opinion. If I could learn to shake off the disdain of what had been the most important alpha in my life, I could certainly disregard this guy.

"You don't smell like your heat is approaching. You don't smell like anything," Coleman said bluntly.

"Watch it," Nico growled, leaning forward and bracing his elbows on the table.

"Come on, Nico. We all just want what's best for Kit. I'm just making sure everything is all as it should be—he's saying she's going into heat, and I've only got the faintest whiffs that she's an omega at all. I'm just checking it's all above board."

"It is," Violet replied, her voice cooler than I'd ever heard it.

"You have to admit, you're a little biased," Jocelyn countered, observing Violet over the rim of her wine glass in a way that strongly reminded me of omega catfights in the schoolyard from my teenage years. "Since she's your friend and all, and we all agree that Kit is more susceptible to Nico's word than any of ours. We just want to make sure she really is the right fit for him, *if*, as she claims, her heat is approaching."

"You tricked me."

I was never going to escape those words, that accusation. Even when I diligently covered my scent, even when I presented myself without the only thing that made me alluring.

Except I didn't really feel as though I could defend myself because this whole thing was a lie anyway.

"What are you even accusing her of?" Nico asked with a dismissive snort. "Ensnaring Kit with a non-existent heat? I'm pretty confident he'd have some suspicions if it never showed up. He doesn't need you white-knighting to the rescue, Coleman."

"You can hardly blame us for thinking she duped him somehow," Coleman shot back harshly.

"Why's that?" I asked calmly, tilting my head to the side and pinning him with my most politely curious look. One thing I'd found in my years of dealing with obnoxious people was that nothing flummoxed them more than being asked to explain themselves.

"What?" he asked, blinking at me, immediately thrown off-balance.

"*Why* is that? Why do you think I 'duped' Kit? It's obvious you don't like me, but what is it about Kit that makes you believe he'd be susceptible to mind games? Is he a particularly fragile, weak-willed man?"

Coleman opened his mouth. Closed it again. Opened it. Changed his mind. It was like watching a goldfish in action.

"Because," I continued, leaving him to his gaping. "That's not the impression I have of Kit at all. Kit has forged his own path in life, pushing past the expectations put on him by his mother and his closest friends. It isn't easy to ignore the hopes and wishes the people we care about have for our lives. It doesn't strike me as the actions of a weak-willed man."

"Kit is *not* weak-willed," Coleman snapped, finding his voice, his face turning an interesting shade of puce.

"Oh, I know. I'm glad we're in agreement."

My adrenaline was pumping, and the people-pleasing side of me was rioting inside my head, but it felt so *good* to stand up to an elitist prick like Coleman. When Fraser had hurled his accusation at me while I stood next to the pool, shivering with just a towel wrapped around me, and all of my dignity washed away with my make-up, I'd said nothing. I was no longer the frightened omega I'd been that day, and I was proud of that.

Unfortunately, Coleman wasn't finished with me yet.

"But I still think you tricked him somehow because I can't think of any reason why he'd be interested in you otherwise."

Ouch.

"Enough." Nico's hand came down on the table with a bang, making everyone jump. "The sooner Kit realises what a drain on him you all are, the better off we'll be. If he spent more time at home, he'd have learned long before now how much he's outgrown you."

"You may think you're too good for us, but Kit isn't a snob like you," Coleman growled. I swallowed thickly, the alpha aggression in the air an oppressive blanket over all of us. While the other omegas look discomfited by it, they were all mated and secure in the knowledge that their alpha would keep them safe. Without that added layer of protection, my fight-or-flight instincts were going wild.

"Come on," Violet murmured, half dragging me out of my chair by my elbow and tugging me towards the house as Nico snarled a response that I couldn't hear over the buzzing in my ears.

I'd heard plenty of worse things over the years from people who meant significantly less to me than Kit's shitty friends. This shouldn't get to me. I shouldn't care about their opinions. I *refused* to care about their opinions.

"I can't think of any reason why he'd be interested in you otherwise."

Violet didn't pause, pulling me through the hallway and up the stairs, hesitating at the door to her and Nico's room before opting for my door instead.

"So Kit can find you," she explained, guiding me to the bed before doubling back to close the door behind her. I doubted he was going to rush around looking for me, but I couldn't quite formulate a reply yet, not while the adrenaline was still working its way out of my system.

Violet paced, alternating between giving me pitying looks and glaring at the door, never one to hide how she was feeling.

"I don't like these people," she muttered, pulling out her phone, her nails tapping frantically against the screen. "I never have. They're rude as fuck, and I'm glad Nico doesn't really bother with them any more. Some friendships deserve to be left at school."

"Agreed," I murmured, my voice shaky. There was something deeply disheartening about knowing these were the kinds of people Kit chose to spend time with. They were a reflection of him, specifically the worst parts of him. The alpha who'd stood in my kitchen and spitballed the idea that I had conspired to trick him into mating me before I'd even met him.

I liked to think he'd learned something from that moment, but this was the healthy reminder I needed that these were the kinds of people Kit surrounded himself with. That those ideas didn't exist in a vacuum, and he'd only addressed the uncomfortable *wrongness* of his words when he'd been confronted with the outcome of them directly.

All good things to keep in mind to counter all the things about him I *did* like. Like his dimples, his wry sense of humour, his talent and ambition, how cute he looked in his glasses, and how he fucked me like an alpha possessed.

"I can't think of any reason why he'd be interested in you otherwise."

Having a mate wasn't on the cards for me anyway, but it wouldn't be Kit even if it was. I was just temporarily useful to him.

"We're not spending the weekend with these people," Violet continued, still busy on her phone. Possibly telling Nico to hurry up and join us. "You are very selfless, Margot. You constantly put others before yourself—which I worry is a side effect of your parents constantly sidelining you for your siblings, but I digress—I'm stepping in today. No Selfless Margot allowed. Kit was wrong to ask you to come here. I'm going to give him the benefit of the doubt that he in no way deserves and say that he probably didn't realise how poorly they'd treat you."

"I don't know. They were pretty rude the first time I met them," I replied absently, smoothing my hands over my shorts to dry my palms.

"Well, that's true. But Kit announced his intentions when he told Coleman you were going into heat and he wouldn't leave you alone."

"That wasn't real," I cut in, my voice a little sharper than I intended it to be. "I'm sorry, I didn't mean to snap. I shouldn't be letting this get to me—"

"You should absolutely be letting this get to you," Violet interrupted. "You are so hard on yourself, Margot. You don't have to be perfectly calm and gracious all the time, you know. No one will think any less of you if you occasionally lose your cool."

I didn't think that was strictly true, though I had lost my temper with Kit when he'd accused me of being a conniving omega, and I had to admit that there was something very freeing about it.

"I'm not going to fight to stay here or anything," I said eventually, letting out a heavy sigh. "I'm not quite that self-sacrificing. Are you looking up train times?"

Violet opened her mouth to answer, but the sound of the front door opening downstairs had us both falling silent.

Kit was back.

Chapter Fifteen

"What's going on?" Kit asked, voice laced with suspicion. "Where's Margot?"

Violet led me towards the landing, both of us pausing at the top of the stairs to listen.

"She's upstairs with Violet," Nico replied, not sounding much calmer than he'd been outside. "Maybe you should ask Coleman what's going on. Better yet, ask him outright what he thinks of Margot. Maybe even what he thinks of *you*, since apparently they all feel like you need group consensus to make decisions."

"What?"

Nico didn't bother elaborating, heavy footsteps already coming up the stairs. He raised an eyebrow at us, seeing Violet and I half hanging over the bannister, but didn't say anything.

"Coleman!" Kit called, heading through to the kitchen, his voice fading as he went. "What's going on? Has something happened?"

"Pack," Nico said succinctly. "If we stay here any longer, I'm at risk of getting myself arrested."

"We never unpacked," Violet said cheerfully, all but skipping back down the hall to get her things, Nico hot on her heels.

I found myself drifting down the stairs, drawn in by the increasingly loud voices coming from outside.

Don't do it. You're not going to like what you hear, I told myself. Kit wasn't going to throw away his friendships over a fake relationship. It was much more likely that this was the moment he came clean, and I actually didn't need to be here to experience that humiliation in person.

And still, I took a step to the right, towards the kitchen.

"You don't know what you're doing—" I heard Coleman say, but his words were cut off by a thump and a sharp spike in alpha aggression that coated the air so thoroughly that I could feel it from here.

I stumbled back, rushing down the hall, slipping on my flats and quietly letting myself out the front door. Whatever was unfolding in the courtyard, I wanted no part of it.

It was a bright sunny day—which was rude because I wanted a dark grey sky to reflect my mood—and I wrapped my arms around my body to ward off the wind chill as I crossed the road to the beach.

I quickly shot Violet a message letting her know where I'd gone, knowing she'd grab my bag, and then hopefully, we could be back on the train to London this afternoon. This whole trip had been a disastrous idea, and I don't know what Kit had been thinking by suggesting I come along. I don't know what *I'd* been thinking by agreeing. Whatever it was, it went beyond my general inability to say no to people, and I wasn't sure I wanted to examine it too closely.

I picked up my pace, heading for the pier to put as much distance between myself and the house as possible, my impractical smooth-soled flats slipping on the pebbles. It was a shame about the company and general circumstances because I *loved* Brighton, and I didn't get to visit as much as I'd like to. The last time I'd planned a weekend here, Michelle had caught the flu and needed help with the kids. And the time before that, Asher had got in a fight with Dad, and I'd gone to take him out for the day for some space.

Of course, the one time I'd taken time for me it had fallen apart.

Then again, this trip hadn't really been for me, had it?

"Margot!"

I paused, scrunching my eyes shut at the sound of Kit's voice, his footsteps crunching over the stones as he jogged to catch up to me. Before he even got to me, I could sense the waves of aggression that were still riding him from the confrontation he'd just had, and that, more than anything, kept my feet firmly planted in place.

Strangely, it wasn't out of fear. With any other alpha, I'd have almost certainly been afraid, but not with Kit.

Never with Kit. With him, all I felt was the urge to soothe, to provide the kind of comfort that omegas were born to provide.

That was a problem in and of itself.

"Margot, are you okay? You're cold." Kit was immediately in front of me, whipping off his jacket and draping it over my shoulders, pulling it tight over my front. The needy omega I thought I'd long since buried was blinking awake, feeling battered and bruised by rejection and needing the comforting reassurance of her alpha's scent and protection.

Except he wasn't *my* alpha.

My subconscious let out a silent whine at the reminder.

"I'm so sorry," Kit was saying, repeating the words under his breath as he rubbed my shoulders and upper arms, warming me and checking me over all at once. I was checking him right back, scanning for any sign of injury or discomfort. "I should have never agreed to this trip, I don't know what I was thinking. I *wasn't* thinking. I've spent so much time away from home that I guess I assumed everyone and everything was the same, but it's not. They're not. That's no excuse for dragging you into it though."

"It's fine," I said, finding my voice. "I mean, it's not fine, but it is what it is. They're just looking out for you. I'm guessing you told them the truth?"

Kit's hands froze, still resting on my shoulders, his forehead creased in a frown. "The truth?"

"About our charade," I clarified. "I'm sure now they know the lengths you were willing to go to just to get them off your back, they'll have learnt their lesson about playing matchmaker."

I had no idea how to interpret the look on Kit's face, and I scrunched my hands into fists inside his jacket to stop myself from smoothing the lines between his eyebrows with my thumbs.

"I didn't... I didn't say that," Kit said eventually, clearing his throat.

"Oh." I paused for a moment. "Did you not think of it?"

His lips twitched, frown smoothing away. "I thought of it. Let's keep walking. Nico and Violet are collecting our things."

"Sure, okay. That sounds good," I replied, still confused. I slid my arms into the enormous sleeves, standing still as Kit buttoned me up and wondering how fluorescent pink my cheeks were from the wind.

Why hadn't he told them it wasn't real? Then again, I supposed it wasn't *that* surprising. He may have been too embarrassed to admit it was all a lie, and we'd be going our separate ways soon anyway. What was a few more days?

"I shouldn't keep you out here in the cold," Kit murmured, more to himself than anything. "I'm being selfish."

"I chose to come out here, remember?" I pointed out, glancing at him. He was being very hard on himself. "And the sun is nice, even if the wind is a little chilly. I have no complaints."

There was a look of frustration on Kit's face, though it didn't seem to be directed at me. "You know, Margot, you can be more... demanding," he hedged. "You're very obliging all the time, and I just want you to know that you don't, you know, have to be," he finished lamely.

That hadn't been what I expected him to say.

"I don't like inconveniencing people," I replied, surprising myself with my candour before quickly shaking my head, dismissing the self-pitying feelings. "And since our charade continues, courting omegas are traditionally not demanding. Me being so would undermine our act. It's only after mating marks that omegas grow more assertive with their alphas."

"Why is that?" Kit tucked my arm into the crook of his elbow, a surprisingly gentlemanly move, before guiding me down the beach at a leisurely pace.

I wasn't entirely sure what was happening.

"Omega nonsense," I replied cautiously, giving a half-hearted shrug. "Instinct drives us to be pleasing and compliant, so you'll deign to notice us. An alpha's instinct—that niggling urge to care for and coddle and satisfy— becomes more pronounced after mating."

"Is that so?" he asked, not sounding particularly convinced.

"I'm not talking out of my ass," I laughed. "I've been a courting omega before, I know how this dance goes. How instincts can drive our actions, can drive us to do things that we wouldn't necessarily do in our right minds."

Kit's muscles tensed beneath my arm.

"When was this?"

I startled at the sharpness of the question, glancing at him out of the corner of my eye. "Years ago. Over a decade now. In the lead-up to my first heat."

"And you changed your mind?"

I snorted. "No. He changed his."

"You tricked me."

I shot Kit what I hoped passed for a breezy smile. It wasn't as though I was heartbroken about what had transpired, not anymore. Not this many years on, seeing who Fraser had become and who'd I'd become. Who I *would* have become if he hadn't called it off.

However, the burn of humiliation hadn't necessarily eased. Strange, how the heartbreak that had felt so soul-crushing at the time was now a distant memory, but the embarrassment of rejection was a living, breathing beast beneath my skin that I'd never been able to vanquish.

"It was distressing at the time, of course. With the benefit of hindsight, I see that he made the right call. He would have made me miserable, and I'm certain I would have made him miserable."

Not that he'd been thinking so altruistically at the time, I added in my head.

"I find that impossible to believe."

The vehemence in Kit's voice took me off-guard. Maybe he thought that because I was obliging, I would therefore, also make a good mate, but no one wanted to be saddled with an unhappy omega, and the life Fraser wanted, the life he had now, would have made me incredibly unhappy.

"Well, perhaps *he* would have been happy enough," I mused. "I wouldn't be the Margot I am now if I'd mated Fraser. I'd have been moulded by his vision of what the ideal mate should do and be. His mate is very content to be at home, surrounded by extended family, with six kids and probably another on the way."

"And you wouldn't be happy with that life," Kit said—a statement, not a question.

"I'd have made the best of it," I hedged. "I mean, I wouldn't have known any different. I was eighteen and fresh out of school. The Margot I am *now* wouldn't want that, but there's no way of objectively looking back in hindsight, is there? I'm coloured by the experiences I've had since, the life I've lived, the opportunities I've missed out on, which are probably just as formative as the ones I've taken."

I shrugged, wondering if there was some alternate timeline where I'd never gone swimming that day. Where Fraser had never seen me less than all done up until *after* we were mated. If there'd been a bond in place already, undoubtedly, he wouldn't have found my appearance so jarring. My scent would have already been blended with his, my ties to him unbreakable.

At eighteen, that had been all I wanted. To bind us together in all ways before he looked too closely at me.

At thirty-two, the idea was horrifying.

"Do you want kids someday?" Kit asked after a long pause.

I'd accepted now that I probably wouldn't have children of my own, but back when I'd envisioned that future for myself…

"I always liked the idea of one. One kid that I could give all my attention to, that their dad could give all their attention to. We'd be a little unit of three, cosy and content in a two-bedroom flat, going on holidays easily when we wanted to, driving around in a little hatchback…"

Perhaps growing up with five younger siblings had affected me more than I thought.

"When I was growing up, I hated being an only child," Kit admitted quietly. "But maybe I just wanted what I didn't have. I don't mind it so much as an adult."

I hesitated, wanting to ask Kit about his dad but not wanting to make him uncomfortable either.

"My dad was an omega," Kit continued, unprompted.

Was.

"Pregnancy is a lot more taxing on alpha females than omega females," I volunteered hesitantly when Kit fell silent again. "Maybe that's why they didn't have more? I can see now why you didn't even blink at Asher being a male omega."

Kit's lips tilted up in a quick, wry smile for a moment before his expression turned sombre again. "I think they would have had at least one more, but my dad died unexpectedly when I was two." His gaze was firmly trained on the crashing waves. "We lived in Cornwall. That's where I was born, where my dad was born. He was a fisherman, practically raised at sea. But even the most experienced sailors have bad days, and the ocean is an unforgiving teacher."

I gave Kit's arm a tight squeeze, and he gently returned the gesture. From the look on his face, it seemed as though his grief wasn't fresh and sharp but an old ache that seemed to have long since settled into his bones, making up the fabric of what made him who he was.

Selfishly, I wondered how long it would take me to get to that point with my tangled emotions about Calum. When would that sharp knife edge of grief dull?

"When did you move to London?" I asked, clearing my throat.

"Almost right away, apparently. I don't remember it, but I'm told we lived in council flats and barely scraped by for a few years—Mum never wanted anything to do with Dad's family in Cornwall, and her own family in Singapore disapproved of her mating him in the first place, so it was just the two of us. She'd always done bookkeeping jobs, and eventually, a kindly employer took a chance on her, and she was able to work her way up. She does pretty well for herself these days."

He sounded ambivalent rather than bitter, which tracked. Alpha children often had a slightly strained relationship with their alpha parent as they came into their own dominance. Usually, it was up to the omega parent to soothe the tensions between them, but Kit didn't have that buffer.

"Why don't you stay with her when you come home? Because of the whole... setting-you-up thing?"

"She doesn't have the space. I went to an alpha-only boarding school from age twelve—that's where I met Nico and the *others*—" Oof, there was a heavy dose of bitterness in that one word, "—and Mum bought herself a one-bedroom flat in a nice part of London right after I went into the dorms. I wonder sometimes if that was why I wanted a job where I got to travel. It meant that the living arrangements never really came up after that."

He shrugged as though that confession had been nothing. As if it didn't explain so much about him.

"What about you? When did you move to London?"

"Right after my first heat." I exhaled heavily. "Like I said, the alpha I'd been courting changed his mind. I went through my heat alone and didn't want to hang around after that, so I applied for university in the city, and I've been there ever since. It really did work out for the best."

"You say it like it's easy, but it must have been awful." The intensity in Kit's voice took me by surprise. Then again, we were friends of sorts, and perhaps he didn't like the idea of me suffering.

"Well, heat is always painful, and the first one is the worst. Mentally, I was in a terrible place already, and then the physical pain started, and it was excruciating. But at the end of those five days…"

The emotions I'd felt back then were locked away in an indestructible box in my mind, and I quickly verified that they were still safely there, unable to touch me.

"What happened at the end of those five days?" Kit rasped, staring at me intently, pulling me to a stop.

I looked up at him, drawing more comfort from those dark eyes than I had any right to. *It's not real. This isn't real.*

"I woke up." It was dangerous to look at him for so long—too easy and too tempting to get lost in whatever this tangle of emotions was—and yet I couldn't look away. "My heat ended, and I woke up and got out of my nest. I took a shower, got dressed, did my hair and make-up. I'd just experienced the most painful moment of my life, and I *survived*.

"Maybe it's denial or an overabundance of confidence, but there was something quite empowering in that for me. I figured that if I could survive that, I could survive anything, and so I carried on. Applied for university, moved away from the town I'd grown up in, learned that there was a life for omegas outside of being someone's mate." I blew out a long breath. "That's why I'm doing all this to get Asher into the Sutton-Harris School. Why I'm willing to stand up and lie in front of my entire family and face whatever fallout and humiliation comes from it. There was no one in my corner when I needed it, and I won't let Asher be in that same position."

Kit's eyes were flaming with emotion, though I didn't have the first clue what that emotion was. I wasn't sure he knew either. For the briefest moment, his hand came up to cup my jaw, his thumb brushing over my cheekbone like I was something precious.

"You're the bravest person I've ever met, Margot."

He pulled his hand away, a faint blush staining his cheeks as he resumed walking, gently pulling me along beside him. *It's not real.*

"I don't know that anyone else would describe me that way," I laughed, trying to navigate us back to safer waters. "Most people in my life think that true bravery would be trying again. That, for an omega, most people think being alone is a fate worse than death. Nico and Violet are really the only friends I have who have never tried to push that line of thinking on me."

Kit nodded in understanding. "For two people who are so happy together, they've never been pushy about the idea of mating. Then again, neither of them was looking for a mate when they met each other."

"Yeah?" I smiled. "I'm guessing you knew Nico back then."

"I was there when they met," Kit replied drily. "It was a forerunner to Bryce and Kane's parties, hosted by some other friends. Nico clocked Violet's degradation kink instantly—I turned around, and he had his fingers in this prim, polished omega's mouth in the middle of the kitchen. Suffice to say, I didn't expect it to lead to a mating and I don't think they did either."

I snort-laughed at the visual, having seen those two in plenty of similar and far more compromising positions since. They really were Couple Goals.

"You don't have to answer this," Kit began slowly. "But isn't heat painful on your own? Maybe that's why everyone thinks you must be miserable without an alpha."

"It is painful, but I'm pretty good at managing it now." I hesitated, torn between mortification at talking about something so intimate but also feeling the need to educate Kit because I doubted he knew anything about heats, based on his track record. He was probably at a disadvantage, having attended an alpha-only boarding school. Most of them framed omegas as accessories to alphas, rather than individuals with wants and needs of their own.

"Because I'm unmated, every heat is like my first," I explained. "It builds over the course of a year or so, and then I take to my nest for a week or so. If I was mated, my heats would be shorter and more frequent."

Kit was blushing even more than I was, which made me feel better.

"I didn't know that."

"Shocking," I teased. "You? Not knowing how omega biology works?"

Instead of getting defensive like I'd expected, he sighed. "I'm embarrassingly ignorant, but I'm working on it."

"I can't tease you about that. There's no shame in accepting what you don't know and trying to change it—the opposite, in fact. A lot of people are too prideful to come to that conclusion."

"Don't give me too much credit, Margot," Kit rasped. "It was wilful ignorance that got me into this spot."

"That same stubborn determination will get you out of it," I replied cheerfully. On reflection, stubborn determination was something the two of us had in common.

"Would you ever consider taking a mate now?" Kit asked suddenly, rushing the question out so quickly that it took me a moment to realise what he'd said.

"I guess... If they were the exact right person," I replied carefully, though historically, the issue had been *me,* not them. "I'm past the point where I feel like I should settle for whoever will have me. My life is wonderful the way it is, I'd only take a mate if they were going to add to that in a meaningful way. If they were going to make me happier than I am alone."

Kit pulled me to a stop again, stepping in front of me and staring intently into my eyes as though he could see into my soul.

"Would you ever consider me?"

"I... what?" My brain seemed to go offline for a moment, just cutting out entirely as I attempted to process his question.

Kit hesitated for a moment, and I wondered if I had, in fact, heard him wrong. That made more sense. That was the only thing that made sense.

"I don't want to scare you off, and I think I'm already dangerously close." Kit shoved his hair roughly off his face, the wind sweeping it right back in front of his glasses again. "I like you, Margot. A lot." He gave me an assessing look, seemingly deciding whether or not I was going to bolt or not. "The things I feel for you... I didn't know I could feel, and saying the words aloud to Coleman has only made me more certain of them. And I know you haven't wanted to take a mate in the past, but I need to know. Would you ever consider me?"

"Consider you... as a mate?"

"Yes."

"Is this a hypothetical question?"

Kit's lips twitched. "No."

My heart was thudding so loud it drowned out the sounds of the crashing waves a few feet away.

"Kit..."

"That doesn't sound promising," he said wryly, though he still had that soft, resigned smile on his face.

"I *knew* this would happen if we slept together," I muttered, taking a deep breath to stave off the impending panic. "It's my stupid scent. It's messing with your head."

"I disagree."

"It *is*," I insisted. I knew that was all it was, I'd done this dance before. Maybe the steps were a little rusty in my mind, but I *definitely* remember how it ended. Or at least how it ended for *me*. Other omegas got to swan off into the sunset with the alpha of their dreams, wearing their mating mark with pride, but that wasn't in the cards for me.

No. Kit was enamoured with me because I smelled good, and that was all there was to it. My natural scent was particularly appealing on its own, and combined with the added sweetness of pre-heat, he didn't stand a chance.

"My slick has confounded you," I muttered to myself. "You're imagining emotions that aren't there. Oh my god, I *did* trick you—"

"You absolutely did not," Kit cut in, all traces of amusement gone. "I should have brought this up before we slept together because I was definitely thinking it. Except you were still pretty mad at me then, and I wasn't sure you'd be receptive to the idea."

"Kit..." I was panicking, I knew I was. I wasn't usually lost for words, but I had no idea what to say except to deny it because he didn't mean what he was saying. This was a side-effect of my scent and nothing more.

Kit cupped my jaw gently, his touch centring me, making oxygen suddenly easier to come by. "It was too soon for this conversation, I see that now. I won't push you, but I am going to prove to you that I'm serious about this."

I brushed my fingers down the back of his hand, inhaling as much of his whiskey and coffee scent as I could, with the salty ocean smell overpowering everything.

"It's just my slick messing with you, okay?" I told him sympathetically. "We won't sleep together again, and your head will clear."

Kit's face split into the most unfairly beautiful smile I'd ever seen. "No, it's not. And no, we won't."

I narrowed my eyes at him, some of my pity evaporating. "Where has all this confidence come from?"

"You." Kit shrugged. "And telling Coleman to go fuck himself. That was long overdue, too. I've never been entirely *comfortable* with my alpha side. It seemed to bring with it a lot of expectations about the kind of person I'd be, the kind of life I'd lived. Mostly I've been content to ignore my designation. Until you."

"Me?" I asked weakly, the ground feeling increasingly unstable beneath my feet, and not just because we were standing on pebbles.

"You," Kit confirmed. "You make me want to be... an alpha. To embrace what I am, because I know my designation helps me give *you* what you need. Suddenly, what I always thought of expectations I realise are privileges. A bonded mate is a gift, not a burden. Changing my lifestyle to accommodate them isn't a sacrifice, it's an opportunity. Does that make sense?"

I opened my mouth before closing it again, totally unable to come up with words to respond to that. It was too... *perfect*. If I for one second believed that Kit was actually interested in *me* rather than my *scent*, that would have been the exact reassurance I'd have wanted to hear. The flawless, comforting argument that he could be the alpha I needed him to be, that being with him wouldn't be giving anything up, but rather gaining something wonderful.

But it wasn't true. It wasn't *real*. It was a mirage created by the temptation of a single omega in pre-heat, and nothing more.

"Hey!" We startled apart at the sound of Nico's voice, turning to find him standing on the pier above us, leaning on the railing and watching us carefully.

I sucked down a lungful of air as though I'd just been underwater, the sounds of the world around me rushing back to full volume.

"We're coming up!" I called out shakily, grabbing Kit's arm and leading him towards the road. "We can continue this conversation later. I'll educate you on the error of your ways," I added, attempting to downplay the seriousness of the conversation we'd just had and the intensity of the emotions I was feeling before Nico picked up on them.

Kit dragged his feet slightly but didn't protest as we headed off the beach. I needed a moment to collect myself, which would be far easier to accomplish with Nico and Violet around to break the tension. Especially with Kit looking at me in that disarming way he'd increasingly been doing, seeing far more than he should.

"Everything okay?" Nico drawled, glancing between me and Kit.

"Of course." I gave him my brightest smile. Nico had defended me in front of Kit's friends—*his* old friends—and I didn't want to cause him any more stress when he'd already done so much for me.

Nico gave me a long look. "I need to apologise, Margot. I lost my cool back there, and I wasn't thinking how all that alpha aggression in the air must have made you feel."

"Oh god, please don't apologise," I said quickly, horrified. "You were sticking up for me, and I'm so grateful for that. You're a good friend, Nico."

"Even so, I should have kept my cool." Nico grimaced. "And Violet's a better friend—while I was raging, she found us somewhere else to stay."

"Oh." I glanced at Kit. "I kind of assumed we'd just take the train back home."

When had he started looking at me like that? His gaze was searing beneath my skin, and I was trying to remember if he'd looked at me like that *before* Bryce and Kane's party or if it was just slick-induced insanity.

It's definitely the latter. Don't entertain otherwise.

How was I meant to go through with my plan to get Asher into Sutton-Harris now? Using Kit had been fine on my scale of moral acceptability when he'd been using me right back. But now that he thought—incorrectly—that he wanted something real...

It changed everything.

"It's your call, Margot. If you want to go home, we'll leave right away. If you want to stay the weekend, just the four of us, then we'll do that." Kit shrugged, as though putting my wishes first was the most natural thing in the world. As though I was the kind of omega people ever put first.

"Violet and I are staying either way," Nico added, his expression turning mischievous. "Once you see the place, I think you'll understand why. It's... one of a kind."

I narrowed my eyes at him. "You really know how to pique someone's curiosity, don't you? Obviously, I have to see it now."

Nico grinned. "Perfect, Violet is already making us all dinner, and we've moved your bags over. Let's go."

Chapter Sixteen

We followed Nico away from the beach and down a few side streets, arriving outside a white brick house with a pale pink door where he let us in using an electronic key code.

"What is this place?" I asked, following Kit into the living room and looking around in awe. It was a rather traditional townhouse from the outside, and the inside retained some of those original historical fixtures, but there was nothing traditional about it.

The walls were all painted matte black and decorated with brightly coloured lewd pictures and sculptures, and every piece of furniture looked ergonomically designed for fucking.

Kit picked up an impressively realistic magenta sculpture of a veiny dick, complete with a knot in full swell, examining it with one perfectly judgemental eyebrow raised.

"Actually, don't tell me," I laughed. "This place has Bryce written all over it."

"You got it," Violet laughed, emerging from what I assumed was the kitchen, leaning against the doorjamb and mixing something in a bowl she had tucked in the crook of her arm. She could make a meal out of nothing, this lady. "This is their little Brighton bolthole, there's just two bedrooms. Both of which are as ostentatious and horny as what you see here, and both of which have wetroom ensuites with a full wall of mirrors."

"We're going to eat dinner together, then we fully intend not to see you until we leave tomorrow night," Nico announced. "We've already put your bags in the upstairs room. Can I help with dinner prep, my love?"

"Please," Violet replied, shooting me a wink as she and Nico disappeared into the kitchen, stupidly cute as always.

"Shall we go look around?" Kit asked, gesturing towards the stairs that led to the upper level.

I chewed nervously on my lower lip. "I don't know. Should we?"

The couch looked pretty comfortable.

Well, no, not really. It looked sturdy and wipeable, which was how I imagined Bryce chose all of his furniture, but it was only a couple of nights. I could rough it.

"What's going through that head of yours?" Kit murmured, watching me closely.

"That you need to be cut off from my slick, and we don't have a great track record of keeping our hands off each other in enclosed spaces," I said tartly, annoyed that we couldn't keep enjoying the no-strings-attached sex that had been absolutely blowing my mind the past few days.

"No, we don't, but I can keep my hands to myself. I never want you to be uncomfortable, Margot." He paused, giving me a loaded look. "Though I think you're overestimating how addictive your slick is. It's fucking delicious, of course—"

"Shhh." I pressed my hand over his mouth. "No talking about how good my slick tastes or you're sleeping on that horrendous couch."

Kit wrapped his fingers around my wrist, pressing a kiss to my palm with a smug smirk as he tugged my hand away.

My stupid belly went all fluttery, and I eyed up the sex bench masquerading as a sofa again before shaking my head to myself.

"We're both sensible adults, aren't we? We understand that we may have got carried away already and that we should reel things back in to avoid hurt feelings." I swallowed thickly. *Would you ever consider me?* It was just my scent confusing him, but 'carried away' suddenly seemed like a huge understatement. "We can share a bed without jumping each other. Right?"

Kit gave me a long, hard stare, and I half expected him to say no.

"Right."

"Right." I nodded, clasping my hands together, filled to the brim with doubt about the soundness of this plan. I was probably going to end up on the couch before night fell out of necessity. "Right, good. Well, we'll just do that then. We're going to have dinner with Nico and Violet and relax, and then we'll both sleep upstairs next to each other and keep our hands to ourselves. That's... Yep. That's what we'll do."

"That's what we'll do," Kit echoed, his voice a delicious rasp that travelled down the length of my spine, awakening all the parts of me that I was trying to put to sleep.

This was going to be a very challenging night.

"Shall we watch a movie?" I asked, emerging from behind the wall that hid the ensuite in my pyjamas and gesturing at the television.

Violet had whipped up omelettes for all of us for dinner, then Nico had practically thrown her over his shoulder and carted her away to the sex dungeon downstairs, which put paid to my plans of using them as a buffer.

And, because this house was basically an upgraded version of the sex dens omegas could hire to get an alpha fix, there was no television downstairs. Everything centred on the bedrooms, which meant we were kind of stuck here.

Movies were good though. Ideally, something with lots of explosions and meathead alpha heroes without so much as a whiff of romance.

"Sure," Kit replied, his eyes lingering a little too long on my bare thighs. *Should have packed full-length trousers to sleep in.*

I darted under the covers, sticking as close to my edge of the bed as possible. Kit was laying on top of the blankets, still fully dressed, his hands resting over his stomach.

It was very inconsiderate of him to not look as stressed about this situation as I felt. He could at least pretend.

I grabbed the remote, turned on the TV and flicked through to the latest instalment of *The Alpha Team*—maybe the worst movie franchise to ever exist—and yanked the cover all the way up to my chin.

"Big *Alpha Team* fan?" Kit asked drily.

I hummed noncommittally. "Captain Bridger can storm my gates any time he wants."

Kit looked disdainfully at the slow-motion shot of said Captain walking towards the camera, gloriously backlit by the rising sun to best show off all those bulging muscles.

These films were dumb as rocks, but I could watch Aaron Tempest walk around all day. Bonus points for when they zoomed in on his biceps.

"Did you know he's from Surrey?" I asked, doing my best to keep the conversation going. "His American accent is so good."

Kit harrumphed, staring narrow-eyed at the screen. We watched for a while in silence as Captain Bridger repeatedly defied all laws of physics, my skin growing increasingly hot underneath all the blankets.

Well, maybe not just entirely from the blankets.

Maybe a little from how unfairly good Kit smelled. I briefly wondered if it would be too on the nose to extol the benefits of scentshield lotion.

"I'm going to shower," Kit said suddenly. I blinked, wondering if I'd accidentally spoken my thoughts out loud.

"Okay. I'll just... be here," I replied lamely, positive I was turning a spectacular shade of crimson. "I mean, I won't look."

The ensuite ran parallel to the bedroom, with a divider wall in between, but if I looked around the corner, I'd be able to see him in the walk-in shower. Fortunately, there was a private lavatory at the other end, at least.

There was also a bathtub on a raised platform right here in the bedroom, but we were both studiously ignoring that.

Kit attempted to discreetly adjust himself as he stood, and I felt an answering twinge of awareness between my thighs.

"Right," he agreed easily, turning to face me and walking backwards to the bathroom. "Hands to ourselves."

What idiot had made up that rule? And why did he look so smug about it?

I groaned quietly the moment he disappeared, slamming my head back against the pillow, the sound muffled by the movie and the running shower.

The dull ache in my pussy that Kit seemed to spark to life by just existing was growing into a full-blown *throb*, and there was absolutely nothing I could do about it, even though I was confident Bryce would have brand-new, never touched, knotted dildos somewhere in this house if I just went looking.

Nope, no, don't think about it. Once the slickgates opened, there would be no stopping the ensuing flood. There were definite downsides to owning an omega vagina sometimes, and almost all of them were related to general decorum.

The rest was clean-up related. Slick was a nightmare to get out of fabric.

I winced as Captain Bridger shot a bad guy in the chest, having never developed much of a stomach for violence. The movie was a bad idea. *I could read a book!*

As quietly as I could, I climbed out of bed, heading for my duffel bag where I'd tucked my e-reader, loaded up with a new financial planning book from a hip, young adviser I'd started following online. As cool and hip as she was, nothing would dehydrate my lady bits faster than money management.

Just as my hand touched the bag, a quiet grunt from the shower had me freezing in place, and that wasn't the only noise I could hear. And the *pheromones.*

No wonder I was getting hornier by the second. Whether he meant to or not, Kit was filling the room with *am alpha, will fuck* energy, and all my tingly omega bits had perked up in response.

Leave, I told myself sternly, closing my eyes for a second. *Go outside and get some fresh, no-fuck-energy oxygen to clear your head.*

I scrunched my eyes together with a grimace as the gusset of my knickers grew damp, flexing my hands at my sides to stop myself rubbing my clit to the muffled sounds of Kit jacking off.

No, I wasn't going to stand for this double standard. If he was going to masturbate in our shared space and fling his hormones around like confetti, then I was too. This was about *equality,* damn it.

Was I going to regret this crusade for equal opportunity masturbating in the morning? Almost certainly. I had the foresight to realise that this would further blur lines that had long since grown fuzzy, but not the strength of will to stop myself.

Why did he have to smell so fucking good?

I crossed the room, leaning back against the wall separating us and listened to the addictive sound of wet skin on skin, Kit's pace seeming leisurely. Occasionally, he let out quiet, muffled groans, and I wondered if he'd clapped a hand over his mouth. Or maybe he had one hand braced against the shower wall and was turning his mouth into his bicep to catch the noises?

I gave up all hopes of not rubbing my clit at that image. Fuck, was he hunched forward? Water running down his back? Over those *glorious* ass cheeks?

I muffled a moan of my own, pressing my hand tightly to my mouth as I rubbed increasingly urgent circles around my clit, building myself higher and higher, my hips rocking of their own volition.

"Margot," Kit called, his voice tinged with alpha growl. "I can smell your slick."

"Yeah, well, I can hear you touching yourself," I called back, attempting to be sassy and sounding like an amateur phone sex worker.

"You said hands to ourselves. I am keeping my hands to myself." He was *outrageously* smug, and I was torn between being offended, and kind of turned on by his gall.

"You know that's not what I meant," I replied, picking up my pace, desperate to reach a peak that was feeling increasingly impossible to get to.

I didn't want my stupid thin, bony finger. Kit was *right* there, smelling like a thick knot and a delicious stretch and *why the fuck was I getting myself off right now?*

"Come here," Kit ordered, careful not to infuse any command into his voice. "I want to watch, and I *know* you do, too."

"Cocky alpha," I grumbled, the ire in my words slightly undercut by the speed in which I shucked my sleep shorts and knickers, walking into the bathroom with just a t-shirt on.

"Shirt off," Kit said immediately, in the exact position I'd imagined him in. My inner thighs were already damp with slick, and I quickly threw off my shirt, heading for the shower before I started making a mess on the floor.

Kit straightened, perfect cock in hand and eyes heated as he watched me approach, standing out of the way of the entry and gesturing to the wide stone bench at the other end of the shower.

I frowned, glancing between him and the seat.

"Hands to ourselves," he reminded me with a lazy smirk, pumping his cock for added emphasis.

"You're not going to touch me?" I all but gasped, a spike of pure omega rage hitting me square in the chest before I shoved it back down. *He's not mine. I have no right to be mad.*

We're not even supposed to be getting naked together at all.

"Not with my hands."

Well, that cured the anger, at least.

"We'll see about that," I replied, sitting on the shower bench and propping one foot up flat next to me, opening my thighs for him. The soft golden light from the wall sconces reflected off my slick-soaked skin, and I made a show of catching a trickle of arousal and dragging it up to my swollen clit. Kit's back hit the tiled wall with a thud, his hand tightening around his cock, the head looking angry and purple and weeping with precum that he was wasting down the shower drain.

I *needed* that cum. In my mouth, in my pussy, I wasn't fussy.

"Omega," he growled, prompting another pulse in my womb and a sudden gush of slick.

Alpha. The word was on the tip of my tongue, a moaned plea for release, for protection, for *everything*, all at once, but I bit it back. His feelings were already complicated enough, and I didn't even want to examine mine.

This was temporary, temporary, temporary.

I wished he wouldn't look at me like it wasn't.

Kit took a step towards me, still pumping his shaft in controlled, deliberate strokes.

"Hands to ourselves," he reminded me, flashing me a toothy smile that I didn't recall ever seeing before. There was no time to analyse it, though, not when he was dropping to his knees with a thud in front of me. "Spread. Let me lick that pretty clit until you're gushing down my chin."

I made a semi-rabid noise of agreement that I was pretty sure I'd never made in my life, propping my other foot up on the bench and spreading myself obscenely for Kit's viewing pleasure.

Kit's back muscles must have been straining as he leaned over me, careful not to touch me with his hands as he lowered his mouth to my pussy, licking up my slick with an obnoxious slurp.

He groaned in ecstasy, briefly sitting back on his heels, his eyes drifting shut. "You taste like a fucking dream, Margot."

"Shh. You're reminding me of all the reasons why this is a bad idea."

Kit snorted. "You give your slick too much credit."

Before I could formulate a reply, Kit got to work, his tongue doing something frankly magical to my clit that had my brain short-circuiting.

I reached for his head without thinking, but I'd only brushed the tip of his hair when Kit pulled away, raising an eyebrow at me.

"You can't be serious about holding me to that?" I grumbled, crossing my arms over my chest. Kit followed the movement, watching avidly as my breasts swelled under my arms.

"I'm very serious," Kit replied confidently, raising an expectant eyebrow at me.

I was sulking, but I wasn't about to cut off my nose to spite my face. I got back into position, creating a V with my fingers that Kit neatly slotted his tongue between, filling the shower stall with the lewd sounds of him licking up my slick before sucking my clit into his mouth.

The sudden movement, the boldness of his actions, the added stimulation of not being able to touch him all sent me over the edge with startling speed and intensity.

Slick flowed out of me in the most generous rush I'd seen outside of heat, whatever he couldn't lap up spilling down Kit's chin.

He groaned, the wet sounds of him pumping his shaft making another gush of slick flow out.

"On the bed, Margot," Kit rasped, the veins in his forearms standing out in stark relief as he fisted his cock.

"Bossy," I murmured, practically salivating over the glistening drop of precum that seemed to be calling my name.

"Are you complaining?"

I pressed my legs together, following Kit out of the shower and accepting the towel he handed me.

"No, I'm not complaining." Even as I roughly dried my body, the top of my thighs remained wet with slick. I definitely wasn't complaining. "Not about the bossiness, at least. A little about the no-hands rule."

Without waiting for a reply, I stalked back into the bedroom and laid down on the bed horizontally, the incredibly unromantic sounds of the action movie still playing in the background as I slid my hand down my stomach to toy with my clit. If I was keeping my hands to myself, then I was going to put them to good use.

Kit paused at the edge of the bed, watching me with hunger written all over his face. "Look at how slick you are. What a pretty, needy pussy."

"Don't get cocky," I breathed. "This is a natural reaction to watching Aaron Tempest flexing his biceps on screen."

Kit paused, eyes filled with challenge. "You expect me to believe all this sweet slick is for an action star you saw on TV? All those sweet moans were for him?"

He was dripping with confidence, and I loved that he was rolling with my teasing rather than getting miffed or losing his temper.

Kit reached for the remote, flicking off the TV. "I think you might be teasing me, sweet, *nice* Margot."

He dragged his cock over my clit, rubbing the fat head in teasing circles over my hyper-sensitive nerves.

"I'm telling you, I'm not that nice." Kit hummed thoughtfully, maintaining his maddeningly slow pace. "I'm not as mean as you, though. Stop tormenting me."

"I'd love to."

"What do you need, an invitation?" I all but snarled, going at least fifty-per cent feral omega in the face of cock deprivation.

"You know what I need. My ego is bruised," Kit teased, his voice all silky smooth seduction.

I snorted, hooking a leg around his hip and attempting to drag him closer. "No, it's not. Why are you so strong?"

To my chagrin, I didn't seem to be moving his dick any closer at all.

"It is," Kit insisted, sliding his cock down, taunting me with the tip. *Is this worse? I think this might be worse.* "Very bruised. Battered, even. It will require some soothing. I don't think I can perform otherwise."

The audacity of saying that while his hard-as-nails cock was *massaging* my pussy, albeit only one inch of it.

"You are such a brat," I whined. "Fine, fine, fine. Every litre of slick—of which there are probably many—that I have produced tonight is for you, you arrogant alpha dickhead. Please fuck me before I lose my mind."

Kit grinned with pure, unadulterated satisfaction, his hands coming to land either side of me on the mattress as he thrust to the hilt.

I cupped my breasts, toying with my nipples. If I was going to keep my hands to myself, I was going to put on a damn good show about it.

"Not that you were ever in doubt, but this is all for you," Kit rasped, the muscles in his arms and abdomen flexing with each movement, his thrusts driving me up the mattress.

I wanted to tease him more, but I'd lost the capacity to speak. My brain had sunk into full omega zone, and I couldn't concentrate on anything but the stretch I was craving from his knot.

"So fucking beautiful," Kit murmured. "I love the way you blush all the way down your chest. Love the sounds you make, the fucking *scent* of you. I could watch you all day."

His words completely undid me. I came with a desperate gasp for air, dragged into an orgasm so intense it felt like I'd drown in it.

So good. How was it always so good with him?

"Knot," I gasped, rocking my hips back, attempting to take Kit's knot.

Except for some unexplainable reason, his fucking *hand* was in the way, wrapped around it the way my cunt was meant to be.

"Nuh-uh, omega. I don't think so. I'd hardly be able to keep my hands to myself if we were knotted together, would I?"

I let out a full-blown gasp of outrage as Kit's movements shuddered to a halt, his cum almost immediately running down my thighs without his knot in place to stop it.

A little bit furious and a lot feral with horniness, I pulled away, crawling around until I was facing him, my mouth level with his still leaking cock.

"Don't be mad, Margot mine. I know how crazy this drove you at Bryce and Kane's party."

Margot mine.

But I wasn't his. With a little time and space, Kit would recognise that too. He'd probably *thank* me for my clearheadedness someday.

For now, I just wasn't going to acknowledge the term of endearment. I'd swoon if I did.

"I'm annoyed that you worked out I had a knot denial kink before I did." I shot Kit a challenging look through my eyelashes before swallowing his still-twitching cock as far as I could, sucking down his cum and the slick on his shaft in one smooth movement.

"Fuck!" Kit rasped, his grip on his knot looking almost painful as he massaged the thick flesh, sending another gush of cum down my throat. "You're full of surprises, Margot mine."

I hummed, suckling down every drop of arousal I could get, only retreating when I'd drained him dry.

"I am. Next time, I want your knot."

"So bossy," Kit teased, cupping my jaw and leaning down to give me a filthy kiss. "Be a good omega, and we'll see."

Chapter Seventeen

None of us had been ready to leave come Sunday evening, and while Sunday *night* had been incredible, driving back to London at six am on Monday after a weekend like that was a special kind of hell.

Kit had reluctantly headed into the city for a meeting with his agent that he'd been putting off for weeks apparently, while I'd headed home with Nico and Violet in time for a nine am conference call.

I'd managed to be mostly on my A game at the start of the call when we were discussing what I needed to hand over before my heat leave began, but now they were discussing a deal that would likely take place while I was away, and my focus was drifting.

The teeny second bedroom that I used as an office was at the front of the flat, overlooking the quiet street. I stared out the window, entertaining the idea for just a moment that I could do this job from anywhere.

That was the whole point of it. I'd been deliberately herded into this particular role because a good omega was at her alpha's beck and call, safely ensconced in the home where their protector didn't need to worry about them.

I'd only ever seen it as a negative. A cruel jab at my singleness even, since the alpha partner I worked under was mated to an omega who stayed home to care for their five children. But maybe I'd been too quick to write off the benefits that came with working from home.

And maybe spending time with Kit, who was so well-travelled—and actually going on a trip this past weekend instead of cancelling to make someone else's life easier—had me entertaining the possibilities.

I still needed a nest. I couldn't live on the road, travelling all the time the way he did. But I could take extended holidays and work from a sunny seaside villa somewhere. Have a change of scenery. Leave the country, so no one could call on me to do anything for them.

That was probably a selfish thought.

"Right, I think that's everything," Reuben said, accepting a coffee from someone off-screen. "Margot, if we don't speak again beforehand, we'll organise a meeting when you're... back in action, as it were."

"Sounds great," I replied with a forced smile, pretending we weren't all now thinking about my heat. How delightful. "Have a good day, everyone."

I signed off instantly, planting my forehead on the desk with a groan. Without a doubt, everyone in the firm would be tittering over that comment at tea break today. I added that to my list of silver linings at being kicked out of the office.

Fortunately, my day improved after that. I finally received some documents I'd been waiting on, and Kit sent me a picture of his lunch after his meeting with his agent that I found weirdly cute in a way I couldn't quite describe to myself.

It was so... domestic?

Throughout my adult life, I'd never had a significant other. I'd never had someone who'd just... send me a picture of what they were eating just because they wanted to share something about their day with me. It was a level of intimacy I'd never experienced before, and it was far more dangerous to my rock-solid emotional walls than anything else Kit and I had shared.

When Kit said he was going to prove to me that he was serious, he may have actually meant it.

Me: Those strawberries look so good.

I tacked on a drooling face emoji at the end before setting my status to 'Away' and heading out of the office. Usually, I preferred to go to the supermarket early in the morning when it was mostly deserted, but I sort of felt like I'd die if I didn't get strawberries that very minute.

The joys of pre-heat.

If there was one thing I'd got good at after so many heats alone, it was identifying the things I could do beforehand to make the five days easier. A craving for strawberries, from past experience, indicated a vitamin C deficiency that my body was flagging before my heat struck.

I grabbed my raincoat and rolling bag on the way out the door, clumsily shoving my arms through the sleeves as I made my way down the stairs. It was a typical spring day—grey and pouring with rain, which at least meant there wasn't a throng of people to navigate through on the high street.

My hood was up and head bowed to stop my face from getting wet, and I let out a muffled shriek of surprise as someone ahead of me grabbed my arm, yanking me into a small loading area lined with dumpsters next to the pizza restaurant.

The metal handle of my bag clattered on the concrete as I yanked my arm free, stumbling back against the concrete wall I'd been steered into.

"You've really been playing hard to get, haven't you?" Jimmy asked, standing between me and the street. "I've been double-checking with your dad, and he keeps saying 'No, Jim, she's not courting anyone, she's just playing games with you, paying some alpha to scentmark her house', but I got to say, you really had me wondering."

He chuckled to himself while my eyes darted around the loading bay, seeking out an escape route, or witnesses, or both. Ideally both.

Unfortunately, the rain seemed to have driven everyone off the street, and Jimmy was doing a solid job of looming over me.

"This may shock you," I said drily, hoping to appear unbothered as I stalled for time. "But my father is actually not the authority over whether or not I'm courting someone. I am, and I *am*, so you may go."

"Careful now, girl," Jimmy warned with a slightly sinister grin. "You know we alphas love a chase. Teddie said you'd be a high-class omega who needed a bit of wooing."

Who the fuck was Teddie?

While he talked, I slipped my hand into my purse, flicking open the small knife I kept in there for emergencies.

"I don't need wooing—"

"Now, now, I won't have any more of this protesting," Jimmy interrupted. Inside my purse, I ran the pad of my thumb along the blade of the knife. "You sent that cute little picture of your toys, I know there's no alpha in your life, and your dad has made his stance on the matter clear. You're going to be mine, omega, no need to fuss about it."

"Fortunately, I'm not a minor and my dad has no say over my life," I replied with a syrupy sweet smile, stepping into his space. Jimmy didn't back up, didn't so much as flinch. Ah, to be alpha, walking around thinking you were untouchable. "You ought to be careful threatening omegas in alleyways, you know. You might come across an old spinster who has enough experience with pushy alphas to threaten right back."

I whipped my hand out of my bag, swiping my bleeding thumb across his mouth. Jimmy's eyes widened in horror as he frantically wiped the blood away with his sleeve, spitting and cursing the whole time, but I was already running, abandoning my rolling bag and relying on the adrenaline coursing through my veins to keep me upright and moving.

In truth, it was barely any blood. At most, it would give Jimmy a headache and a dry throat, and even that was doubtful since he'd immediately wiped it off.

Still, despite what I'd said, I didn't make a habit of threatening alphas with my toxic omega blood, and I didn't feel particularly good about it.

I rushed home, inhaling the faint remains of Kit's scent on the front door from when he'd marked it on Friday before sprinting up the stairs and letting myself into my flat. I made a beeline for the bathroom to clean the small cut before wrapping it in a bandage. A small blot appeared almost instantly, the wound seeping through the bandage, but it would heal before long.

The whole incident had left me shaken. How awful must that omega who Calum had bitten have felt? How *traumatised*? Vaguely, I recalled there were treatment centres that omegas could go to, alpha-free facilities that were meant to offer them respite. Undoubtedly, that was the first place my parents' PI would be looking for them.

Me: Did you ever find out the name of that detective?

I flicked off the message to Chelsea, taking a few deep breaths to get my erratic breathing under control.

Chelsea: Oh! I forgot to look. I'll get onto that.

I don't know why I expected better results from a sixteen-year-old. Chelsea was incredibly smart, but in a very academic way, and at the expense of almost everything else. Real life often got away from her.

Chelsea: Are you bringing that hot alpha from the festival to Nana's party? Asher and I made a bet.

I snorted, some of the tension in my muscles easing. The little shits.

When Mum had announced her pregnancy with Jules and their intention to have another group of three kids close together, I could distinctly recall not being thrilled about the notion. Back then, as far as I was concerned, me, Layla and Calum were the perfect trio and the best of friends, how could they possibly want more?

But after everything that happened with Layla and the alpha that Calum had become, I was definitely glad for my three youngest now. They'd restored my faith in sibling relationships, and I'd have been a lot less happy with my lot in life without them.

Me: I'm not sure yet.

My face heated with long overdue embarrassment when I thought of Kit and I sitting in this kitchen, planning for me to stride into that party and announce that he was accompanying me into my nest for my heat.

There was still *logic* in that idea, of course. But my heart wasn't in it. Even if Kit wasn't suffering the effects of my heady slick, the concept of lying about *that* with *him* specifically wouldn't be sitting well with me.

Aside from that, Nana's party was the day after Kit's awards night. While he didn't strike me as the type to party hard, it was a big event for him, and who knew what kind of shape he'd be in the next day.

Like I'd summoned him with my thoughts, his name flashed on my phone screen.

Kit: I'm downstairs.

He was?

He wasn't giving me much of a chance to rebuild my emotional walls after Brighton, that was for sure. Based on what he'd said on the beach, that was probably by design.

I jogged down to unlock the door, finding him in sweat-and-rain-soaked running clothes that did either terrible or wonderful things to my insides; the verdict was still out.

"Here," he said, passing me a paper grocery back and leaning in to give me a kiss on the cheek.

"What's this?"

"Strawberries."

Don't cry, I told myself sternly, doing my best to give him a valiant smile while my insides cracked in two.

Kit would be such a good mate.

His brain may not know the theoretical aspects of how an alpha-omega relationship worked, but his instincts were steering him along just fine.

Kit had been hovering on the threshold like he wasn't going to come in, but the moment I went to take the bag, his entire demeanour changed.

"What happened to your thumb?" he asked, crowding me in the entryway as he took a step forward, capturing my wrist.

"Just a scratch," I replied hurriedly, attempting to take the bag off him again, though he pulled it back out of reach with an eyebrow raised.

"You're a terrible liar."

"Sorry?" I thought about it for a moment. "No, I'm not really, I'm actually fine with being a terrible liar."

"Margot," Kit warned, giving me his most serious face. "Tell me what happened."

"So bossy." I tutted, not nearly as put off by that trait as I normally was. Kit's brand of bossiness was annoyingly appealing. "You may as well come up—you look about one second away from throwing me over your shoulder."

"I am," he agreed, stepping into the entryway and pulling the door shut behind him.

Without the steady stream of fresh air, I let out a pained groan almost immediately. "This was a bad idea. Your sweat smells *so* good, did you know that?"

Kit's lips quirked as he rested a hand on my shoulder, gently turning me to face the stairs before giving me an encouraging pat on the ass. "I did know. Up you go."

Before I could take a step, he leaned forward, his lips brushing the shell of my ear. "Be a good omega and tell me what really happened to your thumb, and maybe we can play a fun game of keep-our-hands-to-ourselves again."

I glared at him over my shoulder as I climbed the stairs, but I knew it was more of an angry-horny face than an angry-angry face. "*You* can keep your hands to yourself, I make no such promises. Get inside and take your pants off."

Kit snorted. "And you call *me* bossy. You'd make a fearsome alpha, Margot."

"That's the nicest thing anyone has ever said to me," I sighed, unlocking the door to my flat and holding it open for Kit to follow. I made a beeline straight for the sink to wash the strawberries, beyond glad I could satisfy my craving without attempting another trip to the supermarket.

Fucking Jimmy.

Kit sat down on the loveseat, stretching out his long legs in front of him and watching me expectantly.

"You're not going to let this go, are you?" I muttered, taking a bite of a strawberry to give myself a little more time to formulate an answer.

Something about this moment felt important, but I couldn't quite place my finger on what it was.

"Jimmy didn't find my dildo picture very funny, I guess." I shrugged, attempting to downplay it to no avail. Kit immediately leapt to his feet, looking ready to charge out into the streets and chase Jimmy down.

I remembered with perfect clarity the last time I'd purred. It had been the night before that cursed pool party. I'd been sitting on the swinging bench on my parents' patio with Fraser, drinking lemonade while he laid down, his head in my lap because he always liked the way I played with his hair. He'd been stressed about his university application, and of course, I hadn't hesitated to purr for him—that soft, lullaby-like omega purr meant to offer an alpha comfort, the same way theirs offered us comfort.

After that night, I'd never purred again. I wasn't sure I remembered how until this exact moment when Kit needed it. Before I'd consciously decided to move, I was wrapped around him—arms around his neck, legs around his hips, tipping him back onto the couch.

My purr may not have had the same drugging effect that his did, but his taut muscles did relax as his arms banded around my back, holding me tightly in place.

"Margot," he groaned. "Stop being so appealing. I have ass to kick."

"No you don't, I handled it. Hence the itty bitty cut on my thumb. You don't have to take care of my problems."

"I know that, Margot. I know you've got everything under control. I just *want* to. I want to make your life easier."

He's confused by your scent. The purring probably didn't help. Just get through the awards night this weekend and put some space between you, and all these heightened emotions will go away.

And that's a good thing, I told myself firmly. *The best thing. For both of us.*

Chapter Eighteen

After fourteen years, I knew with perfect clarity what to expect in the lead-up to my heat.

First, my scent sweetened. In the weeks beforehand, I was horny as hell all the time. In the final few days—when I *really* had to wrap up whatever I had going on at work, stock up on supplies, fix up my nest, and send out do-not-disturb messages—a low, consistent ache started up in my womb, a teensy preview of the crippling cramps to come. When my body temperature spiked dramatically, then I knew I had to haul ass to the nest right away.

It was such a formulaic process, and I was usually so in tune with my body that it was surprising to realise the low ache in my womb had already started as I climbed out of the car in front of The Ellis for Kit's awards evening. I just hadn't noticed it right away because of the sharper, increasingly urgent pain in my chest.

"Everything okay?" Kit asked, handing keys to the car he'd borrowed from Nico to the valet while I tugged my coat a little tighter around my shoulders, shielding myself from the world.

Everything felt so fragile. *I* felt so fragile. I really wanted to support Kit tonight, but the temptation to stay home and hole up in my nest had almost got the better of me.

I shot Kit what I hoped passed for a breezy smile. "Of course."

It *was*. Or it should have been. The reason it *wasn't* was currently resting a large firm hand on the small of my back, looking like dapper perfection in a tailored three-piece suit, smelling like coffee, whiskey, and dreams I'd long since banned myself from having.

Self-consciously, I fluffed out my loose curls, resisting the urge to check my make-up for the sixteenth time.

"We can leave if you like," Kit said, guiding me through the grand foyer of the hotel to the coat check. I'd been to a law awards dinner here once, though the crowd had been a little more dour, at least at this stage of the night. The woman in front of me had shed her coat and was attempting to find somewhere in her skintight red dress to hide a hip flask. "I hate these things. So much... small talk."

Kit all but shuddered, and I shot him a reassuring smile over my shoulder, needing to look up at him despite wearing my highest ankle-strap heels.

"I'll small talk for the both of us," I assured him, knowing how uncomfortable talking to anyone but his small inner circle made him. "Just keep me supplied with mocktails and hors d'oeuvres. Nothing that tastes like mushrooms," I added after a moment's thought. "Fungi only if it can't be seen or tasted in any way."

"So hard to please," Kit teased, a smile playing around his mouth. It was a curse that he was so handsome. And so nice, beneath his layers of social anxiety, general distrust of omegas that I was slowly educating him out of, and loner tendencies.

When Kit decided to care about someone, he really made them the whole focus of his attention, and he was kind and thoughtful and *addictive*.

That was why tonight *had* to be the end of it.

Technically, my nana's birthday party tomorrow was the last event we'd discussed, but after today I'd have fulfilled my end of the bargain, and I planned on walking away. Walking directly into my nest, in fact, and not leaving until my stupid heat was over, probably weeping self-pityingly the entire time.

Once I emerged, Kit would see me for who I *really* was, rather than the idealised version my pre-heat scent had given him the impression of.

And that would be that.

I pulled out my phone to switch it to silent, noticing I had a message from my sister.

Chelsea: Teddie Reid. He's a private investigator, I found his business card in Mum's purse.

Teddie. I frowned to myself as I turned the sound off, tucking my phone away. Where had I heard that name before?

We got to the front of the queue as I made a mental note to deal with that later, and I shed my lightweight coat, revealing the royal-blue dress I was wearing that I'd bought a few years ago for a work gala. It was elegant rather than sexy, with a fitted top that scooped low in a tasteful way, and thin spaghetti straps to show off my shoulders. The skirt was more flowing, but with a long slit up the front that made it a little less ballgown, and a little more adult evening gown.

I'd purchased it with work in mind, but scanning the room, I realised that in Kit's line of work, I could have absolutely gone for something more glamorous.

Though, with his dark blue shirt, we'd inadvertently colour-coordinated, and that made my silly little omega heart happy.

"You look..." Kit swallowed, shaking his head slightly. "Unreal. I don't even have words. Fuck, I wish I had my camera."

"Do you?" I asked, eyebrows shooting up. Kit didn't photograph people, as far as I knew.

Also, while I looked good for *me*, I wasn't under any illusions. The woman in the red dress, whose flask was half sticking out the top of her tiny clutch, looked like an actual supermodel.

Kit hummed, his slow perusal pausing at the slit that ended just above my knee. "Will you wear this again for me?"

No. I can't see you again after tonight. Or at least not until after my heat has passed. I need space from you, or I'll drive myself crazy.

I opened my mouth before closing it again, giving him a tight-lipped smile that he obviously took as acquiescence. Tonight was a big deal for Kit, and I wasn't about to burden him with my problems.

"Shall we go in?" I asked, wrapping my arm around the crook of his elbow, partly for the comfort of having him close, partly because my shoes were ludicrous death traps that I'd only purchased because I was vain.

"I suppose," he sighed, pulling me a little tighter to his side.

The ballroom of The Ellis was beautiful, in a generic, swanky hotel kind of way—all dark red patterned carpet, cream walls, and gold chandeliers. Round tables had been set up in the centre of the room with tall floral centrepieces, and there was a makeshift gallery along one side of the room that I was particularly eager to get to.

"That's Aaron Tempest's younger sister, Emily," Kit said, tipping his chin towards the woman in the red dress, who'd given up trying to conceal her hip flask and was instead clutching it like a purse. "She's nominated in the Fashion and Beauty category, I believe."

"What a cool family," I murmured, staring for a fraction longer than was polite to see if Emily had any family resemblance to her movie star brother. "Maybe he'll show up tonight to support his little sister."

Kit looked mildly offended that I'd even suggested it. "I hope you're not planning on trading up your date if he does."

"So sensitive," I teased, gently poking him in the side. "You're not still sore about my intense physical reaction to that movie, are you?"

"That was *not* what you were reacting to," Kit grumbled, though his eyes were flashing with mischief. "In fact, I distinctly remember you clarifying as much at the time. Now what were your exact words... I believe the phrase 'many litres' was involved—"

"Stop talking," I laughed, poking Kit's ribs a little harder this time, before he started waxing poetic about my 'litres of slick' in mixed company.

"I rest my case," Kit said, looking altogether far too pleased with himself.

"This really is quite the elegant crowd," I said quietly as we wound through the tables, taking in the small groups mingling around the room. Some of them had very distinctive bohemian artiste vibes, but far more looked like the kind of monied types that I encountered at the charity events my firm hosted to shiny up their reputation.

Kit snorted. "Lots of wealthy patrons of the arts. This night is more for their benefit than ours—they get to show off which starving artists they've beneficently adopted."

"Do you have any benefactors? Any rings that need kissing tonight?"

"Probably, but I have no intention of doing it. There are reps here from the agency, they can handle all that networking shit."

He glanced around the room balefully, as though daring any of the random strangers ignoring us to disagree, before leading me over to the bar.

Kit ordered a mocktail for me and beer for him, and where I expected him to ease off the physical contact, he wrapped his whole arm around my waist and held me tighter.

I tipped my head back to look at him, my lips almost brushing his jaw. "Nervous?"

"Not as much with you here."

"Because I'm your omega shield?" I was aiming for a light, teasing tone, but the words came out embarrassingly breathless.

Kit looked down at me, so close that our noses almost touched. "You're much more than that, Margot."

There was a fluttering low in my abdomen that had nothing to do with my heat and everything to do with *feelings*.

"You shouldn't say things like that."

"I find I can't stop myself where you're concerned." He adjusted his glasses, and the belly flutterings reached crisis point.

"Kit? Is that you?" someone asked, breaking the spell. I sucked down a lungful of oxygen as though I'd just been underwater instead of standing in the middle of a crowded ballroom.

Kit reluctantly looked away, greeting the beta who'd just approached us. His hold around my waist didn't loosen though, putting paid to any ideas I had about running outside for some fresh air.

"Great to see you, man! When was it we last bumped into each other? Lahore, perhaps?"

"Yes, I think so," Kit replied, his voice rough. He cleared his throat, pulling me somehow closer. "Cody, this is Margot. Margot, Cody. A fellow photographer."

"Margot, it's a pleasure to meet you." Cody gave me a brilliant, genuine smile that was so entirely the opposite of how Coleman had reacted to me that it took me a moment to cautiously respond with one of my own. Apparently, not all Kit's friends were total dicks. "I hope tonight won't be too boring for you. I can't even say the food is good—everything is small."

"Well, Kit's company is never boring. And if I get a chance to look at that amazing gallery wall over there, I'll be more than entertained."

"I can certainly manage that," Kit promised, his voice a low purr in my ear. Far too intimate for company, really.

There was a small smile playing around Cody's mouth as he looked at us that had me feeling incredibly self-conscious.

This isn't real. We're just friends. I caught feelings for him by mistake. He only thinks *he has feelings for me.*

"Where are you off to after this, Kit? There was something about a hotel chain wanting photos in France, right?"

Kit was quiet for a long moment, and I gave him a gentle squeeze of encouragement. I didn't want him to feel awkward talking about the future just because I was here.

"I turned that down. Something came up in New York that suited me better. I'm interviewing for it in a couple of weeks."

New York? We hadn't really talked about where he was going after he was finished in London. I supposed I'd assumed Kit was going to Paris like he'd mentioned in passing, and I was a little hurt that he hadn't told me that he planned on going further afield.

Cody gave him a knowing look. "I'm happy for you, man."

"Let's not celebrate just yet, I still have to get the job," Kit said wryly, glancing around. "We'd better figure out where we're sitting."

"Yes, that's a sensible idea," Cody agreed, already scanning the room. He looked back at us, shooting Kit another bright smile. "It's good to see you, Kit. Especially good to see you *happy*."

Kit seemed happy?

I tensed, bracing myself for an emotional blow from Kit that never came. A quiet dismissal, a scornful laugh, *anything*. Something that would put me firmly in my place.

But Kit was perfectly, serenely silent, already guiding me away.

His hand seemed to fit my lower back like a puzzle piece, and I had a sudden realisation that he'd rested his palm there a lot in the time I'd known him. In fact, it was the first thing he'd done when we'd met, way back at that party at Nico and Violet's. For no discernible reason, he'd put his hand on my back.

"Let's look at the photos first since you wanted to see them," he suggested, leading me through the winding paths between tables.

He was so relaxed, and I felt like I was losing my mind.

Fortunately, the pictures were an ideal distraction. The finalists from each category had their nominated work on display, all varying in theme and subject matter and style.

Eventually, we arrived at Kit's contribution—a striking picture of a fishing village in Norway. He fidgeted uncomfortably next to me as I admired the contrast of the bright red houses against the pure white snow, the cosiness of the homes versus the bleakness of the environment. He'd captured it all so perfectly. It wasn't as though this was the first time I'd seen Kit's work—Nico and Violet's house was filled with it—but there was something extra magical about seeing it now and *knowing* him.

"Can we *please* leave?" Kit grumbled, fidgeting despite still holding my hand. "It is an acute kind of misery to look at my own work. You are torturing me."

"Don't be so dramatic," I laughed. "Nico and Violet's hallway is basically a shrine to your work."

"Which is why I always cut through the back garden to the studio," he countered. "Come on, it looks like people are taking their seats for dinner."

They were, but in a very slow meandering kind of way, and there was absolutely no need to rush, but I took pity on him and followed without complaint.

We were sitting in one of the centre tables near the front, our names neatly printed on thick card above our place settings.

And I was sandwiched right between two unmated alphas. Kit on my right, and a Jude Spencer to my left. He smiled broadly as I took my seat, Kit standing behind me to push in my chair, his hands smoothing over my shoulders in a way that felt distinctly proprietary.

"Margot Bailey, a pleasure to meet you. I'm Jude." He leaned forward as he spoke to address Kit as well, who was suddenly looking very glare-y.

"Nice to meet you, Jude," I replied politely, nudging Kit with my elbow. "This is Kit Iyer."

If Kit found it difficult to walk into a room without being immediately accosted by omegas, I couldn't imagine what it was like for Jude. Not that he was *better* looking than Kit—I definitely didn't think so—but he did have that storybook-prince charm, with neat wavy blonde hair, sea-blue eyes, a square jaw and high cheekbones.

He looked like something out of a catalogue, smelled like fresh basil, and every single thing about his clothing and general presentation whispered wealth in an elegant, understated way.

How was this guy unmated?

"So," Jude said, taking a sip of his wine as waitstaff set down starters in front of us. "Are you an artist as well, Margot?"

"Not even a little," I laughed. "I don't have an artistic bone in my body. I sort of feel as though I'm pulling off a great con just by being here."

Jude grinned. "I promise you're not alone. For every brilliant creative here, there are at least two dull corporate types, here to appreciate the general appearance of the work, if not the deeper meaning and technical expertise behind each piece."

I jumped slightly as Kit's hand landed on my thigh under the table, the skin entirely exposed by the slit of the dress.

"Are you one of those dull corporate types?" I asked, attempting to regain my composure as I cut into my butter-poached halibut.

"What gave it away?" Jude asked, flashing me a charming grin. "It's the haircut, isn't it? Even when we're all wearing suits, the artists in the room have an air of effortless cool to them. I think it must be the hair."

Kit's fingers flexed around my thigh, his hand shifting inappropriately higher. I was wearing proper slick-control underwear tonight to keep my scent thoroughly locked down, but I'd never put them to the test before.

Jude leaned around me, catching Kit's eye. "Case in point. The consummate, cool artiste."

Kit all but scowled back at him, which strangely only made Jude's smile brighter. Then again, alphas who didn't know each other could be oddly competitive.

"I'm actually familiar with your work, Kit. I loved the Norwegian series that you were nominated for. Breathtaking stuff."

"Thanks," Kit grunted, not a single ounce of civility to be found.

"Do you have a favourite of Kit's pictures, Margot?" Jude asked. "I'm sure it's hard to choose."

I nearly swallowed my tongue as Kit abruptly tugged my thigh towards him, pulling my legs apart. He looked as though he was about to say something, and I hurried to respond in case he was going to get all alpha-grump on us and ruin a perfectly pleasant conversation.

"It is hard to choose, though there is one photo of Diamond Beach in Iceland that I particularly love. Perhaps, because I was so intrigued that I looked it up myself, and in other pictures—of course, it's still beautiful in the way nature tends to be—there's a sort of haphazardness to it all. A messiness or disorder, perhaps. But through Kit's eyes, through his lens, it was majestic."

Kit had gone incredibly still next to me, and my face heated. Had I said too much? *Revealed* too much?

"He does have a knack for finding quiet majesty in unexpected places," Jude agreed, watching me with an amused look on his face.

"That's a perfect way of putting it." I shot him a grateful smile that he hadn't left me totally hanging out to dry with my fawning.

The faint brush of Kit's lips against my shoulder made me startle, and I turned my face to look at him, our noses almost touching.

The heat in his eyes scorched me to the bone, and tucked my arms in a little closer in the hopes of covering whatever signals my nipples were undoubtedly broadcasting to the beta couple on the other side of the table.

"You okay?" I murmured.

"Not even a little," he murmured, his voice a seductive purr.

"What's wrong?" I reached for him without thinking, resting my hand over his on my thigh.

"I am *exceedingly* jealous. Unhealthily so, probably."

"Oh," I replied lamely, not entirely sure what to make of that. I supposed it made sense—I wasn't Kit's omega, but I was the omega currently in his bed. The omega coating him in my scent constantly. Seeing me around another unmated alpha would probably provoke some possessive feelings.

The idea of Kit around an unmated omega certainly provoked some feelings in me that I needed to work on squashing. Once Kit realised that he'd never really wanted me, that it was my scent luring him in, he'd return to his life of being thrown in front of single omegas all the time, even if he wasn't interested in them.

The idea sent a pang through my chest.

"We won't be staying for the awards," Kit continued in a low voice, pulling me out of my spiralling thoughts.

"No?"

"No. We won't even be staying for dessert. Eat up. I'm booking us a room."

I swallowed thickly, suddenly not at all hungry for the perfectly cooked fish and squid ink risotto on the plate in front of me.

"What if you win? Kit, this night is a big deal for you," I whispered, making one last valiant attempt at being the voice of reason.

Kit gave me a long look before returning his attention to the venison and truffle mash on his plate.

"It was."

I thought we'd been speaking quietly, but based on the brief, knowing smile Jude gave me as he refilled my glass from the water jug on the table, I guessed we hadn't been as discreet as I thought.

"I'll be sure to let you know if you win," he told Kit with a movie-star smile as Kit led me away from the table.

I couldn't quite hear Kit's reply as he guided me past the tables of chattering guests and scraping cutlery, but it sounded as though he said he knew he'd won already.

My head hit the mattress with a thump, Kit yanking my legs out from beneath me until I was flat on my back, industrial strength slick-proof panties off and my legs over his shoulders before I'd even realised what was happening.

A deep alpha purr of satisfaction rumbled out of his chest as he stared down at my bare pussy, a slightly feral glint in his eye that made another gush of slick appear at an almost painful speed.

"Stop staring, start servicing," I rasped, reaching for him. He'd kept his hand indecently high on my inner thigh all throughout the main course, and following through on what he'd started was really the least he could do.

Kit grabbed my hand, interlocking our fingers and holding it over my hips, pinning me in place while he settled himself between my thighs and licked the slick off my skin with an almost savage intensity.

"Mine," Kit growled against my pussy, making my back arch though his arm was still pinning me down, preventing me from going anywhere. "This slick is all for me. Tell me, omega."

I'm in trouble, I thought vaguely, the pleasure coursing through my veins making it hard to think. Hard to appreciate things like consequences and future heartbreaks.

"It's all for you, *alpha*," I rasped, my voice breaking on the last word. On the *rightness* of it. Alpha, alpha, alpha.

My alpha.

With a growl of satisfaction that hit every nerve on the way up, Kit's tongue found my clit, stroking and circling with increasing intensity. I squeezed his fingers, and he squeezed mine back, and it suddenly felt like the most intimate thing in the world to be doing this holding his hand.

The passion and the perfection of it all smashed into my walls like a battering ram, and the orgasm that ripped through me seemed to touch parts of me that had never been touched by pleasure before.

Could my heart orgasm? It felt like my heart was orgasming.

"It's too much!" I rasped, panic gripping me by the throat.

"Shh, it's okay. I'm right here." Kit moved, now gripping both hands over my head, his body covering mine. *Alpha. Safe. Strong. Mine.* "Let it happen, Margot mine."

Before the final waves of pleasure had washed through me, Kit was already sliding his cock through my slick, his fat tip brushing against my hypersensitive clit for a moment before he pushed into my fluttering pussy. He kept his thrusts shallow, a gentle, teasing rock against me, until I dug my heels into his lower back, wordlessly demanding more.

"Don't tease," I whispered, that strange mixture of desire and sharp emotion still warring for dominance in my heart and in my head. "I can't stand it. Not today."

"I'm not teasing," Kit growled, a fierce sound that was all alpha possessiveness and made me melt. "You think I'm not holding on by a fucking thread right now? I'm just waiting for your permission."

"You have it."

"You going to take my knot?" he rasped, finally giving me his whole, perfect cock, the base already growing deliciously thick.

"Yes," I all but sobbed, holding his hands tightly to keep myself anchored to this plane of existence. "I need it. I need your knot."

Too honest. Too revealing. Keep those thoughts to yourself.

Except I couldn't, and neither could Kit. For every mumbled plea I made for his knot, for his cum, for *him*, he met me with one of his own.

"Give me that slick, Margot mine."

"Come for me again, that's it."

And most dangerously...

"Show me that neck."

"Don't lose control," I reminded him, a real frisson of fear running down my spine as he nosed at the unbroken skin at my throat. Fear for *him*. I'd always assumed that if an alpha got carried away enough to bite me outside of my heat, then it was his own fault, and he deserved whatever came to him. But not with Kit. Never with Kit.

"I won't," he promised, pressing his lips chastely against my skin. "Not about to die and go somewhere you're not."

Fortunately, another orgasm crept up on me at that moment, ripping me apart from the inside, but I could at least pass off my tears as pleasure-induced rather than...

It didn't bear thinking about.

He rolled us at the last moment, keeping me firmly draped on top of him as his knot swelled, locking us together. I hid my face against his chest, squeezing my eyes shut and focusing on the feeling of him filling me, stretching me, *fitting* me so fucking well.

"You didn't even take your trousers off," I wheezed, scrambling for safer ground.

Kit let out a low laugh, and I whimpered at the fresh wave of orgasms the movement set off. Knotting was so *intense*.

"And you didn't take your dress off," Kit pointed out. "We're going to reek of each other when we walk out of here tomorrow."

My face grew so hot, I was surprised he didn't feel it through his shirt. The shirt that was probably ravaged by make-up stains by now.

"On second thoughts, I might have to run out and grab us some clean clothes," he mused. "I don't want to share your scent with anyone."

"Probably a good idea," I replied in a strained voice. "Since I smell like I'm going into heat."

Kit growled, and my pussy convulsed around him. "Definitely getting you clean clothes."

"I can't hang around tomorrow. I've got my nana's party, remember?"

"Of course, I remember. I'm coming with you. I'm very much looking forward to announcing to your whole family that I'm accompanying you into your nest."

Shit.

"Obviously, you're doing it for Asher's benefit," Kit added hurriedly, probably noticing my flaming red face. He paused for a moment, his expression turning thoughtful. "To think, when we made this deal, *you* were the one assuring *me* that you had no intention of holding me to that declaration. We've switched positions."

"Kit..." I trailed off, not entirely sure what I wanted to say. Or perhaps, not having the *courage* to say what I wanted to say.

"I'm at your disposal, Margot," Kit teased, running his hands absently up and down my spine, tracing the zipper of my dress and dancing his fingers over the curve of my ass. "Tell your family whatever you like. Do what you want with me."

Now *that* was a dangerous proposition.

Margot mine.

Not about to die and go somewhere you're not.

Show me that neck.

What was real and what was just my scent muddling his senses? The only objective way of knowing was to wait it out. To go into my nest alone, go through my *heat* alone, and emerge clear-headed and clear-scented on the other side.

Just the idea of that gave me phantom cramps, as though my body was punishing me in advance.

"The things you said… Is it just pillow talk?" I rasped, digging deep for the courage to ask, torn between the risk of humiliating myself and trusting Kit not to hurt me if he could possibly avoid it.

Kit's hands froze for a moment, and I braced myself for rejection before his lips brushed the top of my head.

"It's not just pillow talk."

I swallowed thickly, trying to decide if his answer made me feel better or terrified me more.

Even if I took my heat—my *scent*—out of the equation, Kit was still leaving. His lifestyle still wasn't conducive to taking a mate, just like he'd warned—

"Don't panic," Kit ordered gently, wrapping his arms around me and squeezing me tightly. "I meant every word I said on the beach in Brighton. Every word I've said since. I'm already yours, but we're on your timeline here, Margot mine. When you're ready for me, you'll let me know."

Chapter Nineteen

I woke up sticky, hot, and alone.

Strangely, it took me back to the moment I'd woken up by myself in my nest after my first heat, way back when I was eighteen. The only heat where rejection had been the prevailing emotion riding me when I'd come back to consciousness.

He said he was going to get us clothes, I reminded myself. *Don't get all weird about it.*

Shaking off the old ghosts, I climbed out of the soaking sheets and darted for the bathroom, immediately flipping on the shower.

I absolutely reeked of sex, and the travel-size bottle of Om-Guard I'd chucked in my clutch to get me through the dinner was absolutely not going to cut it today. Cranking the water as hot as I could stand in, I stepped into the spray and tipped my head back, letting our combined scents wash down the drain and trying not to feel some way about it.

If there was one thing I'd learned from this experience, it was that friends with benefits did not work between alpha and omega. It was one thing to fuck within the defined constraints of one of Bryce and Kane's parties, but this whole ongoing, spending-time-together thing was an entirely different beast.

"I'm coming in," Kit called, making me jump. I hadn't even heard him come back into the room.

He appeared in new shorts and a t-shirt that had clearly been folded on a display rack before he put it on, judging by the lines. I twisted away, watching him over my shoulder. I must look a fright, I hadn't taken off my make-up last night.

With a *smouldering* look that should quite frankly be illegal, he set down a bag on the counter.

"I grabbed you some clothes, a new bottle of that scentshield lotion you like, and there's breakfast and coffee on the table when you're ready. We've got late checkout."

"Stop that," I ordered, narrowing my eyes at him over my shoulder.

"Stop what?" he asked, baffled.

"Being so..." I gestured vaguely at him, keeping one arm banded over my boobs.

"So... me?" Kit raised an eyebrow.

"Yes. Stop that."

His lips twisted into a wry smile. "Noted. Don't be long, wouldn't want your pancakes to get cold. I ordered you berries to go on top."

I groaned, pressing my forehead to the shower wall.

There was nothing for it. I may not be able to say the words out loud, I may never *do* anything with the information, but I wasn't about to lie to myself.

I'd gone and fallen in love with Kit.

How had I let that happen?! I thought I'd been careful. Was this karma for how laughable I'd once found the idea of developing feelings for Kit? Here I'd been, thinking I was so impervious to love, and the universe decided to smack me upside the head with a giant reminder that no one was above this kind of feeling.

Reluctantly, I scrubbed my face clean before washing my hair and my body twice, then finally conceding I couldn't procrastinate any longer. After drying off, I pulled out the clothes Kit had bought me, snorting at the hot pink boyshort knickers at the bottom of the bag with *What's Knot To Like?* written in glittery silver font across the ass.

Fortunately, the plain black shorts and t-shirt were a little less ostentatious, and there were even slides in my size. Maybe he'd looked at the label on my heels before he'd ducked out? The idea was a little too sweet for my already fragile emotional state, and I quickly shoved it away.

He hadn't bought me a bra, which made sense, but I hadn't been wearing one with my dress last night. Oh well, the shirt was baggy, I'd just be uncomfortable until I got home.

I dressed and slathered myself in the Om-Guard Kit had thoughtfully bought me. Unfortunately, I'd only brought along enough make-up for touch-ups, not a full face. Surely, Kit had caught enough glimpses of me without make-up on that it wouldn't be a big deal, right?

I gnawed on my lower lip, staring at the reflection that hadn't improved with age. *"You tricked me."*

Maybe that was what I needed? Kit to recoil from me in horror and say something that cut me to the quick and put paid to this ill-advised love forever. It was one method that I knew from experience had a one hundred per cent success rate.

Mind made up, I used the hairdryer until my hair was damp rather than soaking wet, hoping my clip-in extensions were next to the bed where I'd roughly yanked them out before falling asleep.

"Done procrastinating?" Kit called. "I'm not rushing you, but your coffee is definitely lukewarm by now."

I took a deep breath and straightened my shoulders, steeling myself for the inevitable pain. *It was really better to get this over with now,* I told myself. Much better to nip this whole love thing in the bud now before it took root. Or flowered. Or whatever it was that plants did.

"There you are," Kit said, looking up at me from the small sun-drenched table next to the window. "The berries look more enticing with each second, so I suggest you start eating."

"Oh. Um, yeah. Okay," I replied cautiously, making my way over to the table. Maybe he couldn't see my face clearly with all the sunlight? "Thanks for breakfast. And the clothes. And the coffee. Just... everything really."

Kit shrugged, pushing the platter of cut-up fruit towards me the moment I sat down, even though there was already a stack of pancakes with berries waiting for me. "Thanks for accompanying me to a boring work dinner."

"It wasn't as though we were there long," I pointed out wryly, taking a sip of my definitively lukewarm coffee. There was no hiding my face now, I was sitting in direct sunlight right across from him. *Any minute now...*

"It was a much better night than I thought it would be," Kit agreed, flashing me a grin filled with mischief. "You're so cute when you blush."

I froze, holding a blueberry halfway to my mouth. "Is that so? I'm a little... underdressed. Compared to usual."

"Mm, it's nice. I like that we can just be together like this. Relaxed. Comfortable."

Fuck my life.

How was I meant to fall out of love with him now?

"Are you looking forward to your nana's party?" Kit asked, making me choke on the mouthful of coffee I'd just swallowed.

Shit.

Nana's party.

My head had been such a mess since the moment I'd woken up that I'd completely forgotten that the party was today. The party that my dad had ordered me to show up to with Jimmy and announce our impending mating. The party where I'd intended to subvert his orders by showing up with Kit and lying just enough to get Asher through the interview stage at his dream school.

That party.

Fuck.

"Margot," Kit prompted after my silence extended into awkward territory.

I blew out a long breath, setting my coffee down and resting one hand on top of the other on the table in front of me, pinning Kit with my most professional expression.

"I know we're not together," I began. Kit raised an eyebrow, pushing his glasses up his nose. "But I'm breaking up with you. I've fulfilled my end of our arrangement, and as we've already established, my slick scent is clearly messing with your head. I'll figure out something else for Asher—"

"That coffee must be getting really cold by now." Kit's tone was mild, that infuriating eyebrow still raised.

"I— what?" I took a sip of my coffee like I was testing it, for reasons that I couldn't fathom even in my own head. Hadn't I been mid-breakup speech?

Kit nodded in satisfaction, watching me. "Do you like me, Margot?"

"I'm trying to break up with you!"

"Yes, I'm getting that impression," he replied wryly. "But do you *like* me? I won't be angry if you don't. I'll drive you home and we'll never talk about it again."

I stared at Kit across the table, looking like a fucking sun-drenched *angel*, the full force of his potent attention trained on me.

Lie, I instructed myself firmly. *For both of our sakes, you have to lie.*

My scent was messing with him, and it wasn't fair to Kit to let this go on any longer.

"All I ask is that you tell me the truth," Kit added serenely, his knowing gaze unwavering.

"Damn it, Kit."

"Want me to go first?"

I sighed before gulping down most of my coffee in one go. Maybe caffeine would help me get through this. "No. You're just going to tell me what you already told me on the beach in Brighton, and I'm just going to repeat what *I* said that day."

Kit gave me a long look before pulling his phone out of his pocket, tapping on the screen for a few moments in silence before sliding the device across the table towards me.

"What is this?" I asked, glancing down at what appeared to be an email, trying to make sense of what I was seeing.

Application Received.

"A job application. Please note the location and the submission date."

I scrolled down, trying to make sense of what I was seeing. It was an application for a fixed-term position at a New York design school.

"You applied for a job at three in the morning?" I asked.

"Which morning?" Kit pressed, sitting back in his chair and observing me.

"The morning... after we had kebabs. After we went out with your friends."

"Former friends," Kit corrected. "And more specifically, the morning after you talked about how you'd always wanted to live in New York. *Long* before I scented your slick, Margot mine. I've wanted to do something different for the longest time, but I didn't know what. I didn't have any sense of direction. Until you."

"I don't understand."

"Don't you?" Kit smiled softly, melting the ice I was attempting to encase my heart in. "I love you, Margot."

For a moment, it felt as though the world stopped turning. I wanted what he was saying to be true *so much*, but how could I trust that it was real? Even if it was, what happened next?

"Don't say it if you don't mean it," I breathed, interlinking my fingers to stop my hands shaking.

"I never would. It's taken me an embarrassingly long time to even understand what these feelings I've been experiencing *were*. I've loved you since you stood in your kitchen with your hands on your hips and thoroughly put me in my place."

"That's all it took? A good bollocking? I didn't realise it was so easy to get the great Kit Iyer to fall in love," I sniffed, a stray tear escaping. I was trying to joke, to play down the seriousness of the conversation, but Kit wasn't letting me off the hook so easily.

"Well, no one else has ever managed it," he said mildly. "In short, if you want to break up with me, it better be because you can't stand the sight of me, Margot. There's no self-sacrificing bullshit happening here, okay?"

"I don't know how this works," I whispered, wringing my hands together. "Where we go from here, what to do. Kit, I'm terrified."

"Come here." He pushed his chair back and I didn't hesitate to round the table, sitting in his lap and burying my nose at his throat. Kit's scent was so soothing that my heart rate slowed from a gallop to a trot almost instantly.

I'd always wanted to live in New York. And while I was happy on my own, I'd be willing to take a mate if they were the *right* mate, and Kit ticked every box I had. And while I was still nervous about my scent influencing him, the job application had calmed my worries somewhat.

So, what was holding me back?

Was it just the idea of change? Or was it something more?

Kit held me tightly, a gentle, rusty purr rumbling up from his chest, lulling me into a peaceful bubble.

I wouldn't like it all the time, I thought vaguely, but the purr definitely had its moments.

"We're going to that party," Kit murmured eventually, giving my thigh a gentle squeeze. "You can tell your family whatever you want about us, about me, but you're not going alone."

"I could just not go at all," I slurred, still a little purr-drunk even though Kit had cut off my supply.

Kit hummed. "I know you'd figure out another way to help Asher if you didn't go, but you'd still regret it I think."

"You're right," I sighed, my head clearing. "But you and I still need to talk about everything. To figure this all out."

Kit pressed a kiss to my temple. "We will. But I get the feeling that your head will be clearer after you talk to your family. This event has been weighing on you for weeks."

"You're not... You're not disappointed?" I asked hesitantly. "You made this lovely declaration, and in return, I told you I was terrified."

"So long as you haven't ruled me out completely, I'm not disappointed. If all I wanted was an *easy* relationship, I've had plenty of opportunities. But I want you. Gloriously complicated you. You're worth the wait."

I wrapped my arms around his neck, clinging to him so tightly it was probably uncomfortable. Kit was everything I wanted. *Everything.*

And maybe, if I was brave enough, I'd be able to keep him.

Chapter Twenty

Kit parked on my parents' street, and I reluctantly climbed out of the car, a bead of sweat already running down my back beneath my floral cotton sundress. I smoothed down the skirt before checking that my hair was still neatly smoothed back in a ponytail and my inoffensive blush-coloured lipstick hadn't smudged. Better not to give my family any more ammo than necessary.

"You look beautiful," Kit assured me, locking the car and coming around to offer me his hand.

For a few silent seconds, I just stared at him. He was clean-shaven for today, his hair perfectly styled into neat waves, and a duck egg blue shirt tastefully unbuttoned just enough to show off his unmarked throat.

He looked *perfect*. So handsome it *hurt*.

In some ways, I'd grown so much from the person I'd been at eighteen. I didn't fixate on my looks every hour of the day anymore. I didn't derive my value or lack thereof from my appearance. I knew I had plenty to offer, no matter what I looked like.

But being back here messed with my head. There was a reason why I didn't visit my youngest siblings at home.

Kit frowned. "Get those voices out of your head, they don't deserve the space they're taking up there. You. Are. Beautiful."

"Thank you," I rasped, slipping my hand into his, holding my head high and heading for the house. He'd already met Chelsea and Asher, so it wasn't as though Jules and Layla would come as a total surprise to him.

Still, in the context of all of us, even without Calum here, the difference between myself and all of my siblings was stark. Wherever possible, I avoided being in the same place as all of them at once for my own self-esteem.

It was stiflingly hot today, the pavers beneath my sandals felt as though they were frying me from below while the scorching sun did its best to freckle me into oblivion from above. *The melting make-up would really add to the effect,* I thought morosely.

I didn't *like* the melancholy nature of my thoughts. It reminded me of Margot from all those years ago, who'd tucked her tail between her legs and ran away in shame. Whatever else was going on, I wasn't *that* Margot anymore. I was accomplished, content, successful in my own right. Perhaps still a little bit of a people pleaser, but I was getting better. I couldn't be the sister Layla expected me to be, but I was a good sister to Jules, Chelsea, and Asher.

And I was loved, though I didn't think I was brave enough to act on it.

Straightening my shoulders, I led Kit past the brick walls and through the open wrought-iron gate, winding through the cars parked on the driveway. From the street, the house itself was hidden by tall, established trees, but I felt Kit's hand tighten the moment he saw the residence proper.

"Wow," Kit said in a slightly strangled voice.

"Yep," I muttered. The house was nearly as old as the village, an enormous red brick monstrosity—complete with parapet—with eight large bedrooms upstairs, big enough to house even our generously sized family.

With a final strained smile at Kit, I pushed open the unlocked door to my childhood home, leading him into the enormous entry hall—all high ceilings and white cornices. As well as the kitchen and dining room, there were three separate reception rooms downstairs, all of which sounded and smelled like they were packed to the gills with guests. The two rooms at the back opened onto a patio and extensive gardens, which is where I was confident I'd find Nana, but we'd have to wade through this veritable sea of disapproving relatives first.

"This place is very... grand," Kit settled on, seemingly struggling to come up with a word that wouldn't offend me, which was hilarious, as I doubted there was much he could say about this house that *would* offend me. It hardly held any happy memories for me.

"It is," I agreed wryly. "And to be somewhat fair to my parents, they reproduced prolifically, so we did need a lot of space. However, they purchased the house for status rather than practicality."

There was really nothing at all downstairs to indicate that children had ever lived here, and that was exactly the way my parents preferred it.

"Margot!" I managed to stifle my dread as Layla appeared, her youngest son in her arms, messily eating a cracker and seemingly getting more on my sister's dress than in his mouth.

Not that it detracted from her appearance in any way. Even with six kids and never getting a full night's sleep in a decade, Layla was still *stunningly* beautiful. Perfectly proportioned, lightly tanned, with all the elegant features that had missed me in the gene pool, and naturally thick dark brown curls. Like all of my siblings, she looked as though she'd just walked off the set of a photoshoot.

"You're *so* late," she hissed. "You were supposed to be here to help set up and watch the kids. What the hell are you playing at?"

"No one asked me to come early," I replied mildly. I'd known they'd expected me to, but just this once, I wanted to be *asked*, the way Layla was always politely asked whenever Mum and Dad wanted her to do something.

"It's not like you have anything else to do," she retorted with a filthy look before turning to Kit with a painfully forced smile on her face. "You're a friend of Margot's, I suppose."

Well, I could hardly hold Coleman against him now after my sister had decided to show her whole ass.

Kit observed her with that slightly unnerving silence for a beat longer than was polite. "I'm a lot more than a friend."

She didn't believe him, and it was written all over her disdainful face. I'd known none of them would.

"I'm Layla, one of Margot's sisters."

"This is Kit," I said after a long silence. Apparently, he wasn't inclined to respond.

"Margot, watch Lincoln for me. Fraser is bored out of his mind talking to Dad's colleagues; I need to keep him company."

Kit stiffened next to me, and I busied myself with taking Lincoln off her hands and distracting him until Layla was out of sight, pretending to eat his cracker and tickling his belly so he didn't bawl for his mother. No need to add more to the list of grievances Layla had for me.

"Fraser?" Kit repeated in a low voice.

I swallowed tightly.

"Yes. And yes. *That* Fraser."

"The alpha you were courting."

"That alpha, yes." I couldn't meet Kit's eye, so I smoothed back Lincoln's soft baby curls instead, glad he looked like his mother. "But I don't think of them that way. He is Layla's mate. Has been for twelve years. A brother of mine, I suppose."

Not that I treated him as such. I had as little to do with Fraser as possible, and he was very happy to reciprocate.

"How?" Kit gritted out. "How did that come to be? Don't," he added with a warning look as I opened my mouth to make a sarcastic birds-and-the-bees joke, eager to deflect from the tension.

With a heavy sigh, I led Kit closer to the front door, away from the crowds in the reception rooms, hoping Lincoln was too little to repeat any of my words.

"Fraser and I started courting when we were teenagers and his family moved in next door. Our parents immediately hit it off—mine were thrilled, since they didn't fancy my chances of finding an alpha who'd be willing to have me on account of my unfortunate face. Don't interrupt," I said quickly, holding up a hand. "I hate everything about this story, and if you interrupt, I won't get through it."

I waited until Kit reluctantly nodded before continuing.

"I'd always been the ugly duckling, you see. This obsession with make-up and how I present myself was imposed on me from a very young age. I never left the house without being 'done up' to my parents' satisfaction." I bounced Lincoln a few times, brushing soggy crumbs off his chin with my thumb. "We went swimming once, a group of us. Fraser's parents have a pool. I got myself all glammed up as usual, and I tried not to get my face wet, but we were having fun, and I guess I got distracted."

My words tumbled into each other as I rushed to get the story out, humiliation-induced nausea churning away steadily in my gut.

"Anyway, my make-up was wrecked, and my hair looked like... wet hair, and obviously my scent—always by far my most, perhaps only appealing feature—was smothered by the chlorine."

"You tricked me."

I finally gathered up the courage to meet Kit's dark gaze. "Anyway, it doesn't bear dwelling on. Fraser ended our courtship that night, claimed I'd used my scent to *trick* him into being attracted to me, and promptly started courting my then-sixteen-year-old sister. He waited two years until Layla's first heat hit, went into her nest with her, and came out mated and an expectant father."

"By which time, you'd already left."

"Oh yes. I was long gone by then, happily settled at uni."

"And your parents?" Kit pressed. "What did they think of all this?"

"As I said, they were very fond of Fraser and his family, so they were relieved that he chose to stick around and make a play for Layla instead. My father told me not to ruin my sister's happiness with my sulking, pointed out that Fraser had always been miles out of my league anyway, and that was the last we ever spoke of it."

I shrugged, not wanting Kit to think I was upset about it. I *wasn't*, not really. There was nothing in the world I'd trade to be in Layla's place. Before her heat had arrived, I'd offered to help her move to London if she wanted to escape and told her that I'd always love her no matter what.

She'd responded by telling me I was a jealous bitch, and that Fraser was humiliated that he'd ever so much as glanced at me. So that was that. The only time I heard from her these days was when she needed something. Usually, a babysitter.

"Anyway, that's enough ancient history. Let's head in. I'd really like to say happy birthday to Nana. I inherited the sickly face and lank hair from her, so she's always had a soft spot for me," I said, attempting to joke though it landed completely flat.

"Margot," Kit said in a low warning voice, gently grabbing my elbow. "I know I said you could tell your parents whatever you wanted about us today, but I'd really like you to tell them that you're inviting me into your nest. I want everyone here to know that you're not alone, that you'll never be alone again, and if they fuck with you, they're fucking with me."

"*Fuck*," Lincoln repeated with perfect clarity.

"Fudge!" I said loudly, looking at Kit with wide-eyed panic. "Lincoln, he was saying 'fudge'. Can you say 'fudge'? Fuuuudge."

"Fuck," Lincoln chirruped, yanking on my necklace.

"Margot!" I stiffened at the sound of my mother's voice from the kitchen. "Margot, where are you?"

"This is a disaster," I muttered, laughing somewhat hysterically to myself as I grabbed Kit's arm and pulled him down the hallway. "We are not done with this conversation, but my fragile self-esteem will be in ribbons if I spend even five minutes with my mother."

Kit growled, sounding like he'd very much like us to stay in place so he could give her a piece of his mind, but let me tug him along anyway. It made me love him just that little bit more.

He was letting me take the lead.

"Where are we going?"

"To see Nana. Mum's scared of her, she won't follow us there."

"Fuck," Lincoln said calmly.

"That about sums it up," I mumbled, hoisting him higher up on my hip as I led Kit through the halls and around the edges of one of the reception rooms that led out to the back garden.

With each step I took, carrying Fraser and Layla's child who I'd maybe met once, with Kit walking as close to my side as he could without tripping me up, a strange sense of calm descended over me.

No, not strange.

Not at all, actually.

It was the same sense of calm confidence that I carried around with me each day when I went to work, when I ran errands for the Clarksons, and spent time with Michelle, and went to yoga with Violet.

Because that's who I *was*.

I was a calm, confident, *capable* woman. It was only this place, these people, that made me feel like I wasn't.

And I didn't want to feel like that anymore.

Unsurprisingly, Nana was holding court already, surrounded by her ancient cousins and siblings, a glass of wine in her hand that I'd bet money was just there for decoration. Like me, she'd never developed a taste for alcohol.

"Margot!" she exclaimed, waving me over with a frail hand. "My sweet girl, how are you? Look at you; just arrived and that daft sister of yours has already lumped you with one of her infants."

"Nana," I chided, leaning down to give her an air kiss. "It's really no bother. Layla has so many to keep an eye on."

Nana snorted. "Young Asher has been entertaining all of her spawns but this one for the past hour. Now, who is this handsome young alpha you've brought with you? Quite the strapping lad, aren't you?"

Kit bestowed his most charming smile on her, and though Nana was well past her heat years, I could have sworn she gave a little omega preen.

"I'm Kit. It's a pleasure to meet you; Margot speaks so highly of you."

"Well, of course she does. No one else in this family treats her worth a damn." Nana and her cronies cackled, and I pressed my lips together to stop myself smiling. In this family, it was the older generation who were liable to be the most disrespectful and cause the most mischief. It was thanks to them that Fraser never felt entirely comfortable at these events, more than a decade later. "Now, tell me, are you serious about my granddaughter? She doesn't need another flighty alpha wasting her time," Nana warned.

"Nana! That's a little forward, don't you think?" I laughed, hoping some of my great-aunts would join in. Of course, they all left me hanging, the witches. I'd had low expectations for how well Kit meeting my family would go, but this was definitely more awkward than I'd anticipated.

Nana looked thoughtful for a moment. "No, not really. I'm ninety years old, in case you've forgotten, young Margot. If I keel over dead tomorrow, I want to know that I'm leaving you in good hands."

"Margot is always in good hands," Kit replied smoothly, making my pulse kick up a notch. "Her own. I've never met a more capable, self-sufficient person in my life. She handles every burden that comes her way, as well as everybody else's."

I blinked quickly, pushing back the unwelcome swell of tears that accompanied his words.

Nana smiled softly. "That she does. Margot has been that way ever since she was a wee girl, bouncing smaller babies on her hip since she was old enough to toddle to give their mothers a break. But what are *your* intentions?"

"I'm very serious about your granddaughter. I was serious about her before I was even conscious of it. Before I even realised how incredible she is, how lucky I am that she gave me the time of day."

Nana grinned, plucking Lincoln out of my arms with surprising strength and speed, and gesturing for me to move closer to Kit with no subtlety whatsoever.

"If I'm a very lucky man," Kit continued, wrapping an arm around my waist. "Margot will invite me to her nest. Perhaps even move to New York, where I have a job opportunity, though I would move back to London if that's what she wants."

"Oh, but Margot has always wanted to live in New York! Isn't that right, Margot?" Nana was practically glowing with approval.

"Well, yes—"

"And you sit at home all day for your job, don't you? Surely you can do that anywhere?"

I snorted. Nana had always been somewhat derisive of the whole work-from-home concept. 'Back in her day,' people actually *went* to work, so she liked to say.

"Maybe. I'd need to talk to them—"

"Details, details," Nana said with a dismissive wave before extricating her sapphire brooch from Lincoln's grip. "What's holding you back, Margot? It's long past time for you to be happy."

With Nana asking me so bluntly, the vague worry that I hadn't been able to clearly define became obvious. "There are people here depending on me. Even if I stay in London..."

If I took Kit as a mate, he would always be my first priority, the bond would ensure it. I wouldn't be able to offer as much of myself to the other people in my life I cared about, and that was a big decision to make.

"Margot," Nana said softly, eyes filling with sympathy. "My sweet, you can't live your life for everyone else."

A throat cleared from somewhere nearby, and I knew without looking that it was my dad's. I'd always had a knack for sensing the weight of his disapproval, even from a distance.

"Margot," Dad said flatly. "I believe we had a deal, but you don't appear to have upheld your end of the bargain."

I ignored Dad for a moment, turning in Kit's arms to face him. He stroked my cheek, and while it was the briefest touch of contact, it settled the storm in my head almost instantly. That was the power an alpha had over their chosen omega. "What do you need?"

I melted a little in his embrace. "Just for you to be here. That's all I need."

"Of course. You put everyone else first. My job is to put *you* first. Go be selfish, Margot mine. I'm right behind you."

Steeling myself for confrontation, I slipped out of Kit's arms and moved across the terrace to where my dad was waiting with a furious frown on his face.

"Lewis..." Nana warned from behind me, though one hard look from Dad quelled her. For all Nana disapproved of his decisions, Dad could still wield a hefty dose of alpha dominance that she couldn't shrug off.

As a general rule, I tried to avoid standing directly in the line of Dad's scornful gaze. He was an enormous alpha, with the shiny oak-coloured hair that five out of six of his children had inherited, as well as the super thick dark lashes gene that had also somehow managed to skip me. If my parents were betas, Dad would have done a DNA test on me just to be sure.

That was a joke he'd been very proud of making in front of everyone I knew at my seventeenth birthday party.

"What are you playing at?" Dad hissed the moment I was within earshot. "Who the fuck is that? Poor Jimmy—"

"Poor Jimmy, nothing," I interjected, keeping my tone low and perfectly polite. I didn't want to cause a scene at Nana's party. "You said show up with an alpha. Kit is an alpha. What the hell were you playing at telling Jimmy to come and court me? Giving him my address and my phone number? Does my safety mean *nothing* to you?"

Dad's face went a spectacular shade of purple, and my neck strained from the effort of keeping it straight rather than bowing my head in submission.

"You were perfectly safe with him. Jimmy is a good alpha, and he's been suffering alone for years while his mate bond fully disintegrated. He *deserves* an omega. You will apologise to him and invite him to your nest."

"Ignore him," Kit countered instantly, his voice infused with his own alpha command to counter Dad's. I locked my knees to stop them buckling, the weight of an alpha bark making me tremble. Kit was suddenly at my back, holding me to him, keeping me steady.

I wasn't a minor. I obviously wasn't my father's claimed omega. He had no right to command me to do *anything*.

"Watch your words," Kit warned darkly, his scent winding around me like a comforting blanket. "Margot wants to handle you herself, and I support anything she chooses. But I will *not* tolerate you using your bark on her."

Dad's nostrils flared as he glared at Kit over my shoulder. Out of the corner of my eye, I could see Asher jogging towards us, shaking off one of Layla's errant children as he went.

I inhaled deeply, focusing solely on Kit's coffee and whiskey scent. He was the only alpha I'd ever entrust with myself; he was the only one I'd even considered giving the gift of my omega submission.

"Did you say things like that to Calum? About *deserving* an omega? That would explain a few things," I added sarcastically, feeling increasingly hot and out-of-sorts after being barked at.

Dad glared at me, his eyes settling on Asher for a moment before he straightened, his expression suddenly smug.

Here we go, I thought to myself, feeling oddly detached. *He's going to play his trump card.*

"Announce to everyone here that you're inviting Jimmy to your nest. Follow through, let him claim you, and I'll grant my permission for Asher to go to that ridiculous school you two keep going on about," Dad pronounced, gesturing magnanimously at my shell-shocked brother. "Provided he passes the interview stage, I suppose."

"Margot," Asher began, already shaking his head furiously. "No, I won't go. Not like this."

I shot him a reassuring smile before returning my attention to Dad. "I don't accept your deal. I don't need to. You're going to let Asher attend the Sutton-Harris School, regardless."

I may not have got any of the looks in the family, but I'd definitely got the brains.

I was *smarter* than my dad. I didn't have to play this game with him. Dad spluttered an indignant stream of refusals, but I was done letting him control the conversation.

"No alpha *deserves* an omega. That's a lesson you should have passed on to your oldest son. So unless you want me to make an impromptu speech about exactly what happened to Calum—with a side of explanation on who your new friend Teddie Reid is—" *Thank you, Chelsea, for your excellent information gathering skills* "—then you'll graciously give Asher permission to attend the interview for Sutton-Harris, and send him off with your full support come the start of term for him to finish his education there."

Dad looked stricken, glancing around to make sure no one had heard me, while Asher twisted to grin at me, his eyes lighting up.

I frowned, twisting back to look up at Kit. "Did I mention the part where Teddie Reid was convicted for stalking an ex-girlfriend and sentenced to nine months in prison? Quite the company for a respectable alpha like my dad to keep."

"Is that so?" Kit murmured.

"Mm. Also that he's Jimmy's *cousin*. So there's a very good chance that I wasn't just a convenient omega for Jimmy to set his lonely heart on, but I was probably also meant to sweeten the pot a little. What a charming notion for a father to come up with, no?"

I patted Kit's arm because he didn't look particularly thrilled to be playing along with the conversation now. He was back to glaring at my dad with murderous intent.

"You're blackmailing me," Dad stammered.

"I am. Not nice when people play god with your life, is it?"

Asher sidled up next to me, somehow almost as tall as me already, and rested his head on my shoulder, nuzzling me slightly. It was a movement that was one hundred per cent omega comfort and only served to annoy Dad more.

"I had two too many children," Dad muttered, amazingly *not* talking about the alpha son who'd sent himself into an early grave by assaulting an omega. "You are always so *difficult*, Margot."

I thought about arguing. I really gave it a decent cost-benefit analysis in my mind while I watched the vein in his temple thud to the beat of the jazz music playing inside the house. In the end, I came to the enlightening conclusion that it wasn't worth it.

It wasn't *worth* it.

It wouldn't make a difference. Dad had never attempted to understand me before, and he wasn't about to now.

"Oh, and that one is my oldest daughter." Dad laughed, gesturing at me, standing at the back with baby Asher on my hip at the picnic we'd just rocked up to with his colleagues. "Bit of a trial run, her. We got it right with the rest of them, though."

No, he wasn't worth my energy.

He startled—probably at the slightly unhinged smile of peace spreading across my face—and a weight I didn't know I'd been carrying seemed to vanish from my shoulders.

Kit had been *so* right about me needing this closure. I was going to reward him with the sloppiest blowjob ever for anticipating my needs so well.

"Great, I'm glad we got that settled," I announced, wrapping an arm around Asher's waist and giving it a squeeze. "I'm going to leave now because frankly, I don't want to be here. Sorry, Nana," I added over my shoulder.

"Nothing to apologise for," she replied cheerfully. "Did you all hear that? My sweet Asher is going to that fancy art school in London—didn't I always say how talented he was?"

"Thank you, Margot," Asher whispered, wrapping both arms around my waist and holding me tight, sandwiching me between him and the needy alpha at my back who didn't seem in any rush to let go. "You're my fucking hero, did you know that? Now get out of here before the vein in Dad's temple explodes. I have to go explain to Nana that I've only got an interview, and I'm not actually in yet."

I ruffled his hair. "You'll get in."

The moment I released Asher, Kit's lips brushed the shell of my ear. "I'm so fucking proud of you, my magnificent, beautiful, *brave* omega."

"Your omega, hm?" I whispered, my voice catching. My heart was beating like crazy, and my face grew incredibly warm, and it wasn't just from the sunny weather.

"I'm choosing to be optimistic."

Asher gave us a knowing smile that was frankly a little unsettling coming from the sibling that I still occasionally thought of as an infant as I pulled Kit away from the crowd, guiding him around the side of the house, not willing to risk running into any other family members at this point.

We didn't even make it to the gate before Kit had me pinned against the wall, his hips pressed firmly against mine, yet his hands on my jaw incredibly tender.

"Shall I put you out of your misery?" I teased breathily, gripping the front of his shirt.

"Between the smackdown you just delivered to your dad and the torment you're putting me through now, maybe you are a bit of a shark."

"You finally get it," I laughed. "I hope that's not too off-putting for you, because I would really like you to join me in my nest—"

"Yes."

He barely got the word out before his mouth was on mine, pressing me harder against the wall, his tongue stroking mine.

"Wait, wait, wait," I gasped, pulling away. Kit pressed his forehead to mine, breathing heavily.

"What is it?"

"I haven't told you I love you yet. And I do. I love you."

A shooting pain ran through my lower abdomen, and I clutched at my dress, sucking in a sharp breath. *No.* No, this was not happening now. It was too early. I had a few days left, at least.

Didn't I?

Kit watched my movements carefully, leaning in to inhale against my skin but finding nothing. I'd been even more liberal than usual with the Om-Guard, and I was wearing some *industrial* underwear that was feeling more constrictive by the second.

"It's too early," I insisted out loud as Kit pressed a hand to my forehead.

"If you were on your own," Kit pointed out gently. "But you've had a very willing alpha in your bed, and I'm not going anywhere. My pheromones are probably messing with your schedule." Kit shot me a slightly sheepish look. "Violet gave me a book on omega biology and told me to educate myself."

I made a mental note to give Violet a fruit basket or something the next time I saw her.

"You're probably right." I breathed through another cramp, one hand clutching my middle and the other still wrecking Kit's nice shirt. They were the bearable-but-still-uncomfortable cramps of heat setting in, a biological alarm blaring, telling me to hustle back to the safety of my nest.

"But we're not done *talking*," I whined—an actual whine, all omega. "We need to talk about your job, and my job, and the future—"

Kit wrapped an arm around my waist, already ushering me towards the gate. "I love you, Margot, and you love me—you said it, no takebacks. The rest is just details, okay? We'll figure it out. But right now, you need your nest."

Nest. Yes. That sounded delightful.

"I need my alpha," I added, my voice barely above a whisper.

Because that's what this was. Heats had always just been an inconvenience, but it wasn't *just* that. It was a biological imperative. It was my pussy demanding a knot, my womb demanding his seed, and I'd never been more aware of those things than I was at that second.

"You have me," Kit replied firmly, steering me through the gate and away from my parents' home. "I would be honoured to accompany you into your nest. Trust me to take care of you, Margot. Trust me to love you, and cherish you, and protect you, and see you through your heat safely. Through *every* heat safely."

"I do. I trust you. Alpha."

Chapter Twenty-one

KIT

The fact that Margot had been through heat fourteen times before was our saving grace. She kept her eyes determinedly shut in the passenger seat, taking deep, steady breaths and kneading at her lower belly with strong, sure fingers. She didn't look comfortable, but it was apparently enough to keep the worst of the pain at bay.

My pain was just starting. It was actually very fucking uncomfortable to drive with a hard-on, I decided. And the *knot*. Fuck my life. Usually, it only made itself known when I was about to come, but things apparently worked differently when the rut hit. I'd never experienced it before to know.

"Are we nearly there?" Margot rasped, her eyes still kept tightly closed.

"I'm just pulling onto our street. Just a little longer."

She made a terse sound of agreement, and I fought the urge to press the pedal all the way to the floor just to get us there three seconds faster. *Must get my omega home safely. Get to the nest. She needs the nest.*

I threw open the door the second I cut the engine, vaguely aware that I'd done a terrible parking job. It was fine; Nico and Violet were going to come by soon to stock the fridge and take the car back. I'd already messaged them and they'd promised they'd handle it.

My job was Margot. Whatever she wanted from me, whatever she needed from me, I would provide.

My omega.

Finally. *Finally*, mine.

I only had myself to blame for how long it had taken to get to this point, but I found I couldn't regret it. Margot and I both had hangups about mating that we'd needed to address on our own before we could truly be ready for each other.

The idea that I could have missed Margot because of my own stubbornness was fucking terrifying. Because I *had* been ready for a mate. I'd already been contemplating making a big change, feeling the need to put down some roots, but hating the pressure put on me by everyone else in my life who thought they knew better than I did what I needed.

I hadn't just wanted *any* mate.

I'd been waiting for the right omega. An omega who was confident and driven, sexy and kind. Margot was *everything*.

"Nest," she demanded, voice barely above a rasp, the moment I opened the passenger door. I leaned across her to unclip the seatbelt, pausing at the crook of her neck to inhale the first hints of her delicious scent. She always smelled good, but nothing like this, and this was only a *taste* of what her scent was underneath all that de-scenter.

My gums were already aching.

No, too early, I told myself firmly. I'd be deep in the rut by the time it was safe to bite her, and it suddenly struck me as unfair that neither of us would have clear memories of a moment that would define the rest of our lives.

Then again, maybe it hurt and not remembering was a self-preservation tool.

Margot moaned faintly as I helped her out of the car, scooping her into my arms and kicking the door shut behind me. *Unsafe, unsafe, unsafe.* There was no one else on the street, but my grip on her tightened anyway, as though an alpha would leap out at any moment and snatch her away from me.

I'd never understood why my alpha friends were so grabby with their omegas—honestly, it looked like their mates should be claustrophobic with how close they kept them—but I got it now.

I completely got it now.

Margot fumbled with her purse, eventually pulling her keys out, and I was forced to put her down and use my slightly steadier hands to unlock the door. The moment we were on the small landing at the base of the stairs that led up to her apartment, a switch seemed to flip.

I'd thought my omega was in heat before, but the slightly feral glint in her eye as she glanced at me before bolting up the stairs told me that I had *no* idea what an omega in heat truly looked like.

She was very clearly running for her nest, but my alpha hindbrain only registered the running part. With a growl that seemed to startle me more than her, I was running up the stairs two at a time, pinning her against her apartment door.

Margot let out an appreciative moan as the bulge in my jeans dug into her ass, her entire front pressed up against the door.

"Omega," I growled, vaguely aware that I was rocking my hips against her. "Nest."

She let out a full-blown whine, and I remembered that I was the one holding the keys. *Idiot.* The moment I got the door open, I had Margot inside and pushed up against it, frantically tugging off her clothes with plenty of enthusiastic assistance. Her skin was hot to the touch, her hands alternating between taking off her clothes and grabbing every inch of my body she could reach.

"Alpha," she whispered, sighing in relief as I ripped off the thick pre-heat underwear and tossed them aside. "Alpha, alpha, alpha."

Without the physical barrier in the way, the rich scent of Margot's need filled the apartment, making my mouth water. It still wasn't quite right though, I thought, nosing the column of her neck as I kicked off my own trousers, a growl rumbling through my chest. The lingering smells of other people who'd touched her clung to her skin, and the scentshield lotion made her delicious natural vanilla scent smell sort of soapy and off.

No, no. This wouldn't do.

"Nest," Margot demanded.

"Shower," I countered, steering her into her tiny bathroom.

She growled—a fierce, demanding, bratty sound that went straight to my dick, but I didn't back down. The wrongness of her scent, the smell of others on her skin, would be bothering her too. She just wasn't lucid enough to pick up on the nuances of her irritation right now, which was fine.

That was my job.

I quickly turned the shower on, divesting us of the rest of our clothes before grabbing one of the cloths Margot used for removing her make-up and wetting it under the shower stream.

She stilled, staring up at me with a slightly stubborn tilt to her chin, and waited. Ignoring the throbbing ache of my cock, the syrupy sweet smell of Margot's desire, ignoring everything else, I slowly began massaging away the make-up, dropping light kisses on her bare skin as I went.

I wasn't entirely oblivious. I'd known that Margot had some hangups about me seeing her without make-up on—which I finally understood after she'd told me about the incident at the pool—but I'd hoped that *not* bringing attention to them was the best way of offering her reassurance.

Maybe that had been the right call. Maybe it hadn't. We had our entire lives for me to learn the best way of keeping my omega happy.

"You are beautiful," I murmured, kissing the tip of her nose before carefully wiping off her eye make-up and pulling her into the shower. "So fucking beautiful. I can't wait to wake up next to you each morning, Margot mine. I'll remind you when you're able to focus on something other than my dick."

I grunted in surprise as Margot wrapped her hand around my cock, taking my words as a suggestion rather than a jest.

"Fuck," I rasped, my abs contracting as she began working my shaft at the perfect tempo, a hungry gleam in her eyes as she stared at the bead of precum welling at the tip. "Okay, let's get you washed before I go into rut and keep you in the shower for your whole heat."

She wasn't listening.

I grabbed the body wash, breathing hard as I washed every part of her I could reach while she gave me the best fucking hand job of my life.

"Margot," I warned, my shoulders hitting the shower wall while my hips seemed to move of their own accord. "Let's go to your nest. You can play with me all you want in your nest—"

Too late.

Her knees hit the floor with a thud, mouth open and tongue extended to catch every drop of cum she could. Margot's eyes drifted closed, a blissful look on her face as though she'd never tasted anything better, and my hindbrain roared to life.

Nest. Fuck. Knot.

Claim.

I shut the water off, roughly grabbing a towel and pulling Margot to her feet, attempting to dry us both whilst simultaneously rubbing myself all over her, driven by instincts as old as time to cover her in my scent.

We tumbled through the flat, both grabbing frantically at each other, rubbing skin against skin, our skin still damp. A near-constant flow of slick ran down Margot's inner thighs, bathing my cock each time I rubbed against her.

Her usually sharp toffee-brown eyes that missed nothing were hazy and unfocused, though they kept returning to me as if to assure herself that I was still here.

I groaned at the scent of her nest, pushing the button to close the electronic door behind me. *Fuck.* The pure, unadulterated *Margot* of this room nearly had me falling to my knees. She didn't have time for the intense revelation I was experiencing though. Margot grabbed my wrist, dragging me towards the edge of the bed with surprising strength and all but throwing me onto the mattress sunken into the floor.

And then she pounced.

I captured her nipple in my mouth the moment she landed on me, her sharp nails digging into my shoulders, a layer of slick coating everything from the bottom of my ribs to my mid-thighs as Margot ground down on top of me, covering me in the same scent as her nest, marking me as belonging.

Patience, I told myself, rocking my hips, desperate to feel her slippery cunt gripping my knot. But this was important. This was symbolic. This was a *gift*. And I'd reciprocate with my teeth.

Soon.

At the thought, a rusty purr rumbled out of my chest, and Margot practically melted over top of me, laying her upper body on my chest and nosing affectionately at my throat.

"Such a good omega," I told her, cupping her ass cheeks and thrusting into the slippery warmth between her thighs. "So sweet, so good. That's it, mark me more, Margot mine. Give me your scent."

She was writhing on top of me, attempting to notch my cock at her entrance, impatient for a knot. But—according to my research—heat was a marathon, not a sprint. The more prepping I did now, the more comfortable the next few days would be.

I rolled us over, pinning her with a palm in the centre of her belly when she attempted to climb back on top of me.

"Not yet," I chided, grinning at her feral little omega growl. "Got to stretch you first. Got to make that cunt ready for me. Going to be knotting you for days, my omega."

"Knot," Margot mewled, attempting to wriggle free from under my palm.

"Soon," I promised, wrapping my free hand around my shaft, needing to take the edge off so I could tend to her properly.

This was going to be over very quickly, I thought to myself, my fist bumping my burgeoning knot with each stroke. Margot was all but salivating at the combination of my pheromones and precum filling the air, her vanilla scent growing headier with each passing moment.

"My omega," I growled, angling my hips to cover her perfect glistening cunt in hot splashes of cum, immediately releasing my cock to massage it around her clit before pushing it in her pussy.

Margot bucked her hips wildly, but my hand pressing her to the mattress was unyielding as I added a second finger, alternating between scissoring, thrusting and curling them inwards, prepping her for days of hard fucking.

As eager as I was to bury myself in her pussy and never leave, I didn't want Margot to wake up after her heat ended with any pain beyond tired muscles.

With a filthy squelch and a gush of fluid, I thrust in a third finger, rubbing the heel of my hand against her clit with each pass.

Margot came with a shudder and a whine, her slick making a sizeable damp patch on the sheets beneath her. Her inner walls squeezed and massaged my fingers, and I stifled a groan at the memory of how fucking good the movement felt around my knot.

As she slowly came down from her high, some of the crushing tightness around my fingers eased, and my cock throbbed in time with Margot's rocking hips, a silent message to my brain that it was time. That she was ready.

I withdrew my fingers, hooking Margot's legs over my elbows and sliding my cock home in one smooth, soaking motion. Margot exhaled instantly, a mixture of relief and ecstasy on her face.

"So beautiful," I growled, my movements wild and frantic, gums already aching. There was no gentleness here, no finesse. I fucked Margot like I'd die if I didn't, each thrust shoving her up the mattress.

Claim, claim, claim.

Margot's palm covered my mouth as I approached her throat, lost in a haze of desire but still aware enough to look after me. With an impatient growl, I sucked her fingers into my mouth, using them to distract me while I fucked her into one orgasm, and then another.

I was thirsty.

The thought was a semi-lucid one.

Margot was curled around me like a vine wrapped around a tree, and I disentangled myself as carefully as I could, reaching outside the nest for the mini-fridge and grabbing a bright blue sports drink.

I sat up, downing half the bottle in one go before caramel eyes flashed open, pinning me with a furious glare, accompanied by an impatient omega growl.

"Drink," I ordered, pressing the drink bottle to her lips.

Margot turned away petulantly, rolling onto all fours and crawling up my body, licking the tip of my cock as though it was the only sustenance she required.

I captured her chin, dragging her face up and holding the bottle to her lips again.

"Drink," I repeated, infusing my voice with the alpha command I'd never used until her.

Margot's eyes flashed with annoyance at being denied what she wanted, but she did drink as instructed.

This was what it was to be an alpha. This was why I had the bark I'd never had any use for.

To care for my omega.

And then Margot deep-throated my cock, and any trace of lucid thought fled me.

Sticky. The sheets are sticky.

I peeled a section of saturated fabric away from my skin, baring my chest to the cool air. Margot squirmed at my side before throwing a leg over my hips, wriggling up over my body and sinking down onto my cock without even opening her eyes.

"Omega..." I rasped before the rut pulled me into its clutches once more.

A coppery taste filled my mouth, chasing away the sweet slick that had been coating my tongue.

This new flavour was bitter and tangy. Unpleasant.

And yet...

I felt something like victory flow through me, making my blood roar in my ears and my knot swell in my omega's warm, clenching cunt.

My omega.

My *claimed* omega.

Chapter Twenty-two

As always, I regained some control of my brain by day five. My pussy still ached, craving the stretch and fill of a knot, but it was a more manageable throb. I was still a leaking mess of slick, but it had slowed to a trickle.

And it wasn't just slick leaking out of me.

I wasn't alone in my nest. And I had an aching mark on my neck to contend with. Kit pulled me tight against him the moment I moved, his mouth closing over the now-sealed bite mark, tracing it with his tongue. A jolt of alarm ran through me that he hadn't even *checked* that it was fully closed. My hormones were wearing off and with it the neutralising effect that made my blood safe. He had to be more careful.

"Calm, omega," he soothed before breaking into a purr, his lips brushing featherlight kisses down my shoulder. There was a rough quality to his voice, and judging by the way he fitted his cock between my slippery thighs without so much as a 'How do you do?', he was still very much feeling the effects of the rut.

I let out a breathy moan as he angled his hips, the blunt head of his cock nudging my clit. My legs spread of their own accord, the dull throb of need morphing into a raging, greedy inferno in two seconds flat. Was this what it was always going to be like having Kit in my nest each night? He thrust into my fluttering pussy in one perfect swoop, his knot already thickening the base of his cock, and I decided I didn't mind so much. I'd happily wake up in a puddle of slick with an aching cunt every morning if it meant he was there to take the ache away.

"My omega," Kit mumbled, hooking his elbow under my thigh, opening me to him. I arched back against him, my fingers finding my way between my legs to play with my hypersensitive clit.

Fuck me.

Was this what having a mate was like? No wonder everyone was so hung up on the idea. He moved his arm higher, dragging my leg with it, so he could pinch my nipple gently between his fingers. My thighs were screaming, every muscle on the border between pleasure and pain, and I couldn't get enough of it.

"Keeping you in this nest," Kit rasped. I whined as he rolled me onto my front, his body covering my back, arms moving to either side of my head so he didn't crush me. "Keeping you on this knot."

"Alpha!" I cried, attempting to meet him thrust for punishing thrust while he fucked my body farther and farther up the mattress. He was wild and unabandoned, completely lost to his lust and without the usual carefulness that always held him back ever so slightly in the other times we'd fallen into bed together.

Or fallen onto a washing machine together. Or over the back of my couch together.

Could he feel how much his rough, wild movements did it for me through the bond? Did he know that I loved it? That I loved him?

I slipped my hand beneath my body, rubbing my clit furiously and tipping myself over the edge as Kit's knot swelled. He came with an alpha roar that sent my whole body into the most glorious kind of submission. I was safe. I was protected.

I was loved.

I closed my eyes and went back to sleep.

The next time I woke up, I was lucid.

And sticky.

So very sticky.

Kit snored softly next to me, and I carefully extricated myself from his grip, letting him sleep. I doubted I'd been so considerate in the worst of my heat—the poor guy was probably exhausted.

Silently, I snuck out of the nest, tiptoeing down the hallway to the bathroom, cringing at the trail of our combined fluids left with each step. Heat with a partner was even messier than heat alone.

A little gift basket tied with a blue bow sat on the bathroom counter, and I was filled with a rush of affection for Violet. Who knew what she'd heard when she'd stopped by, but I didn't feel embarrassed, particularly. I'd been their support person for her last few heats, and they were frankly so open and constantly attached to each other that it hadn't seemed that different from the way they usually were.

As much as I wanted to take advantage of the face mask I could see in the basket, getting clean was a higher priority. I turned the shower on as hot as I could manage it, bracing myself against the tile wall with one hand as I got in and let the water wash away the evidence of the past few days.

Well, most of it.

My free hand rubbed absently at the mating mark that I hadn't quite gathered the courage to look at yet, my heart pounding in my chest.

I was claimed.

It was heady and incredible. And more than a little overwhelming.

The day I'd gone into heat had been intense, from the moment I'd woken up in that hotel room, hot and sticky, to the moment I'd gone into my nest, also hot and sticky.

The memories of that day came to me in broken bits and pieces as I washed cum out of my hair, and I made a mental note to call Asher later and check that he was okay before arranging his interview at Sutton-Harris.

There was a sudden spark of warmth in my chest that made me gasp, and I realised it was the bond. Kit must have woken up, and the bond had come online accordingly.

It was a strange, beautiful feeling that would definitely take some getting used to.

There was a small frisson of panic in my chest that without the sweetness of my pre-heat scent, Kit might not... like what he saw.

And I was annoyed with myself for even contemplating it. I was more than the sum of my myriad of issues, and I was choosing to believe that when Kit told me he loved me, he meant it.

Right?

Right.

I blew out a long breath, grabbed the soap and scrubbed until my skin was pink and raw.

The bathroom door swung open, and I jumped, dropping my loofah on the shower floor in surprise.

"Kit?"

He didn't say a word, just stalked into the shower, crowding me against the wall and pressed his lips to mine. *Oh*, I thought vaguely, gripping his forearms. *I guess he's still in rut.*

By the time we broke apart, we were both breathing heavily, and I waited for Kit to hoist me up against the shower wall and fill me with his knot again.

I was a little sore, but definitely not opposed to the idea.

"Don't fucking do that; you scared me to death," Kit said eventually, letting out a heavy sigh and kissing me on the forehead. "Just wake me up before you get out of the nest next time. I won't mind."

I blinked a few times, scanning his face.

"Are you... are you not in rut?"

Kit frowned. "No. Are you still in heat?" I shook my head. "Oh, good. Not that I didn't enjoy it, but I really need to eat, and I'm sure you do. After we get this shampoo out of your hair," he added, lips tilting up into the most delicious half-smile. I'd been washing my hair?

Kit guided me back under the water, and I tipped my head up to stare at his face while he carefully massaged my scalp, carefully rinsing the shampoo out of each strand. I waited for the shyness to kick in, the lingering insecurity borne from him seeing my make-up-free face, but it never did.

One hand came to collar my throat, his thumb tracing the outline of my mating mark as he let out a satisfied purr that had my shaky knees knocking together.

"Mine," he growled, eyes flashing with alpha possessiveness.

"And you're mine," I whispered, running my fingers down his chest to where the mate bond would be. "Are you happy?"

"Happier than I've ever been in my life."

I blew out a long breath. "We've never really discussed it outright, but you don't... you don't wish I was, you know, beautiful?"

I was vaguely aware that I was acting more than a little needy, but I was hungry and tired and my hormones were doing the conga around my head. Nothing was coming out right.

Kit blinked at me, his brow slowly pulling into a frown. "You are beautiful."

"I know I'm not. And I'm fine with that—really! I am—you're just so handsome, and I'll never have a pretty face—"

"Margot," Kit interjected, somewhat exasperated. His hands came up to cup my jaw, thumbs brushing my cheeks. "This is the face of the woman I love. There's not a single thing about it, or you, that I would change."

"Okay," I rasped, nodding. A stupid tear trailed down my cheek, and I hoped he thought it was water from the shower. "I'm sorry. I don't know why I feel so... vulnerable."

"Because *this* is vulnerable. It's new and it's overwhelming, and heat has taken a lot out of you. We've both been alone a long time, Margot mine. We're bound to hit some speed bumps on the way, but we're on the same team, okay? Always. So long as we're together, there's no obstacle we can't overcome."

I exhaled heavily, the combination of his words and the warmth of the bond centring me. "I love you."

Kit smiled softly. "And I love you. Now, let's get some food and fluids in you, then we're going to take a nap."

"We need to talk about New York."

"We will," he agreed. "But I'm going to take care of you first."

Chapter Twenty-three

"You really didn't have to do all this," I told Violet, pulling her into a tight hug. "Honestly, neither Kit nor I felt particularly strongly about even having a mating party."

"You say that like it's a good thing instead of an absolute travesty," Violet laughed, still gripping my forearms as she pulled back, giving me a watery smile. "I'm going to miss you so much. Nico and I have decided to try for a baby at my next heat, and I selfishly want you to be here if we're lucky enough to conceive. There's no one in the world I trust more than you. Well, except for Nico, that is."

I gave her a smile that was equally as tremulous. "You guys are going to be the best parents. And New York is only a red-eye away; you know we'll both be on the first flight back to meet your little one."

"Maybe even with a little one of your own?" Violet teased, waggling her eyebrows.

I snorted. "Not just yet. We went and got the postcoital contraception shot the day after my heat broke. We want to spend a little time, just the two of us, first. Besides, New York could be temporary. Kit may hate teaching, in which case we'll come back to London and regroup."

I wasn't worried about where the future would lead us, not anymore. We were Team Iyer, and we were unstoppable.

Kit's arm banded around my waist, tugging me gently out of Violet's grip. "I'm jealous. Humour me."

"You're jealous of Violet?" I laughed.

"I'm jealous of any and all recipients of your attention, Margot mine. It's probably unhealthy. You should really tell me off. You know I only listen to you."

"You guys are syrupy sweet," Violet sighed, pressing her hands to her heart. "I knew once you met, it would be love at first sight."

"You did not." I shook my head, laughing silently.

"I did!" she insisted. "Ask Nico. I've always said that, ever since I met you, Margot. I never expected Kit to stay out of the country so long, it was driving me crazy to wait."

Kit squeezed my waist. "I'm glad you didn't say anything, Violet. Just the idea that I might have avoided Margot just because I didn't like being set up makes my chest ache. We could have missed each other."

I turned in his arms, pressing a soft kiss to his lips. "I like to think we would have found each other anyway. Eventually."

He didn't look particularly comforted by the idea, holding me just a little closer than he was before. For a guy who hadn't known the first thing about omegas, who hadn't shown the slightest amount of interest in having a mate, Kit was an incredibly devoted and surprisingly romantic alpha.

"Your guests are arriving," Nico called from down the hall. "Margot, your three youngest siblings and your Nana are getting out of a cab."

"Oh good, they're here." I went up on my tiptoes to give Kit one more quick kiss before disentangling myself, ready to greet my four favourite family members. My parents were still furious with me, and Layla had sided with them—a turn of events that shocked no one—so I hadn't bothered inviting them tonight.

It was incredibly freeing, *not* being the bigger person, *not* keeping the peace, *not* putting my own wants and needs second in order to placate people who would find fault in me no matter what I did.

Kit grabbed my hand before I could walk away, tugging me back for a longer, deeper kiss. "I hate sharing your attention."

"I know, you're a real brat like that."

He snorted. "You bring that out in me, Margot mine. Enjoy tonight, before I squirrel you away to New York and keep you all to myself."

"I'd point out the multitude of red flags in that statement if you hadn't already invited my siblings to come and stay with us over winter break," I laughed, rolling my eyes affectionately before softening my tone. "You're already the alpha big brother they always wanted but never had."

Not even when Calum was alive.

Kit couldn't quite hide his own emotions at that. He *loved* having younger siblings, and even his mum had taken a liking to the three troublemakers.

"I love you, Margot."

"Not as much as I love you," I replied solemnly. I didn't think it was possible. What I felt for Kit seemed too big for words, too big for my body sometimes. He was everything.

Kit shook his head, a small smile playing around his lips. "At least a hundred times more."

Epilogue

KIT

There was no point pretending I wasn't listening to Margot's conversation with her youngest siblings. The open-concept, industrial-style apartment we'd been living in for the past year was many things—picturesque, well-located, aesthetically pleasing—but sure as shit wasn't soundproof. When she had confidential work calls from London, I ended up just leaving the apartment entirely to give her some privacy.

"I'm so excited," Asher was saying, his voice much lower and more adult-sounding these days. *"You're sure it's okay to come and stay, right? Mum says you'll hate it, and I'll be in your way."*

"Mum doesn't know what she's talking about," Margot replied dismissively, making me smile. It had taken some convincing to get Margot's parents to agree to let Asher spend the summer with us here in New York, but we were pretty confident her dad was still a little bit scared of her, so we pulled it off.

We'd have happily had Chelsea too, but she'd opted to spend the summer at Oxford, doing a biology course. It wasn't evident at first because Chelsea was shy and incredibly modest, but apparently beneath all of that, she was a secret science genius.

"Are you positive you're still enjoying school?" Margot asked nervously as I climbed the stairs, letting myself into her office. My scent and the bond announced my presence. "If you're not, you know you're always welcome here. I'm sure we can get you into Kit's school. Nepotism keeps these great institutions alive."

Margot twisted in her seat, shooting me a mischievous grin over her shoulder.

"It's college, sweetheart."

"Details, details. Hey, I've got to go, kid. We've got a date at an absurdly swanky restaurant—there was a waitlist and everything."

Asher sighed dramatically. *"New York has made you even more bougie, Margot. Love that for you. See you in a couple of weeks!"*

"You're fretting," I pointed out as she hung up, noticing the bond twisting anxiously in my chest.

"I know, I know." Margot sighed. "I just want him to be happy."

"Asher is incredibly happy." I leaned down, kissing the top of her head. "Thanks to you. You worry too much. It's because you're such a nice person."

"I am *not* nice," Margot retorted primly. "I'm very mean. The meanest."

"Mmhm."

"I am! Get out of the way—see, very mean of me—I need to put my make-up on. What if we see famous people tonight? I saw Aaron Tempest is in New York filming his latest action movie."

I tugged Margot out of her seat with a growl, pulling her against me and slipping my hands down to grip her ass. "Is that why you want to go out tonight, hm? You want a shot at seeing your true love, Aaron Tempest?"

We both knew I was teasing her but my cock was stirring in my dress pants anyway. It was a running joke that usually led to me fucking Margot senseless, declaring her love for me while she was stuck on my knot.

Margot tutted, her eyes still full of trouble. "We don't have time for your alpha nonsense right now, Kit. We have a reservation. You're going to have to blow my back out when we get home."

"You little minx, are you riling me up on purpose?" I laughed, pinching her ass. "I'll get you back for this."

"I'm counting on it," Margot sing-songed, darting away to get ready. "But you know you have nothing to worry about. You know you're the love of my life."

Damn right I was. And that feeling was entirely mutual.

ACKNOWLEDGEMENTS

THANK YOU SO MUCH FOR READING MARGOT AND KIT'S STORY! IT'S BEEN FLOATING AROUND IN MY BRAIN, DEMANDING ATTENTION, FOR MONTHS NOW AND IT'S SUCH A REWARDING FEELING TO HAVE IT OUT IN THE WORLD. I HAVE PUT A LONG PREORDER UP FOR THE NEXT BOOK IN THIS SERIES, EXCESS, THOUGH THIS MAY MOVE FORWARD. EVERY BOOK IN THE ON THE SHELF SERIES WILL FEATURE MAIN CHARACTERS AGED 30+, AND THEY CAN BE READ AS STANDALONES IN ANY ORDER.

I HAVE TO THANK THE WONDERFUL STEPH FROM RAWLS READS EDITS FOR DEV EDITING AND LORIE FOR PROOFREADING—YOU GUYS ARE THE DREAM TEAM, IT'S SUCH A JOY TO WORK WITH YOU. THANK YOU ALSO TO RACHEL AND RORY FOR BETA READING, I APPRECIATE YOU BOTH SO MUCH! THIS BOOK DEFINITELY WOULDN'T HAVE HAPPENED WITHOUT THE EMOTIONAL SUPPORT AND GENTLE (MOSTLY) ENCOURAGEMENT FROM FELLOW WRITERS AND FRIENDS, AND I ADORE EACH AND EVERY ONE OF YOU.

AND, AS ALWAYS, MY BIGGEST THANK YOU GOES OUT TO YOU, READER. IN AN EXTENSIVE LIBRARY OF SMUTTY, FUNNY, WONDERFUL EBOOKS, THANK YOU FOR TAKING A CHANCE ON THIS ONE <3

COLETTE XX

ABOUT THE AUTHOR

Colette Rhodes is a paranormal romance author from New Zealand. She loves to write about love in all its forms, and adores imperfect heroes and heroines who find perfection in each other. You'll often find her trying to justify her degree by including ancient history and mythological influences in her work.

If she's not writing, then you're almost certain to find her reading—ideally with a cup of tea in hand and a scented candle burning to match the mood.

Keep up with Colette here:

coletterhodes.com

@coletterhodes_author

ALSO BY COLETTE RHODES

STATE OF GRACE:

Run Riot

Silver Bullet

Wild Game

Dare Not

Saving Grace

SHADES OF SIN:

(MF monster romance)

Luxuria

Superbia

Gula

ON THE SHELF:

Scheme

Excess

THREE BEARS DUET:

Gilded Mess

Golden Chaos

LITTLE RED DUET:

Scarlet Disaster

Seeing Red

KNOTTY BY NATURE:

(RH omegaverse with T.S. Snow)

Allure Part 1

Allure Part 2

EMPATH FOUND:

The Terrible Gift

The Unwanted Challenge

The Reluctant Keeper

DEADLY DRAGONS:

The (Not) Cursed Dragon

The (Not) Satisfied Dragon

STANDALONE:

Dead of Spring (MF - Hades & Persephone retelling)

Blood Nor Money (RH - vampires)

Fire & Gasoline (MF - wolf shifter fated mates)

Colette Rhodes
ROMANCE AUTHOR

www.ingramcontent.com/pod-product-compliance
Lightning Source LLC
Chambersburg PA
CBHW061650190726
48289CB00006B/1814